NIGHTSTALKERS

NIGHTSTALKERS

BOB MAYER

47NORTH

Text copyright © 2012 by Bob Mayer

Published by 47North
P.O. Box 400818
Las Vegas, NV 89140

ISBN-13: 9781612185835
ISBN-10: 1612185835

DEDICATION

To our grandson: Riley Kiran Cavanaugh
1/4/2012

CHAPTER 1

Roland fired the M-240 from the hip—not approved procedure for accuracy, but he was a former Special Forces weapons man with three combat tours, and every 7.62-millimeter round went directly at the seventeen-inch screen of the laptop. The golden iris emanating from the screen sucked the bullets in like a raging ocean absorbing rain, without the slightest ripple or effect.

The laptop rested on a boulder at the foot of a mesa fourteen miles outside of Tucson. A generator was stuttering nearby, providing power to the laptop and having supplied energy for the initial opening of the phenomenon protecting the computer. Roland was still in his jump harness, having just completed a high-altitude, low-opening parachute drop through the night sky.

"Confirming a Rift," Roland yelled into his throat mike. "Six Fireflies are out."

Moms's unflappable voice replied in his earpiece. "Roger. Inbound."

Roland released the trigger after wasting a second fifteen-round burst, knowing bullets were now useless against the Rift. His head was on a swivel. He'd spotted six golden sparks come out of the screen just before his feet hit the ground, and who knew what they'd gotten into? The Rift was Doc's problem now. The Fireflies were the real danger.

The Snake came roaring in, wings rotating from horizontal to vertical, jet engines pulsing, almost eerily silent as the thrust passed through sound dampeners. Doors slid open on both sides of the delta-shaped aircraft and fast ropes were tossed out. Four figures slid down. The fast ropes were released and the Snake rose to over-watch height. A door slid open at the nose of the Snake and the chain gun extended into firing position.

Racing from the discarded ropes, Moms—the team leader— led the way, her MP-5 submachine gun at the ready. Nada was on her right with his sub, along with Burns armed with an M-203, and Doc brought up the rear, carrying a military-hardened laptop of his own along with a small dish transmitter.

"Eagle," Moms ordered the pilot, "get a Wall in."

The Snake banked and raced in a clockwise circle, five hundred meters around the Rift, firing down probes every three hundred meters of the circumference. When the last one was in, they were activated, forming a Wall around the area of operations, and the Snake returned to over-watch.

Out of the corner of his eye, Roland caught movement as he shrugged off his parachute harness. He wheeled as a coyote launched at him from twenty meters away. An unnatural leap for a coyote and plenty of distance for Roland to stitch it with a solid burst. But close enough that the rounds weren't enough to stop a creature taken over by a Firefly. The bullets barely slowed the coyote's flight.

It landed on Roland, teeth snapping, claws ripping at his body armor.

Moms and Nada fired at the coyote on top of him, making the Delta Force live-fire training for hostage rescue in the Kill House at Bragg look like child's play. Every round hit the beast, not a one scratching Roland.

The combined force of the fusillade knocked the coyote off Roland and he rolled in the opposite direction, bracing for what he knew would be next.

"H.E.," Burns warned as he fired the forty-millimeter grenade launcher underneath the rifle barrel of his M-203. The high explosive round hit the coyote's center of mass, blowing a huge chunk out of the creature's chest and stunning it for the moment. It had been dead since Roland's initial burst, but the Firefly still had enough to work with.

"Doc, forward!" Moms ordered. "Nada, cover him. Burns, finish it. Eagle, we got one in a coyote, scan for anything living."

Doc—a short, balding man with thick glasses—was completely out of place among the military personnel blasting away with weapons all around him. And yet he ran toward the growing golden iris in front of the offending laptop. He dropped to his knees and opened up his own computer. He scrambled to connect a FireWire cable to the dish.

Roland ignored Doc, firing his M-240 at the coyote, but despite the damage, the remains of the coyote came toward Roland.

Burns fired again, and this round blew the remnants to shreds. Roland slid the machine gun on its sling over his shoulder and grabbed the pistol grip attached to the tank of napalm on his back, pulling it out of its asbestos sheath. He flamed the remains, charring it to ashes.

A golden spark of light, four inches in circumference, lifted from the corpse, then disappeared into a wisp and then nothing.

"How many?" Moms was at Roland's side as he slid the flamer back into its holster and readied the machine gun once more.

"Six. One down."

"You certain?" Moms asked as the two went back-to-back to gain 360-degree coverage. Nada was hovering over Doc, head turning to and fro.

"Yes."

A new voice came over the team's net. "Got two hot to your west, moving in tight to each other toward you," Eagle reported from the Snake, hovering a hundred feet overhead. "Targeting. Looks like more coyotes. I've got a Wall surrounding you at five hundred meters."

The chain gun mounted in the nose of the Snake let loose, firing thirty-millimeter depleted uranium rounds. At a rate of over ten rounds a second, Eagle was not only hitting the two targets with the heavy rounds, the pyrophoric nature of the bullets caused what they hit to burst into flame as the uranium cores released their built-up heat. Eagle fired for twenty seconds, saturating the target, knowing he had to do more than kill them—he had to destroy them.

"Nothing warm, but be careful," Eagle announced into the sudden silence as he finished firing.

"Status, Doc?" Moms asked. "I don't want any more Fireflies coming through."

"Getting the frequency." Doc's fingers were flying over the keyboard. His focus was on the data on the screen, ignoring the battle raging about him. He sounded a little puzzled. "This one's a little different somehow."

"Roland, ready the flame," Moms ordered. "Burns: with Nada, and secure Doc."

Roland moved to Moms's left shoulder, five feet away, as she headed toward where Eagle had chewed up the ground with his firing.

Roland slid the machine gun on its sling over his shoulder and grabbed the pistol grip for the flamer.

"Intriguing!" Doc's exclamation caused everyone to shift attention to him.

They could immediately see what had caused it: the golden iris was expanding and pulsing. "That's new," Roland said.

"It's bad," Nada said, but then he said that about pretty much everything.

"We're fucked," Burns added.

"A little faster please, Doc," Moms said. "On task, people."

Moms moved into the kill zone, Roland at her shoulder, and they mentally tallied body parts.

"Two dead?" Moms asked, which was polite, since she wouldn't specify the number if she wasn't certain.

"Two," Roland confirmed as he incinerated the remains with the flamer.

"Did you see the Fireflies?" Moms asked.

"No," Roland said, "but Eagle tore them into such tiny pieces, they had to have dissipated before we got here. You saw what was left."

Moms frowned. "Eagle, did you have observation?"

"I was watching," Eagle said. "I definitely saw one Firefly dissipate and they were moving as a pair. It was hard to see with all the rounds hitting."

"We've got three left," Moms informed the team, which wasn't needed, but she was a worrier. Not as much as Nada, and in a different way. "Eagle?" As she spoke, she was leading Roland back toward the rest of the team. He shifted from flamer back to machine gun.

"Got one small hot spot about thirty meters to your south-southeast. Real small, but it's moving fast, back and forth, not advancing. It's—" Eagle paused. "Hopping? I can't get a lock, but I could blast the area."

"Negative," Moms said. "We couldn't confirm something that small when you're done."

Moms moved in the direction indicated, Roland at her side. He spared a glance at the Rift. The golden iris was now about fifteen feet tall and three feet wide. The Rift was bigger than any he'd ever seen or any Nightstalker had recorded since the team was formed in 1948. Which was a lot of years and a lot of—

"Focus," Moms said, as if reading his mind. "Range?" she asked Eagle.

"Fifteen meters. Straight ahead on your track." There was a pause, then he guided them with each step they took. "Shift left, more left. Right one-quarter. Half left."

Roland spotted it and fired instantly. "Rabbit!"

His burst struck with the first three rounds, but then the bunny leaped out of his field of vision and the rest of his rounds raced out into the darkness.

Moms was firing and he spun, seeing her tracers arc hard, which meant the target was moving fast—very fast—around them and she was a fraction slow shifting to nail it.

"Incoming, Nada!" Moms yelled. She ran back toward the rest of the team with Roland.

Burns had the M-203 at the ready, but hitting such a small, fast-moving target with the grenade launcher…He fired and the grenade flew past Moms and Roland, barely missing them.

Nada, having spent thousands of hours in the Kill House as a member of Delta Force in his previous life—as if any of them had a previous life—fired his MP-5 on semiautomatic, finger pulling the trigger as fast as he could twitch it.

Every round hit the rabbit, but failed to stop it as it launched with unnatural speed toward Doc, who was still focused on his computer screen and data. But Nada was fast, too, dropping the MP-5, letting it fall to the end of its sling, and whipping out the machete sheathed over his left shoulder with a single rapid motion.

The bunny was less than two feet from hitting Doc and sinking its incisors into his neck when the machete sliced it in two. Moms and Roland arrived. The rear half was motionless, but the front half was scrabbling at the desert sand with its front paws, still trying to reach Doc, surprisingly long teeth snapping.

Roland had already shifted to the flamer and he fried the front, then the rear half. Through the flame, a golden spark rose, then dissipated.

"Now would be good, Doc," Moms said as she dropped an empty magazine and slammed home another one full of nine-millimeter rounds. She was staring into the light. "We don't want whatever's forming in there to come out."

The *whatever's forming* got everyone's attention. The iris was now twenty feet high and five wide. The laptop generating it was barely visible inside the Rift. And behind the laptop, in a depth not of this world, something dark and ominous was beginning to take shape.

"Oh shit," Burns said. "We're totally fucked."

"Shut up," Nada said.

"Eagle?" Moms asked.

"You're the only thermal images in the radius," the eye in the sky informed the team on the ground.

"Inanimate?" Moms wondered.

Roland, Nada, and Burns scanned the surrounding terrain, trying to figure what object a Firefly could have gotten into: boulders, cacti, lots of sand and sage.

"Nothing that could move," Nada said.

"They like machines," Roland noted. "The generator?"

"Faster, Doc," Nada said, an edge to his voice no one on the team had ever heard before.

The rattlesnake came up out of a hole in the ground less than four feet from Doc. It sunk its fangs into his upper right arm and reared back for a second strike, aiming for the neck.

Nada's machete was quicker.

Roland burned the head and the still writhing body.

The Firefly dissipated.

"Synced!" Doc announced as he hit the enter button on his laptop, seemingly unaware he'd been bitten.

Nothing apparent happened for a moment.

Even though there was a sixth Firefly still loose, the entire team lost discipline and stared into the Rift. Whatever was forming, a ten-foot-high, somewhat human-shaped—but not quite—figure seemed to shiver with rage...then the golden iris snapped out of existence. The laptop that had been the source of all of this was dark.

"Security!" Moms yelled. "Eagle?"

"Nothing."

"Give me a perimeter." Moms tapped Doc on the shoulder. "You've been snakebit."

Doc shook out of a thousand-mile stare at where the Rift had been. "What?"

"Rattler got you on the shoulder," Moms said. "Do you have antivenom in your med kit?"

"Yes." Doc blinked, then winced. "Well, damn." He had more pressing things on his mind, though. "But the Rift, that was different. I'll have to check the data."

"This shit is getting old," Burns muttered as he walked around the laptop, eyeing the generator suspiciously. "What if the Firefly is in it and blows the gas tank on that thing?"

"Burns." Nada's tone completed his order: Shut up.

"I'm just saying—"

Burns screamed as the fourteen-foot-high cactus to his right sprayed him with needles.

Moms, Roland, and Nada fired in concert, chewing up the plant.

"Cactus!" Moms yelled, alerting Eagle.

The plant fired back with more thorns, causing them to dive for cover behind the boulder on which the laptop rested. Roland grabbed Doc, who had just given himself an injection of antivenom, covering him with his own body.

Burns was still screaming, writhing on the ground, the thorns having torn into his skin in dozens of places not protected by body armor. His arm, leg, and face were shredded on his right side.

"Frag!" Nada yelled, throwing a grenade over the boulder, over the cactus and behind it, hopefully keeping Burns out of the fragmentation as it exploded.

"Stay down, Doc," Roland said, letting go of the scientist even as he readied the flamer.

Eagle fired a short, two-second burst from the Snake. The rounds tore up the plant as Roland got to his feet and charged. He pulled the trigger, projecting a stream of napalm, raking the tall plant from base to top. He kept the trigger pulled until his tank ran empty.

The Firefly fluttered up out of the flames, then was gone.

Moms ran over to Burns, who was bleeding badly. "Doc, can you help?" Burns was not only punctured in dozens of places, but some of the thorns had sliced right along the skin, leaving flaps of loose flesh dangling.

Doc nodded. "I'm a little woozy, but yeah." He knelt next to Burns.

"Get these fucking thorns out of me!" Burns cried out.

"Technically," Doc said, "they're spines, not thorns. Cacti have—"

"Doc," Moms said in a quiet voice as she shook her head.

"Right." Doc got to work, hitting Burns with painkiller.

Moms pointed at the laptop. "Secure that, Roland. Nada, shut down that generator and rig it for destruction."

Moms watched Doc working on Burns and mentally gave him a couple of minutes before the combination of venom, antivenom, and mission shock put him out of commission. But he was doing fine for the moment, pulling thorns—check that, spines—out of Burns and stopping the bleeding. They'd both live.

Moms was tall, just short of six feet, with broad shoulders but surprisingly narrow hips and a nonexistent ass. She had short brown hair with a tinge of premature gray streaking through it. She appeared the outdoorsy type. One could picture her riding with the Marlboro Man, owning a ranch somewhere in Texas—which wasn't too far off the mark, except she came from one of those dark, desolate farmhouses you see on the horizon while racing across Kansas on I-70. The kind of place Truman Capote would only pay attention to if everyone inside had been slaughtered.

Roland came up to Moms with the laptop, its lid shut, a metal thermal blanket wrapped around it.

"Where's its owner?" Moms asked.

"Saw him get snarked into the Rift like they all do, just as the Fireflies came out. I was a couple of seconds too late. So he's on the other side, wherever that is." He reached down and picked up a cap with the Arizona State Sun Devil mascot on the front. "This is all that's left of him."

"Anything else come out of the Rift?" Moms asked.

"Not since I put eyes on it," Roland said, "and near as I could tell, the ASU kid who programmed it only got the Rift open just before it took him."

"So just the six?" Moms pressed.

"Yes, ma'am," Roland said.

Moms slapped Roland lightly on the shoulder. "Good job, soldier."

Roland, all six-four, two hundred and forty pounds of trained killer, shifted his feet uncomfortably like a freshman at the senior dance, laptop in one hand, the carrying handle of the smoking machine gun in the other, the nozzle of the flamer red hot in its asbestos sheath on his hip. The livid scar that ran along the right side of his head from the temple to above and behind his ear went red.

"Eagle, retrieve your probes. We're wet." She looked at the team sergeant. "Nada, how's the Satcom link?"

Nada went from putting the demolitions on the generator to checking the com link on Burns's wrist. "Got banged up—nonfunctional."

"Eagle, get me a Satcom link to the Ranch."

"You've got it. Live now on channel four."

Moms switched her throat mike to the new channel.

"Ms. Jones, we are wet here."

The voice that replied was old and had a vaguely Russian accent forced into speaking American for a long time. "And?"

"Two wounded, one MIA scientist, six Fireflies destroyed." Moms paused. "There was something different about the Rift."

"Tell me in debrief. Come home."

The channel went dead, and Moms switched back to the team freq. "Eagle, land."

Creating a minisandstorm, the Snake settled down on its landing gear forty meters away as the chain gun retracted into its compartment. The back ramp opened as floodlights set above it lit up the area and Eagle stepped out, surveying the battlefield, a stretcher in his hands. He was a tall black man, completely hairless, and the entire left side of his head was scrolled with burn scar tissue from an IED in Iraq eight years ago.

Nada was helping Doc to his feet. The venom was taking its toll despite the shot, but he'd gotten Burns stable.

"Let's get our people on board," Moms ordered.

Nada half-carried Doc to the Snake, while Roland and Eagle tenderly placed Burns on the stretcher and carried him up the ramp.

Moms's were the last boots to step on board. Eagle climbed forward into the cockpit and was closing the back ramp as she got in the copilot's seat. He began powering up the engines.

"Next time," Doc mumbled, "I think I'll have the FireWire connected *before* we land."

"You think?" Roland said.

"We need to coordinate our firepower more efficiently," Nada said.

"Idiot scientists need to stop playing with shit they don't understand," Eagle observed as he twisted the collective and pushed forward on the cyclic. The Snake lifted.

Below them the generator exploded.

"All right, enough chitchat," Moms said. "Let's get back to Area 51 and the Ranch."

Moms looked over at the team's wounded communications man, then reached back and tapped Nada on the knee. "We're gonna need a new commo man."

Nada sighed. "You know how long it takes Ms. Jones to find someone."

"I hate fucking Rifts," Burns muttered, then passed out.

CHAPTER 2

Area 51 is in the middle of nowhere on the way to nowhere. Worse, in most of the nowhere it's on the way to, no one would survive long. To the west is the Nevada Test Site where the government—in the form of the United States Department of Energy— exploded 739 of the 928 nuclear tests it conducted over the years. Uninhabitable would be kind. No living thing being able to cross and survive long is more to the point.

To the north is the Nellis Range, where the government in the form of the US Air Force regularly drops bombs, big and small. Like most good pilots in the military, they often deliberately target anything moving out there, usually cattle or deer, since any kill is a good kill. The government pays the ranchers around the area a stipend every year for livestock that wander into the kill zone.

The deer are out of luck.

For most who cared, UFO enthusiasts among the most likely, the key to Area 51 is the world's longest runway set on the dry bed of Groom Lake. Every day a plane carrying contractors from Las Vegas lands on that runway depositing workers for the facilities built into Groom Mountain and hidden from the probing eyes of satellites.

The Nightstalkers did not take the daily flight to and from Vegas.

Area 51 itself would have been much too public a place for the Nightstalkers to be headquartered, although the huge perimeter, the inaccessibility, and the built-in security were all certainly enticements. The forerunners of the Nightstalkers had only been based at Area 51 because the scientists who conceived most of the problems they had to deal with were based at Area 51. Along the way someone realized that if everyone knew about Area 51, then it wasn't the best place to keep the covert team. The unit had changed names many times, always at least one step, and hopefully a lap, ahead of scrutiny. Now the Nightstalkers simply stayed in the vicinity to use that great buffer of security to the west, along with being able to tap the resources of the classified facility. And, of course, because they also had to be close enough to go in and take care of the problems that occasionally cropped up from some experiment gone awry in one of Area 51's many labs.

The new location, when they moved out of Area 51 proper, had been initially dubbed the Ranch, and that stuck.

So the Ranch was across the road. Right across Extraterrestrial Highway, a.k.a. Nevada Route 375. The curious who came out there always looked west, where the base was. No one ever looked east, toward the Ranch. On private land. Registered in county records to the actual current owner: Ms. Jones.

This made the location even more secure than the government facility across the way, because Nevada's Stand Your Ground Law, dating back to the Wild West of 1871, allowed Ranch security to gun down anyone who crossed its boundaries into the private property and represented what they considered a threat. The big, spray-painted plywood *NO TRESPASS: WE WILL SHOOT YOUR ASS* signs around the Ranch carried a lot more weight than the fancy red-and-white metal warning signs posted around Area 51, where the occasional interloper got a six-hundred-dollar fine.

The main part of the Ranch was, of course, hidden underground. Inside the complex—inside the Den—Eagle and Roland were needling MacGyver, a.k.a. Mac, about missing out in the "Fun Outside Tucson," as the latest mission had been labeled on the flight home. Mac had been off getting trained up in some other secret facility on the latest in demolitions, and Eagle told him they could have used the Holy Hand Grenade of Antioch on the killer rabbit, which drew blank stares from Roland and Mac and a sigh from the older man.

In reality, the two men were on edge and Mac was humoring them, while they all pretended not to listen to what was going on in Ms. Jones's office next door and stared aimlessly around their dreary surroundings. The central room they were in had originally been called the Bunker. It certainly fit the moniker. Depressing, gray, steel-reinforced concrete walls, curving to a popcorn ceiling that had another twenty feet of concrete pressing down on it. The Den was the center of the facility, the team room. Besides Ms. Jones's office, Moms and Nada's Command Post (CP) was adjacent to it along with the weapons room and the team living quarters.

Unfortunately "bunker" had sounded too last-days-of-Hitler and someone had started calling the room the Zoo. As in *The Spy Who Came in from the Cold*, when the Cold War was still chilly. But then that era passed and the allusion faded.

So it had morphed from Zoo to Lions' Den, in a time when perhaps a fiercer leader than Ms. Jones reigned, but that was too much work to sustain, so now it was just the Den.

It was a heavily fortified Den, though, surrounded by layers of security that would make Fort Knox weep with envy, so it always struck each new man as weird that the door to Ms. Jones's office was a flimsy, hollow-core affair, poorly hinged, leaving an inch opening above the floor. The reality, though, was that the office was more a sanctum. At least that's the way every team member thought of it. It was Ms. Jones's sanctum, one from which she had never come out. Each member had only been in once, to meet her when they had been in-processed.

Only Moms, occasionally with Nada, got to go behind the door more than once. This was one of those times.

The weird thing was that the flimsy door and the inch gap let every person in the Den hear every word spoken in the office. But only the conversations with Moms, occasionally Nada, and the in-briefs of new personnel, from which the existing team members could generate the newcomer's team name. Because other than when someone from the team was in the office with Ms. Jones, there was never a sound. One would think Ms. Jones talked on a phone, or radio, or to herself occasionally, but such utterances were never heard. There was never the creak of a desk chair, or even Ms. Jones breaking wind.

Some even speculated Ms. Jones wasn't real. She was a holographic image with a voice. After all, they could agree that during in-processing all they had seen was someone—or something—sitting in a darkened chair on the other side of a massive aircraft-carrier-sized wooden desk that had absolutely nothing on top of it. Forced to squint into lights aimed forward from above and behind the desk, lights that made one long for the days of the Gestapo and bootjacks, it was impossible to determine who or what was in that big chair.

So, for someone so secretive, one wondered why she would allow every word she spoke to every guest to be heard by every team member in the Den.

And eventually each new team member silently realized what the others had already figured out: there were no secrets inside the Nightstalkers. Anything discussed in there with anyone was information the entire team was privy to. Ms. Jones might have her own secrets, but she made sure the team had none among its members.

As Ms. Jones got the debrief going, Roland and Eagle stopped needling Mac for being away updating his demolitions expertise—"Doc and Burns coulda used some help in the Fun Outside Tucson" was the last thing Roland said before silence descended and they listened in.

Ms. Jones: "You said the Rift was different. How?"

Moms went into a succinct, efficient description of how the iris had expanded beyond any recorded in the history of the unit; and she gave her best recollection, better than anyone else there, of the thing that had been growing inside the Rift and appeared ready to come out.

Ms. Jones: "An intelligent being?"

Moms had no idea. Nada had yet to weigh in, because no one weighed in unless Ms. Jones invited them.

Ms. Jones: "So the Rift was becoming something else?"

A long pause caused the three men in the Den to exchange glances. Mac raised an eyebrow at Roland and Eagle. Both shrugged.

Ms. Jones: "Ms. Moms?"

Moms: "I believe so."

Ms. Jones: "Mister Nada?"

The team sergeant hefted his weight: "Yes, ma'am."

Another long silence drifted through the Den.

Ms. Jones: "A portal, perhaps."

There was no question mark in the tone, so there was no answer to the statement.

Ms. Jones: "This is not good. We must have that computer's hard drive analyzed."

Nada dared speak up: "Doc is laid up for a while, ma'am. Snakebit."

Ms. Jones let out the rarest of nondialogue cues. A sigh.

Ms. Jones: "We'll have to outsource it to someone on the Acme list. I'll have it taken care of by Support. Now proceed with the mission from drop to completion."

Moms proceeded in full detail, without hesitating, glossing over nothing, as if she were reading from a teleprompter. Moms was like that. She could pull together the chaos of a firefight into a coherent story better than anyone.

Ms. Jones interrupted four times, with specific questions, but it didn't break Moms's narrative. That is until she got to Burns getting wounded. Nada jumped into the breach.

Nada: "He got a load of cactus spikes in his ass, ma'am."

Ms. Jones: "Thank you, Mister Nada."

As if it was the most normal thing in the world to be attacked by a fourteen-foot-high cactus.

Moms picked up the fumble and continued onward until the team had landed back here. She fell silent, and all three men in the Den leaned forward to hear what Ms. Jones would have to say about the whole mess.

Ms. Jones: "The priority, of course, is the change in the Rift. Twenty-seven Rifts and they've all been exactly the same. As far as we know."

Mac looked at Roland and Eagle and he could tell by the looks on their faces that they agreed completely.

Ms. Jones had not been idle while the team flew back. "I checked on the graduate student who ran the Rift program. A Mister Henry Craegen. Working on his PhD in physics. Nothing stands out in his background, but I'm having our Support field agents run a detailed background check to find where he might have found the bootleg copy and how he might have altered it, but I believe the hard drive will yield the most useful information."

A short pause. Then Ms. Jones: "Now about Mister Burns."

Everyone on the team was Ms. or Mister to Ms. Jones. Perhaps, somewhere in the distant past, that was how she had gotten her own moniker. It made the whole nickname thing seem kind of stupid, but it was as stupid as a lot of the other weird stuff they did. They did know part of her story, as it was integral to the lore of the team: she'd been a nuclear engineer in the control room the day Chernobyl blew. That explained the accent. Whatever else had happened to her was a matter of speculation. She'd gotten hit by some bad shit, there was no doubt of that. So bad no one got to see her.

Doc had been the one to float the hologram idea, speculating her voice was piped in while her real body was lying in some intensive care place surrounded by machines and kept alive by tubes, because Doc liked to imagine shit like that was real, and he swore the thing in the chair had flickered for a moment during his in-briefing. Most speculated she was some disfigured, shriveled remains of a human being whose mind could still cut like a knife, while the body was confined to a chair or bed.

How someone from Chernobyl's control room ended up being in charge of the Nightstalkers was a mystery, but Eagle had commented it was about as likely as a muscle-bound weight lifter from Austria ending up governor of California.

In other words, who the hell knew?

Ms. Jones: "Ms. Moms?"

Moms explained Burns's wounds, which was Moms being nice, since it wasn't what Ms. Jones wanted to hear. "Burns suffered severe lacerations of the face, arm, and leg. Basically everywhere on that side where he wasn't protected by body armor. He was fortunate not to have lost his right eye. A spike missed it by a quarter inch, went into his skull, and medical says they're going to have to leave part of it in place as it's touching the optic nerve and pulling it might cause more problems than leaving it alone. His body will just have to heal around it."

"Does he still have vision in the eye?" Ms. Jones asked.

"Yes."

Ms. Jones: "Mister Nada?"

Nada went into a long (more than two sentences) explanation of combat fatigue and how it happened occasionally that a guy lost it on a mission. And might even want out.

The last part caused each of the listening men to look into their own psyche for a moment. They had all been special before coming to Nightstalkers: Green Berets, Rangers, CIA, Black Ops—it ran the gamut. The fact that Ms. Jones picked them meant they had something that went beyond special, into unique. The thing was, none of them were exactly sure what made each one unique.

Ms. Jones: "You believe Mister Burns should be separated, Mister Nada?"

Nada: "I never really trusted him."

Mac snickered because they all knew Nada wouldn't trust a Girl Scout leading a nun across the road. He'd figure there was an angle to it, and it wasn't a good one. In Nada's world, the Girl Scout would throw the nun under the bus, then steal her rosary beads and hock them, using that—along with the money from her cookie sales—to feed her gambling addiction. But Roland frowned at both the snicker and the comment. He knew Nada meant something deeper, something real. Because the funny thing was, no one on the team had ever really trusted Burns. Well, they had at first. You had to. But something had been brewing between Burns and the rest of the team for a while.

Ms. Jones: "Mister Burns was an experiment on my part. I was trying something different and I take responsibility for the decision and the result."

Mac choked down another snicker because Ms. Jones always took responsibility for everything on the team and even Mac couldn't laugh at that. They all knew she had their backs.

A record-setting second sigh came from Ms. Jones.

Ms. Jones: "Mister Burns will be out-processed."

Moms and Nada were silent; the decision had been made.

Ms. Jones: "It could have been worse."

All three men in the outer room—even Mac, who hadn't been there—were nodding, because they all implicitly knew Ms. Jones knew what "worse" was.

Then Ms. Jones began speaking, almost like Moms, except she wasn't detailing *a* mission, she was talking about *the* Mission. It was pretty close to what she'd told each of them individually when they in-processed and it was similar to what they'd all heard when they'd volunteered and made it into whatever high-speed unit they'd come from. It had a catch phrase in those elite organizations: Why We Are Here.

That's why Roland and Eagle and Nada, and even Moms—though she wouldn't admit it—had known Burns was done when he'd been screaming with an ass full of spikes: "Why am I here? Why the hell am I doing this crazy shit?"

They all knew why they were here and they all knew Ms. Jones was repeating it as much to them as to Nada and Moms.

Ms. Jones: "We are here because the best of intentions can go horribly awry and the worst of intentions can achieve exactly what it sets out to do. It is often the noblest scientific inquiry that can produce the end of us all. We are here because we are the last line of defense when the desire to do right turns into a wrong. We are here because mankind advances through trial and error. Because nothing man does is ever perfect. And we are ultimately here because there are things out there, beyond mankind's current knowledge level, that man must be guarded against until man can understand those things. We must remember this."

During the in-brief, she'd then ask each prospective team member: "Can you live with that?"

And they'd all said yes. But every once in a while that yes turned into a big NO, like it had with Burns.

Roland, Eagle, and Mac jumped to their feet as the flimsy door to Ms. Jones's office opened and Moms and Nada walked out.

"You get all that?" Moms asked as she shut the door behind her.

The three nodded.

Nada went over to Mac. Nada was a short, muscular fireplug of a man. He was of Colombian heritage, the dark skin on his face pocked from a childhood sickness. Short gray hair rose straight out of his head as if even his own hair was afraid of the dark thoughts that ran through his brain.

He tapped Mac on the shoulder. "Don't laugh when we're talking with Ms. Jones, okay?"

Mac nodded. It had just occurred to Roland, upon hearing that speech again through the door, that Ms. Jones not only had their backs, she also listened to them over their shoulders to see which way they were facing.

Then Moms and Nada went into the team CP and their door slammed with a solid thud. Whatever they discussed between them stayed in that room.

CHAPTER 3

TWO WEEKS LATER

On the other side of the world, Staff Sergeant Winthrop Carter was not at all where he wanted to be. The officer had lied. For reenlisting, Carter had been promised a slot into Special Forces Assessment and Selection at Fort Bragg, and after passing that—and passing it as he knew he could—he'd be in the year-long Special Forces Qualification Course. And after passing that—and he knew he would—he'd be assigned to the Tenth Special Forces Group (Airborne) and *then* he should have ended up back here in Afghanistan. And in between graduating and deploying he'd have been paid the bonus that had been the entire purpose of reenlisting for SF in the first place.

It wasn't that Carter didn't want to be in a combat zone. This was his fourth tour, having already done one with the First Cav Division and the last two with the Ranger Battalion, but this assignment was bullshit. Besides the fact he hadn't been given his Q-Course slot yet.

What was the point of being a soldier if you didn't serve in combat? But as a Green Beret, not as a glorified taxi driver, carting about some burned-out, drunk-ass lieutenant colonel in a

Humvee, visiting outposts manned by joint US–Afghan forces, filling out paperwork so some guy in Washington could brief some other guy in Washington so that they could dump all the real data anyway, and make up data to give to the people who made the decisions so they would make the decisions they had wanted to make in the first place.

At least that's what Colonel Orlando had groused to Carter on the second day of their journeys together; after several sips from his CamelBak, which Carter knew held something other than water, since the colonel had the same smell Uncle Ray had back home in Parthenon. That's Parthenon, Arkansas, zip code 72666, the last three numbers a dark, unintentional joke by the United States Postal Service that so aptly applied to the place. Parthenon was just an intersection along crumbling Route 327, which ran from nowhere to nowhere. So people only got on it when they got lost looking for somewhere else. Or they came for the meth. Uncle Ray drank to stay off the meth, so it seemed a reasonable deal in Carter's mind. To Carter, Colonel Orlando drank because he was doing a job that could get him killed, which in the long run mattered not in the least in the strategic picture. But pretty much everyone in the 'Stan was doing a job that could get them killed, and drinking in a combat zone wasn't something Carter thought highly of, not that a staff sergeant got to tell a colonel that.

Carter drove cross-country, paralleling the dirt road ten meters to their right, sustaining the jolts and slams of the rough terrain in exchange for avoiding the possibility of an IED ripping their armored Humvee to shreds. Several times he came upon wadis too steep to negotiate and he'd go farther into the country-side searching for a way across. Orlando took these detours with a roll of his eyes and another sip from his CamelBak.

"Geez, son!" Orlando yelled as Carter slithered the vehicle down a particularly treacherous slope, then gunned it up the far side with teeth-rattling jolts. "We can get killed as easy rolling over as getting blown up."

"Yes, sir," Carter said. *Yes, sir. Sorry, sir.* He'd learned those long before the army. There was no such thing as *No, sir*. Not to Pads; his father had prepared Carter well for the army. Not intentionally.

Orlando checked his watch. "Frequency switch. Two-four-seven."

Commo man. He'd been given the designation in the Ranger Battalion, even though his MOS, military occupation specialty, was 11B—infantry, the queen of battle. He'd been sent to all sorts of special schools for commo in the past year that he had never requested, but the one school he'd requested seemed further and further away. He switched the frequencies as the colonel called in to their next destination to let them know they were arriving and to kindly not shoot up the friendlies.

Carter was of average height and lean, whipcord thin, the result of a childhood of hard work, not much food, and constant tension. His face was all angles, but he had the deepest blue eyes, as if there were something gentle deep inside all that exterior hardness.

Carter spotted the brown walls of the next compound they were to inspect. Guard towers crowned each corner of the ancient outpost, the snout of a fifty-caliber machine gun poking over the top of each. Generations of soldiers had passed through the gate of the outpost. Americans. Taliban. Mujahedeen. Russians. British. And on through the extensive invasion roll of Afghanistan. Alexander the Great might have pissed on the place for all anyone knew.

The square facility had twenty-foot-high mud and stone walls, each forty yards long and narrowing from ten feet wide at the base to four at the top. Inside, as per every other compound they'd visited, were headquartered a dozen American military advisers and a contingent of Afghan soldiers. The size of that native contingent varied depending on how bad the local economy was: the worse the economy, the more signed up. Some even stayed more than a few weeks. Most left, went to the next region over, and signed up again, taking the enlistment bonus. *At least* they *got what they were promised*, Carter thought.

Like Vietnamization a generation before, Afghanization—or whatever they were calling it, the system of turning control of the country over to the locals to fight against locals—wasn't going to work. The colonel knew it, his boss knew it, his boss's boss knew it, they all knew it all the way to Washington, but the president was bringing the boys back, and one had to put a positive spin on it.

"I used to do real work," the colonel groused as Carter finally pulled them onto the dirt track, making a beeline for the gates.

"Yes, sir." *I did, too.*

The colonel shot him a look. "Son, you've got no idea of some of the real shit that goes on."

"Yes, sir."

"You know why you didn't go to SFAS and got assigned to me?"

That got Carter's attention. "I do not, sir."

Colonel Orlando shook his head. "Forget it." He laughed. "Nada would probably give very low odds on you."

"What are you talking about, sir? Who is Nada?"

The colonel didn't respond.

"I needed that bonus, sir, for getting through SFAS. My family needed it." Pads would have smacked him for speaking up like that, but Carter was hot, tired, and bored.

The colonel shrugged. "Shit happens. Things never turn out like you think they're going to, Sergeant. You would do well to remember that."

The wooden gates swung open on rusty hinges. Just before he drove through, Carter felt the hair on the back of his neck tingle. Just like it used to before Pads came in, stoked out of his mind on the meth, swinging whatever was handiest. Carter had always tried to stand in the way, but it was Dee—as the oldest—who always took the worst of it.

Carter looked over his shoulder at the dusty landscape behind them but didn't see anything to warrant the feeling. Then they were through, the gates shutting closed.

Waiting for them was a captain sporting the Green Beret that Carter had so desperately wanted. Behind the captain stood two dozen new Afghan recruits in the semblance of a formation, most of them picking their noses or spitting, whatever bored men did when forced to stand somewhere they really didn't want to be.

Carter stopped the Humvee and got out. The captain saluted Orlando and began to walk him around, giving the spiel given a hundred times by captains to colonels, which was *everything was working just great*. Most of the SF team was out on patrol with a bunch of the Afghan recruits, so only a handful of Afghan soldiers were maintaining security.

Carter leaned against the front grille of the Humvee, feeling the heat from the engine matching the heat from the sun overhead. He still couldn't shake the feeling of unease. He scanned the walls. A single Afghan lounged in each tower, supposedly manning the fifty cal, except they were nervously looking inside the compound rather than out.

That wasn't right. The veins in his neck pulsed as his heart surged. He readied his M-4 rifle.

"*Allahu Akbar!*"

Carter wheeled, bringing up his M-4. An Afghan soldier came dashing out of a dark doorway and was running toward Colonel Orlando and the captain and the recruits behind them. The pockets of his combat vest bulged with explosives, and he was crisscrossed with wires, a Christmas tree festooned with C-4 instead of lights. He had his right hand up in the air and a clacker in his hand, a dead man's switch that would ignite the explosives as soon as he let it go. He was already close enough to take most of the recruits, Orlando, and the captain out if he set it off.

Carter had the armored Humvee between him and the bomber. The sergeant dropped the weapon on its sling and sprinted around the protection, faster than the Afghan, faster than he'd ever run in his life. He wrapped his arms around the bomber, one hand clamping down on the Afghan's hand and the dead man's switch.

The two tumbled to the ground, Carter on top. His hand was steel on the Afghan's own and the dead man's switch, and he pressed his other forearm across the man's neck. The bomber was staring up at him, eyes losing focus as Carter choked him out.

When the bomber was unconscious, Carter carefully peeled the man's fingers from the clacker, keeping it depressed. He unscrewed the firing wire before tossing it aside. Then he stood, drawing his pistol, and pointed it down at the bomber, finger curling around the trigger.

* * *

"Easy, son." Colonel Orlando placed his hand over Carter's gun.

The Green Beret captain knelt next to the bomber. The Afghan recruits were nowhere to be seen. The guard towers were unmanned.

"Might as well put a round in him, sir," Carter said. "Once a man commits to that, he's gone over."

Orlando smiled as Carter holstered his pistol. "Once a man commits, he commits. Why didn't you just take the cover of the Humvee?"

Carter shrugged as if the question made no sense. "Wouldn't have been the right thing to do, sir."

The bomber blinked into consciousness and, surprisingly, the captain helped him to his feet.

Carter whipped his pistol back out.

"Easy," Orlando said once more. "He's on our side."

Carter blinked. "What?"

"A test, son, a test."

"I could have killed him."

"I disabled your M-4," Orlando said, "but not your pistol. Which is why I had to stop you."

"You disabled my weapon in a combat zone?" Carter's face was red with anger.

"Don't worry," Orlando said. "The SF team from here has a perimeter set up around us and everyone in here was vetted. You were perfectly safe. One of the parts of the test was to see whether you would try to shoot him with your rifle—in which case you were making a dumb decision and killing a bunch of other people—or if you'd simply save your ass by using the Humvee as a shield, in which case you were making a smart but self-centered decision. You picked door number three. Very few people pick that door."

Orlando reached into a pocket on his combat vest and pulled out a satellite phone. There was only one number it was programmed to call.

It was answered on the first ring.

"Yes?" the vaguely Russian voice answered.

"He passed, Ms. Jones," Orlando said.

"I'll have transportation waiting at Bagram. You get him there. You stay with him the whole way until you get him to the Ranch."

"Got it."

There was a moment of silence. "Good work, Orlando."

"Thanks, Ms. Jones." *And I'm fine too, you bitch*, Orlando thought but didn't say as he turned the phone off. A vein was bulging in Carter's neck and Orlando knew he was going to have one angry man next to him for a journey around the world. A man to whom he could explain nothing.

CHAPTER 4

TWO DAYS LATER

It started with the pretty postdoc who was the point of contact at the University of Colorado.

The Courier had been up all night partying at one of the frat houses, only two years removed from college himself. Or, more accurately, two years removed from his single year of college. After being kicked out of college, he doubled down on that year sucking dirt in the Marines, including a year at Bagram Air Base on the perimeter guard post, shooting at a whole bunch of nothing and basically being bored to tears. The stories he'd told the wide-eyed rich kids at the party were true—that is, if the older grunts who'd told the stories to him in the first place had been telling the truth.

So at the end of his year in 'Stan, when the contractor came calling with offers of big bucks and lots of time off for combat-experienced Marines (they considered a year in-country combat experience, so the boredom counted for something), the Courier had signed on the dotted line and kissed the Corps good-bye. The deal had turned out sweeter than he'd expected. They didn't send him back to the 'Stan but rather to the Depot.

Like any other gig, though, there were drawbacks. One was the implant. The gruff retired gunny sergeant who'd taken him through Depot processing at Area 51 had told him it was a minor physical procedure—he wouldn't feel a thing—and the actual device only had to be worn during the time when he was working. During his two months off for every one on, why, no problem, he could leave it at the Depot. That was where guys like him, the Support for a bunch of high-speed people called the Nightstalkers, were stationed. Underground on the Area 51 military reservation in the middle of no-fucking-where, Nevada. It sounded a lot cooler than it was, both figuratively and literally.

The gunny hadn't been totally up front. The actual procedure was sticking some long, really thin wire into his chest. It left the tiniest of nubs sticking out just center and below his left nipple. That wasn't coming out as long as he was in Support. Then when he came on duty they strapped a belt around his chest that had a matchbox—scratch that, he wasn't old enough to have used matchboxes—an iPod Mini–sized device right over the nub and connected it to him.

When he'd asked what the device was for, the old gunny had told him: "So we can track you and make sure you're okay. We don't want nothing to happen to you, sonny-boy."

So, okay, for one month's work and two off, he could deal with it. And, of course, for the pay. That was ten large every month, even the ones he wasn't working. The Tea Party would have a fit.

They gave him some guns, a souped-up armored van, a thick binder full of what they called "protocols," and a handheld device the gunny called an Invoicer (the way he said it indicated it was capitalized, like a lot of stuff around the place). It contained his deliveries for this tour of duty.

"Like a FedEx driver?" the Courier had asked.

The gunny had just glared at him for a moment, then shook his head. "Read the Protocols, sonny." The gunny had looked about as if the walls had ears. "You do good on Support, there's a chance you make the team out at the Ranch. They're short one body on the 'Stalkers. Been short a while. Ms. Jones is real picky about who makes the team."

What are we, back in high school? the Courier thought but did not say, having had experience with gunnies in the Corps.

The key to being a Courier, the gunny explained, was to keep a low profile. A single panel truck, a single man, playing it cool, wouldn't draw attention the way a clearly armored vehicle and escort convoy would.

Whatever, the Courier thought.

There were eight deliveries, all around Colorado, Utah, Idaho, and Nevada. Pick this up here, drop it there. Then the next, and the next.

He'd gotten briefed, along with other new Support personnel, by some Nightstalker people with weird names: Moms and Nada and Doc. Moms told them to be very, very careful, and Nada told them to read the Protocols very, very carefully and then follow them exactly to the letter, and if they had any questions, any at all, there were no dumb questions, to call on the sat phone they were each issued.

The Courier knew from high school there were dumb questions. Those were the nerds who never got laid.

At least in high school. He wasn't experienced enough to know the inverse of that formula as one got older.

The last guy, Doc, had some really scary shit to say about bugs and viruses and nukes and stuff that would kill you, which the Courier wasn't sure how to take. According to this Doc guy, looking the wrong way could cause you to get some disease and die a horrible death.

At first he'd felt really cool, driving the van with all the guns and high-tech gear. After the seventh time, though—loading a sealed locker full of who the hell knew what in the vault in the back, driving 387 miles from some computer tech place in Boise, ID, to Dugway Proving Grounds in Utah (he knew the exact mileage because one of the Protocols required him to fill out all these little boxes on the electronic invoices and two of them were start and end mileage of each run, as if he were going to detour to Malibu or some such; plus he had no doubt the van GPS and the damn thing plugged into his chest were also recording everything)—it began to get boring.

He hauled ass for invoice eight, looking forward to the promised time off, with pay, after delivery. Vegas. That's what was on his mind as he tore through the Rockies on I-70 at ninety miles an hour. Six hundred and twenty-four miles to Boulder. Protocol said don't speed, but they'd given him a badge and a very official-looking card with his photo on it, that the gunny had told him would make any local law enforcement fuck off, because he was working for the FEDERAL government, even though technically he was only contracted. That technicality made a difference, a big one. Federal employees took something called the Oath of Office, the very first law enacted by the very first Congress, so those Founding Fathers had felt it was important. Courier got ten large each month instead and signed a contract. Either way, he got into Boulder a night early.

And partied.

He was sure there was something in Chapter 40 of the Protocol (it was pretty damn thick) about not partying the night before a drive, but he'd read what he needed to and skimmed the rest. He'd make the pickup the next day right on time.

And he did. Wearing fresh khakis, his Glock nestled inside his leather jacket, he checked the file once more before he entered the Biochemistry Building at the University of Colorado. He recognized the Point of Contact in the courtyard outside the building from the picture in the file and she looked better in person than the drab photo that must have been taken for her student ID. He walked over.

"Hey."

That drew him the withering smile pretty girls reserve for "not now, I'm busy" until he pulled out his badge and ID.

"I hear you've got something for me, Ms. Debbie Simmons."

Her eyes grew wide. She looked around as if there were spies hiding behind the bushes. Which the Courier found humorous because they weren't in the bushes, but rather hundreds of miles overhead with a clear line of sight. His first platoon sergeant in the Marines had told him no one ever looked up. He had been referring to snipers in trees, but once the Courier got to Nightstalkers' Support, old Nada, in his briefing, had modified that to include what you couldn't see way up there circling the planet. The unblinking eyes in the sky.

She swallowed and nodded. "Follow me."

They entered the building and she walked past the elevators, which the Courier found odd, and opened a fire door. They began to troop up the stairs, which was when the Courier became rather intrigued with her ass. He tried to make small talk, but she was in crisis mode and everyone knows that people worried about their careers seldom flirted. Instead they tended to talk and explain.

"I don't know why I got stuck with it. I just did the lab work. The professor did all the real work on the project. And the professor was insistent that no one have access to her data."

The Courier could give a shit, and her taking one step at a time was hurting his knees. He wanted to bound up at least two, if not three at a time. She kept explaining as if the Courier hadn't read the Invoicer, or been briefed by Moms and Nada and Doc.

He and the others had been grilled with Nada "what-ifs": *What if you can't locate the Point of Contact? What if the Package is breached? What if gravity as you know it ceases to exist...*

Or, as everyone in Support called it, the Yada-Yada from Nada. But never when he was around.

"The problem is, well, the professor, she must have gone on sabbatical, at least that's what the dean said. Sort of. And I got stuck with it. So we brought it over in the safe it came in and up the elevator and into the most secure lab."

If you got an elevator, why are we taking the stairs? the Courier thought.

"I followed the rules in the book the professor had."

The Courier felt heartened that he wasn't the only one who had to follow Protocols.

"It's locked up here, because the bio people have the most secure areas." Simmons literally shivered. "It scares me, some of the stuff they work with."

"Why are we climbing the stairs?"

"I use the stairs for the exercise," she explained. That explained her tight body, but also a sense of narcissism to include him in her workout routine while he was on a job.

"Everything should be all right and up to date," she continued as they made it to a door with a big 6 stenciled on it.

The Courier wanted to tell her Nada's theory during his lecture about *should be*, which Nada had said often translated to *what the fuck?*

"I don't really see the big deal," Simmons prattled on as she led him down the hall to a door with all sorts of warning signs and big biohazards symbols. "It's pretty small."

He decided to show the college girl up, with a tidbit of knowledge he'd had hurled at him during the Support briefing by Doc. He tapped the closest yellow sign. "The engineer who developed the biohazard sign said: 'We wanted something that was memorable but meaningless, so we could educate people as to what it means.'"

He remembered that because it was one of the dumbest things—among many dumb things—he'd been told, not even realizing his remembering actually validated the engineer's point.

She stopped talking for a moment and stared at him as if he had two heads. "The professor has never taken a day off since I've known her. She's always like ice; nothing bothers her, but this," the girl nodded at the steel door, "this bothered her. Why would the professor take a sabbatical now?"

"Right," the Courier said, not really listening to her, eyes on her breasts. Figuratively, wishing for literally.

Shaking her head, Simmons entered a punch code and the door slid open.

They walked over to another door that required a second punch code, as well as a retina scan this time, so he knew they were getting close to the Package.

There was a safe inside the next room.

An old iron safe, like Butch and Sundance used to rob.

She pulled out a rumpled piece of paper and began twirling in the combination and he stifled a laugh. He could see Nada's long hand in this last line of bullshit.

"So the Package is all right," she said with enough degree of uncertainty that even the Courier realized why the government was taking this particular thing away from the university boys and girls. "So you can see the problem?" she asked, indicating she had no clue what the problem was. She swung open the heavy door and pulled out a small metal box.

For the Courier the problem was that his knees were killing him.

She was anxious to pass the problem over to him. "I don't know why the dean was so upset, since he had to have given the professor the sabbatical."

The Courier tuned her out once more. He didn't see any opening to the box. There was a set of numbers etched on the side after the letters *ASU*. He checked his Invoicer. Bingo. "Okay." He held out the Invoicer. "Sign here, here, and here on the screen and I'll be off."

"The professor was really, really upset about getting this in the first place," Simmons said as she scrawled with the electronic pen. "She said it should have never been sent here. She said someone named Doc should have been responsible, not her. And certainly not me," she added as if he didn't get it.

"Someone is taking care of it. Now. Me." The Courier grabbed the Invoicer from her and hefted the Package under one arm. It was light, for which he was grateful.

"What about the safe?" Simmons asked, looking as if she had to take the thing home.

"Not on my form."

"I did everything correctly, right?" Simmons asked. "You'll keep it safe, right?"

She seemed overly concerned about something for which she was no longer responsible, even the Courier could see that. "I work for the government," he said. "This is my job. It's taken care of."

He didn't say good-bye. Not that it mattered: she didn't do small talk, yet she talked too damn much, he thought as he took the elevator down. He unsealed the back of the van and secured the box in the vault that took up half the rear, the rest being full of weapons and other military equipment.

He got in the driver's seat and accessed the onboard computer. He synced the Invoicer, indicating a positive pickup, and waited for the machine to tell him his next, and final for this tour, destination.

Area 51 Archives.

The GPS calculated the route in seconds. Seven hundred and seventy-seven miles.

"Hot damn," he muttered as he started the van up.

Not far from Vegas at all.

* * *

To Carter, it just looked like an old deserted filling station out in the middle of the desert. Colonel Orlando was driving the battered Jeep, which was the latest in a bunch of strange things to happen ever since he'd been "tested" back in the 'Stan.

Since then, Orlando hadn't said two words, ignoring every question Carter had thrown at him, and using the defense of that silver oak leaf indicating his rank to treat Carter like the staff sergeant he was.

Except after landing at some incredibly long runway in the middle of Nevada, the colonel had gotten in the driver's seat of this old beat-up Jeep that had been waiting for them. A colonel driving for a staff sergeant wasn't normal, even for the elite army. They'd been bumping along for over an hour now, leaving the runway and the hangars and the guards and all that far behind.

Two minutes ago, Orlando had turned off the hardtop road onto a dirt road, passing a plywood sign spray-painted none too steadily with the warning *NO TRESPASS: WE WILL SHOOT YOUR ASS* along with a skull and crossbones also crudely sprayed onto the wood next to the words. Now the old gas station was ahead on the right and Carter could see three guys shooting a beat-up basketball at a metal rim set about eight feet off the ground on a leaning light pole. He knew right away they were Special Ops, even though two had long hair. It was the same way at Bragg, where you could always tell the difference between guys in the Eighty-Second Airborne, not exactly slouches, and someone in Special Forces. They looked different because they were different.

The three didn't even look over as Orlando screeched the protesting brakes of the Jeep, bringing them to a halt a hundred yards short of the station. Carter saw the reason. Two men had materialized from spider holes, weapons at the ready. Carter blinked as a red laser designator wavered over his face, settling in between his eyes. Shifting his glance to the left, he saw Orlando also wore a red dot.

A third man, who must have been in a hole, too, came up from behind. He held some weird device and flashed it in Orlando's eyes. It beeped, and since the colonel wasn't shot, Carter assumed that was a positive beep. All three wore ghillie suits with black fatigues underneath and no sign of rank or unit, so Carter figured they were contractors. He'd seen a ton of them in the 'Stan and Iraq. The guard started to go around the rear of the Jeep—not crossing the line of fire of the others—when Orlando spoke up.

"He's the new one."

The guard nodded, looking vaguely disappointed for some reason, as if Carter were stealing his role in the school play. "Proceed, Colonel."

Orlando put the Jeep into gear, the clutch protesting loudly.

One of the three, a tall black man whose left side of the face was terribly scarred, took a long shot and it flew past rim and pole into a pile of old tires, sending them tumbling. A rattler came buzzing out, trying to see who'd interrupted its late-day nap.

"Yo!" one of the others, a big hulking guy with what Carter initially would have called an honest, happy face, yelled. "Eagle got a snake."

"I hate fucking snakes," Eagle said.

"Tell Doc about snakes," the third guy said with a Texas drawl. He was a young Tom Cruise look-alike, handsome in a way that initially irritated almost every man who met him.

"Fuck you, Mac," Eagle said to him as he drew a Mark-23 from under his T-shirt and fired, hitting the snake in the head, and firing again, hitting the stump.

"No one would think you were any army of one," Mac said. "Afraid of snakes." He stepped over the body and retrieved the ball. "We used to eat rattler back home in Texas. Tastes like chicken."

"Bet you had to eat rattler," the big guy said, with all seriousness. "My mom used to make us pine bark soup flavored with pine needles."

"You had one fucked-up childhood, Roland," Mac said. "We ate it 'cause we liked it."

Carter got out of the Jeep as Orlando did. Now that he was closer to the big man, he could see that thing deep in Roland's eyes that belied his genial face. The man was a killer.

The three finally decided to notice the newcomers.

Eagle nodded at Orlando. "Colonel."

"Eagle. Roland. Mac." Orlando nodded three times, like he was blessing them or asking permission to pass, it was hard for Carter to tell. "Been a while."

"It has indeed, sir," Eagle said. He looked at Carter. "Must be an officer. He isn't covered in shit."

Orlando was the only one who got it, and he laughed as he got back in the driver's seat. "You gentleman have a fine rest of the day. Until next time."

Carter hastily grabbed his duffel out of the back of the Jeep. And then the colonel was gone in a cloud of dust. Carter stood there, uncomfortable in the late-day sun, duffel bag weighing on his shoulder, his camos drenched with sweat. He knew they were reading the cues on his fatigues: Ranger Tab, left shoulder; Ranger Regiment scroll, right shoulder, meaning combat service with the unit; Combat Infantry Badge; Master Parachute Badge; Free-fall Parachute Badge; Scuba Badge.

Most people were impressed.

These were clearly not most people.

"Where do I report?" Carter asked.

"Get a grape soda," Mac said as the other two turned back to the basketball and their game.

"I don't want a grape soda." Carter regretted the words as he spoke them.

Mac laughed. "Buddy, no one wants a grape soda, but one time me and this hot little cheerleader, all we had was some Jack and some grape soda, and it worked then. It'll work now," he added, nodding toward the rusting soda machine leaning against the side of the station.

Carter went over. The peeling labels indicated he could get Dr. Pepper, Pepsi, Orange, or Grape. Twenty-five cents. He reached for his pocket, then realized he didn't have any change. Before he could turn, Eagle called out.

"Just push the button. And make sure it's grape. You don't want the orange, trust me."

Carter hit the grape button.

With a hiss of escaping air, the soda machine slid to the side and a stairway beckoned, cool air blasting out.

Carter hesitated.

"You got eight seconds," Eagle added as he took a shot. "Or it will shut on you."

Carter scooted down the stairs and the door slid in place above him. He caught his bearings for a second, then continued down. He reached a landing, noting the unblinking eye of a camera staring at him. There was someone at the other end of that camera and Carter shivered for a second.

There was a steel door facing him, one that just screamed "try and blast me open and let me laugh at you." The door slid aside and a gray corridor beckoned. A figure filled the corridor. Short, built like a power-lifter, dark skinned with an acne-scarred face, gray hair, and an attitude that said he was the one who ran things. The well-worn handle of a machete poked over his left shoulder from a sheath on his back and he had an MK-23 strapped to his right hip, tied down with a strap around his thigh.

Carter stiffened to attention as the door slid shut behind him.

"We don't do that shit here," the man said.

The door behind opened once more and the three who had been playing basketball pressed by, paying Carter no heed.

"I'm Nada."

Nada? Carter thought. "I'm—"

"I know who you think you are," Nada said, "or else you'd be a pile of ashes back there on the landing."

Eagle laughed as he looked over his shoulder at the end of the corridor. "Best to forget who you were and focus on who you will be."

"That's real fucking Zen-like," Mac said.

"Follow me," Nada ordered. "And drop that bag. You won't need any of that shit."

They went down the hallway and into a large circular room with dull gray walls. There were several tables in it, along with whiteboards, flip charts, corkboards for imagery, and a row of lockers. The three from outside were stripping off their soaking shirts.

"You're meeting Ms. Jones," Nada said, stopping in front of a surprisingly flimsy and ill-fitting door, the antithesis of everything Carter had seen since entering the complex. "You listen to her very carefully."

The door to the left opened and a tall woman in fatigues stepped out. The way Nada shifted his posture, Carter realized with surprise that he answered to her, so he stood a little straighter.

"I'm Moms," the woman said.

Moms? Carter was trying to take it all in.

"I was just telling him to listen carefully to Ms. Jones," Nada informed her.

Moms nodded. "Listen to her offer. Then you get to say yes or you get to say no. There's no shame, no blemish on your record for saying no."

"No is the easy way," Eagle yelled from across the room.

"No is back to the world," Mac added.

"Hush," Roland scolded the other two. "Moms is talking."

Moms put a hand on Carter's shoulder. "You understand?"

"Yes, ma'am."

Mac laughed. "He ain't got a fucking clue."

Moms nodded at Nada. He rapped on the flimsy door, rattling it on the hinges. Then he swung it open and indicated for Carter to go in. "Take the seat in front of the desk. Do not get out of the seat until dismissed, then come straight back out here. Anything else and I'll kill you."

He said it so matter-of-factly that Carter only realized he was serious after taking three steps into the room. A hard plastic chair faced a massive wooden desk. The smooth surface of the desk was unmarred by any phone, computer, or knick-knack. Behind the desk was a huge wing-backed chair, the occupant completely in the shadow cast by the large lights pointed directly at the plastic chair.

Carter sat down, hands on his knees, feeling like he'd been called into the principal's office and he'd done something really bad—like burn down the school.

The voice startled him, not only with the accent, but the suddenness. "You do know, of course, that someone has to man the walls in the middle of the night? The walls between all those innocents out there who lay their heads down on their pillows every evening, troubled by thoughts of such things as mortgages, or their pet is sick, or their child is failing in school? The normal things people should worry about. There are even those who have grave, serious worries, such as just being diagnosed with pancreatic cancer and given weeks to live. But the things we, here, worry about, they are far graver than any of those worries."

Carter didn't know if she was really asking or if it was a test, so he followed Uncle Ray's advice and said nothing.

Ms. Jones continued. "Someone has to worry about those things that go bump in the night, and let me assure you, young man, there *are* things that go bump in the night."

Like Pads going after Dee, Carter thought. He knew there were bad things in the night.

As if reading his mind she continued. "Of course you sort of do, given your background. You did very well in the test with Colonel Orlando. You did very well in the Ranger Battalion and in your combat tours. You did very well in Ranger School. Surprisingly well, considering everyone thought you had been flunked after speaking back to that Ranger instructor. You were a wash-out. A recycle. Yet somehow when they printed out the roster for graduation, there was your name on it. Everyone was quite surprised. Including the graders who had flunked you."

Carter sat straighter in the chair. He'd known someone would come after him about that sooner or later. "I earned my Ranger Tab," he said defensively, throwing aside all the advice he'd grown up with, just like he'd done that hot day in the Florida swamp with the asshole RI. "I earned my combat patch in the Ranger Regiment. There's many who wear the tab who never served with the Regiment."

"Oh, yes," Ms. Jones said. "You earned the tab. The computer said so. The interesting question is how the computer could have said so when the data the—I believe they are called RIs?—put into it flunked you."

Silence fell over the room as Ms. Jones waited. Carter fidgeted, not sure which way to go, just knowing he was at a critical juncture not only in his career but in the rest of his life.

"Truth doesn't set you free," Ms. Jones said. "It just keeps you alive in the Nightstalkers."

Carter blinked in surprise. "Task Force 160? I thought they were at Campbell and—"

"Not *those* Nightstalkers," Ms. Jones said with a hint of frost. "When Task Force 160 was formed in 1981, we switched *our* name to Nightstalkers also, because it's always best to have a cover behind some other classified unit. As you just indicated, it works for misdirection. We prefer to be a shadow inside of a shadow."

"What were you called before that?" Carter asked.

"That is not important," Ms. Jones said. "And, as a bonus, Nightstalkers was appropriate. As I told you, we're the ones who man the walls against the things that go bump in the night. Do not make me repeat myself. How did you pass Ranger School when you should have flunked?"

"I cheated, ma'am."

"Very good," Ms. Jones said. "How?"

"I knew they were gonna flunk me for sassing back at that RI. But he made a comment about my sister, and he didn't even know I had a sister. Got two actually. So I snuck out the night before graduation. Everyone else was wiped out. The last night, after the last patrol, after the entire course, everyone reaches their limits and just collapses."

"But not you."

"I knew they were gonna flunk me." Carter flushed as he realized he'd repeated himself. "I couldn't flunk. I needed to graduate."

"For the tab?" This time it was a question.

Carter swallowed, but he was too far down the alley of truth and the walls were closing in. "No, ma'am. I needed the pay bonus."

She didn't ask what for, which surprised him. "How did you cheat?"

"I snuck out. Went to the command shed. Stole a smartphone they use for commo. Hacked into the system. Changed my grade."

Ms. Jones waited.

"Then I got all the score sheets. Took them over to the admin shed. Scanned every one on me. Photoshopped all of them and changed mine to passing. Took them all out into the swamp. Roughed them up and stained them like the originals. That took a while, as I had to dry them off afterward to make them look real. Put them back."

"They knew you cheated."

Carter remembered the uproar, the RIs swearing the forms with their signatures weren't right, that the computer was wrong. The sheets were wrong. "Yes, ma'am."

"But they graduated you because the computer said so and they were afraid you would appeal and lawyers would get involved and it would be a mess. Easier to move you on."

"Yes, ma'am."

"What a sad state the army is in when an RI just can't flunk a student with his word as a soldier and that a computer can overrule him. It's a recipe for disaster. I predict you'll see a similar disaster like that if you say yes to my question. Which, of course, is why you're here."

Then Ms. Jones gave the *why we are here* speech. When she was done, she simply asked: "Can you live with that?"

Carter hesitated, which he knew was bad, but he had to ask. "Ma'am, I reenlisted for Special Forces. And—"

"For the bonus, not because you particularly wanted to be a Green Beret, correct?"

"Yes, ma'am."

Ms. Jones remained silent and Carter was tempted to tell her why he needed the bonuses, but he knew Dee would have told him a man doesn't beg. He only gets that which is his due.

Finally Ms. Jones broke the silence and there was, strangely enough, approval in her voice. "You send all your money to your family. To your older sister, Dee. Correct?"

"Yes, ma'am."

"To look after your younger siblings."

That was not a question.

"Your father blew himself up recently cooking methamphetamine, correct?" Ms. Jones did not wait for an answer. "And the county is going to seize the family house and land for back taxes. You need not worry, young man. Your land and house will not be seized by the government. The exact amount of money that you should have gotten in your reenlistment bonus for Special Forces will be sent to your sister. Understand, though, that unlike our Support, who are contractors—a move I was completely against but was overruled on—we are not mercenaries in the Nightstalkers. We are soldiers. You have sworn an oath."

"Yes, ma'am."

"Your answer?"

"Yes, ma'am."

There was the grinding sound of a shredder operating in the darkness. "That was your service record. Winthrop Carter no longer exists," Ms. Jones said. "You may go and learn what name options the team has chosen for you."

He got up and went to the door. It swung open before his hand touched the knob and Nada was waiting for him, pulling him into the Den, the door swinging shut behind. On one of the whiteboards five names were written, each in a different color:

Slick

Know

Cheetah

Fred

Kobayashi Maru

"Gentlemen," Moms said. "Please read your choices and explain where needed," she added with a quizzical glance at Eagle.

Roland spoke first. "I think we name him Slick. 'Cause what he did in Ranger School was, well, slick." The big man flushed red.

Moms was next. "I think we call him Know. Because we all know the *n* in Ranger stands for Knowledge." She said the old joke with a smile to take away any possible sting.

Mac was standing next to a plastic garbage can. "Shoot, we call him Cheetah, 'cause that's what he is. Fast and smart."

Nada was frowning, but that was Nada's usual look. "Fred. Every team needs a Fred."

"My choice," Eagle began, "is—"

"We ain't using two damn words," Nada interrupted. "You know the rule. One name. An easy word. And one that won't confuse us, so I think Know is out, sorry, Moms."

"It's okay," Moms said, meaning she'd never been in.

Ms. Jones's voice came through the door, surprisingly vibrant. She always sounded perky during the name-choosing ceremony. "What did you write, Mister Eagle?"

"Kobayashi Maru," Eagle said. "I know the rule about one word and—"

"I believe," Ms. Jones said, surprisingly interrupting Eagle's attempt at explaining, "I know where you are going with this. From the old American television series *Star Trek*. I watched it as a child in the former Soviet Union. Yes, we had a television. The test that was lose-lose, where choosing either way was wrong. And Captain Kirk cheated on it by reprogramming the computer. Very interesting."

There was a silence as they waited on Ms. Jones to make her ruling now that she had all the entries.

"The thing I liked about what our new team member did," Ms. Jones said, "was not reprogramming the computer. Any fool can reprogram a computer. Even the Photoshopping of the score sheets was to be expected. But he did all of them, not just his own. So they would all look alike and his wouldn't stand out. And weathering them. That was the nice touch. Welcome to the team, Mister Kirk."

"Hot damn!" Mac exclaimed, a can of Pearl beer in each hand. He tossed the first to Moms, the next to Nada. He pulled and pitched until everyone had a cold brew in hand. He popped the tab and everyone else did. "To Kirk."

"To Kirk," the team echoed.

"I like it," Nada said after taking a deep draft of the beer. "Short. One syllable."

Kirk was a bit overwhelmed as his teammates came by, slapping on his shoulder, calling him by his new name. When Mac came up, Kirk clanked cans with him.

"Thanks for the brew, Mac. I didn't think they made this in the can anymore."

"They don't," Mac said. "My daddy owned a piece of the company before it got broke up and he got a warehouse full outside of San Anton'.'"

"You got a daddy?" Roland said, smiling.

Mac's face went hard. "Yeah, I do, and he's a right mean son-of-a-bitch."

Roland flushed red and he tried to stutter out an apology, but couldn't gather the right words; he was better with guns than words. Moms reached out and placed a comforting hand on Mac's shoulder, which he shrugged off angrily. She glanced at Nada and he gave the slightest shake of his head.

Then Mac suddenly smiled and the room lit up. He ran around Roland's massive form and the big man reacted slowly, because he was only fast in combat mode, and Mac jumped on his back. "Lookie there. Roland made a funny. Someone alert the news." He poured his can of beer over Roland's head while the big man halfheartedly slapped at him with his massive paws.

Nada shook his head. "Fucking *F-Troop*."

"What's *F-Troop*?" Roland asked, Mac still on his back.

Ms. Jones's voice came through the door loud and clear. "Another classic television show of the sixties. A western comedy. Very amusing about a bunch of misfits cast together." She made a strange sound, and Nada started for the door thinking she was choking…and then everyone realized it was Ms. Jones laughing.

After an awkward pause, everyone started chatting again. Mac slid off Roland's back and passed more beers out.

"What would you have done with the beer if I'd said no?" Kirk asked Mac.

Mac laughed. "Drank it anyway."

"No one says no," Eagle said. "That's why she's Ms. Jones. She picked you."

For a surprising third time Ms. Jones cut in. "And do you know why I picked Mister Eagle, Mister Mac?"

Mac didn't hesitate. "He's a fucking great pilot, Ms. Jones."

"He is indeed," Ms. Jones confirmed. "But great pilots are easy to find. He's also a superb navigator. The combination of those two is still relatively common in the big scheme of things."

Moms looked at Nada questionably. Nada just shrugged.

Ms. Jones continued. "Did you know that London cab drivers have a larger hippocampus on average than most other people so they can memorize the maze of streets upon which they ply their trade? Eagle has a hippocampus that puts theirs to shame. That is why he has arcane knowledge such as the Kobayashi Maru and the Holy Hand Grenade of Antioch as well as his technical skills. He also has quite a bit of useful knowledge in his brain."

Now it was Eagle's turn to flush, the scars on the left side of his face pulsing darker with blood.

Moms stood close to Nada and whispered so only he could hear. "Something's wrong. Ms. Jones has never spoken this much."

"I know," Nada said. "We're screwed."

Ms. Jones finished: "Drink your Pearl, gentlemen and Ms. Moms."

Kirk stared at the can of beer in his hand. "How'd she know we were drinking Pearl?"

* * *

In the darkness of her real office, lying in her hospital bed, Ms. Jones listened through the speaker as the team wrapped up the naming ceremony with more beers. She turned off her microphone and the holographic image generated by the machine in the chair in her office.

And she worried about things she had no control over and things that others couldn't even conceive of.

Because that's why she was Ms. Jones.

CHAPTER 5

The Courier made it through the Rockies and just past Salt Lake City at dark. He pulled into one of those huge truck stops to get gas, pee, and grab some coffee and something to chow down on. He gassed up, parked away from any other vehicles, got out, then set the three separate locks and alarm systems on the van before heading over to the bright lights of the station.

As he was peeing he noticed the condom machine on the wall, which naturally got him thinking about the tight ass on that student at UC. Daddy probably footing her bill through school, while people like him ended up in the 'Stan. Conveniently forgetting, of course, that his father had paid for his solo year, then yanked the plug when he ended up with four incompletes.

He was still thinking about the student's ass, and not the realities of his own life's shortcomings, as he made his way back to the van. He laboriously pushed the codes that disarmed and unlocked the thing, then got in. He perched his cup of coffee on the dashboard. There was no cup holder. The computer that ran through the GPS display took that slot. She'd had a nice rack, too, he remembered as he unwrapped the hoagie he'd bought. He was just about to take a sip of coffee when a rap at the window caused him to slosh some over the side and onto his pants.

"Damn!"

With his free hand—his off hand, as his gun hand was still holding the coffee—he scrambled awkwardly for the Glock. He was a contortionist for a moment, trying to put the coffee back down and trying to get the gun, which was still in his holster and not in his lap, where it was supposed to be as per Protocol when in the vehicle, when he saw that the rappee was a cute young girl with long, dirty-blonde hair hanging out of a knitted wool cap and a lollipop dangling out of the corner of her mouth. If he'd thought it through, he, like anyone else with common sense, could have come up with Nada's Yada about pretty young hookers at truck stops: *They don't exist.*

He didn't think it through. Not that way, at least.

He ceased all activity and took a deep breath. He placed the coffee carefully on the dash and pulled his other hand out from under his jacket.

"What?" he mouthed.

She indicated for him to roll down the window.

Bulletproof, he thought. *Doesn't roll down. Ever.*

He shook his head.

She pouted.

He tapped the window, made a rolling down gesture, and slashed his other hand across that, indicating, he hoped in truck stop language, that the window was indeed incapable of being opened.

She pointed past him and looked over his shoulder, while his hand—the correct one this time—was going for the gun. But he saw no threat behind him. He looked back at her quizzically.

She smiled and slowly pulled the sucker from her mouth. Then she pointed at it at him, and then past him at the passenger seat.

It didn't even take a year of college to figure that out.

Then she signaled with two fingers and then a zero.

Twenty bucks?

The Courier thought of that smart-assed college girl.

He glanced down at the muted GPS display. Area 51 was 429 miles away and then he'd have to debrief, fill out a shitload of paperwork, and drive two hours to get to Vegas.

Too damn far and too long.

He nodded, and she walked around the front of the van.

As she did so, he pulled the Glock out and placed it on his left side, within ready reach. He took out his wallet, removed a twenty, and shoved the wallet farther down on the left side of the seat. He wasn't stupid, after all. Hookers were known to rob people. Let her try and she'd be in for a surprise.

Thinking of pulling the Glock on her excited him as much as watching her climb in the door as he shoved it open for her. She tossed the sucker over her shoulder as she squirmed in.

She smiled, didn't say a word. She took the twenty and leaned over into his lap.

College girl would have still been talking, he thought.

She unzipped him. Her hand was cold, but exciting enough, and he thought once more of the Glock, of putting it against her head as her lips closed on him. He leaned back, fingers closing around the grip of the Glock, eyes half-closed.

She pulled her mouth off him with the same slow movement she'd done with the lollipop.

He looked down. She smiled up at him with wide, innocent eyes as she shoved open the driver's door.

Stunned, the Courier looked to his left, into the visage of a human monster. The man's face was terribly scarred, with lateral marks across it as if he'd been flayed. The man smiled as he jammed the icepick into the soft spot on the bottom of the Courier's jaw, right up into his brain.

He was dead before the Glock hit the floor.

The girl screamed and scrambled back against the passenger door.

"You said you were robbing him! Not killing him!"

"I am robbing him," Burns said. He had a silenced Beretta in his off hand and he fired a round right between her eyes, following it up with a second bullet, sticking to Nada's Yada to always double-tap in the head and make sure they're dead.

CHAPTER 6

Two beers were all the Nightstalkers were allowed, although Mac snuck four. Moms was firm about that rule in the Den, but it was her and Nada's turn to in-brief the newly minted Kirk. Roland, Mac, and Eagle ambled off to their little rooms—cells almost—to catch some Zs while Kirk cleaned up before going into the CP. New guys always cleaned up. It was the same in every unit around the world.

As Kirk tossed the last can into the trash, the door to the Den from the outside corridor hissed open and a short man with glasses walked in. He spotted Kirk and smiled.

"Good day. I am Doc." His voice was almost musical with a strong trace of his parents' Indian accent. He held a finger up to his lips as Kirk was about to reply. He looked at the whiteboard. "Let me guess what Ms. Jones picked."

He frowned as he read the list. "Know is out, naturally. A pathetic attempt at humor in some way, perhaps by Mac or Moms. Slick would be Roland. He wants a Slick and he does not care who it is. Ah, Cheetah. That would be Mac since Fred is Nada. Nada thinks every team needs a Fred and we are never going to have one. So Moms did Know. She never wants to name anyone. As if she does not take enough responsibility."

Kirk waited patiently as Doc unraveled the naming mystery that was only a mystery to him.

"So that leaves Eagle with Kobayashi Maru, and Ms. Jones almost always goes with him, but I do not see it this time. Kobe? Maru?"

"Kirk."

Doc blinked, cocked his head, and then nodded. "Ah. Got it. *Star Trek.* So you are a cheater, no disrespect intended, a former Ranger, and Ms. Jones chose you. As good an intro as you can get. Welcome to the Nightstalkers."

"Thanks, Doc."

"Nada did get to name me. He broke his Fred rule and said every team's medic had to be called Doc, and Ms. Jones went along with him." Doc sighed. "I am indeed a medical doctor, by the way, so come to me with any ailments or concerns. But I also have four PhDs in—"

The door to the CP cracked open and Nada stuck his head out. "Yeah, Doc, we know you're a multiple professor of whatever and wherever, but we need the new guy. And welcome back."

"Thanks, Na—" But the door was shut. Doc's shoulders slumped. "I suppose since I missed the naming ceremony I missed my two beers?"

Kirk nodded and reached into the other can, pulling out two cold ones. Doc sat down with a sigh and popped open the first. "When will these uncouth savages learn about champagne or wine?" he asked no one in particular. He then looked back at Kirk. "It is best not to keep Moms waiting."

Kirk went to the door and knocked, barely making an audible thud in the steel. It seemed Nada had been on the other side waiting and opened it immediately, escorting him in. The walls of the CP were covered with maps, satellite imagery, and printouts of things Kirk couldn't make sense of in his quick glance about.

Moms sat behind one desk, Nada taking his place behind the other. They were standard government-issue gray desks and they faced the door from opposite corners of the CP. Surprisingly, a plump armchair was in the center facing them.

Kirk suspected a trap, perhaps no support in the seat, and sat down gingerly. But the chair was firm. Even comfortable, which further aroused his suspicions.

Moms started. "Every unit I ever went into, when I met the CO, it was always a series of warnings. Don't fuck up. Don't do this. Don't do that. Behave. And I've walked into a lot of units in my time. Your experience?"

Kirk ran his career reel through his head. "The same, Ms. Moms."

"Save the Ms. shit for Ms. Jones. There's no Ms. or Misters here. I'm Moms. That's it. You're Kirk. He's Nada. I heard Doc out there. Just Doc. Got it?"

"Just Doc. Got it."

Moms smiled slightly. Kirk noticed a bend in her nose and knew it had been broken and badly set a long time ago. Dee's nose had the same crook. From Pads's fist. Kirk pulled his mind back to the present as Moms continued.

"The ceremony outside is real. The people are real. We're very happy to have you on the team." She glanced to her left. "Right?"

"Oh, yeah." Nada was pulling open a drawer in his desk and glanced up. "Thrilled beyond words."

"If you notice, we don't wear rank, we don't have patches or tabs or badges. I know you're proud of them, but we don't do that stuff. We don't do medals, we don't do plaques or memorials or any of that. But you are still in the service, okay?"

Kirk nodded.

"We work for Ms. Jones. Who exactly she answers to, we don't know and we don't have a need to know. She did the 'things that go bump in the night' shtick, which she alternates with some other stuff for new people, but officially Nightstalkers is on call to deal with extraordinary emergencies. That includes incidents involving nuclear, chemical, and biological material. Doc will get you up to speed on what you need to know in that area and our special gear to deal with contingencies. A lot of the times we bring scientists with us. Nada interrupted him, but putting it simply, Doc is a genius in a whole bunch of fields I can't even pronounce."

"Yeah," Nada snorted. "I remember you wrote Genius on the board when he in-briefed with Ms. Jones."

Moms ignored him. "Doc has what we call the Acme list, after that company the Coyote always bought his stuff from in the Road Runner cartoon."

This time Nada actually laughed as he started piling up binders on his desktop. "Yeah, Mac wanted to call him Road Runner. Beep beep. He's always interested in figuring shit out. Keep an eye on him with that. You can get killed while figuring shit out."

Moms continued. "The Acme list contains the names of a whole bunch of scientists who are on call to the government. We Zevon them—"

"Excuse me?" Kirk said.

"Zevon," Moms repeated. "It's an alert ring tone on their phones. You'll understand soon enough; hopefully not too soon."

"Good luck on that," Nada muttered as he took out an alcohol pen and began thumbing through a pocket-sized acetated pad.

"Working with those from the Acme list can be a pain—"

"Working with Doc can be a pain," Nada said to himself, checking the binders against his small pad.

"—but they're the experts. They tell you don't touch something, don't touch it. They tell you to flame something, flame it. They tell you to run—"

"You're fucked," Nada said.

"True," Moms said. She stared at Kirk as if reading him. Seeing how he was taking it. She must have liked what she saw. "Okay. There is an event that's our primary mission, and actually prompted the founding of this unit many years ago. Something you've never heard of."

"Join the rest of the world," Nada said.

"Rifts and Fireflies," Moms said.

Kirk blinked and hoped for amplification.

"No, I can't tell you what a Rift is," Moms said, deflating his hope. "No one can."

"Not even Doc," Nada added.

"But Fireflies—" Moms began.

"We kill," Nada finished for her.

"Fireflies come through Rifts," Moms said. "Anywhere from one to fourteen, which happened back in '68 and is the record."

"*That* must have been a motherfucker of a firefight," Nada said enviously.

"Doc will give you more info on this topic," Moms said, "but simply put, Fireflies are things that come through Rifts, and our best guess is that they are some sort of energy being or probe that can take over an animate or inanimate object." She stopped because of whatever she was reading on Kirk's face.

"They can go into things and animals," Nada tried to explain. "And take them over. So anything around you can be under the control of a Firefly." He thumped his desktop. "A Firefly could get into this desk, then slam shut the drawer when I put my hand in to get something. With enough force to chop my hand off, 'cause they enhance whatever they're in. You kill an animal they're in, it ain't enough. It's got to be flamed to cinders. Roland does most of the flaming. Once the creature is reduced to pretty much nothing, the Firefly floats out of the body and dissipates."

"They can't jump from one place to another," Moms said. "Once they go in they're stuck—"

"Until we obliterate what they're in," Nada said.

"They can't go into people," Moms said.

"Not that we know of," Nada warned. "Or yet. Whichever."

That one stopped Moms for a second, then she went on. "If they get into an inanimate object, then we have to blast it, break it down, crush it, blow it apart—whatever—depending on what the object is. There is a critical point at which the object no longer has what Doc calls a sufficient level of integrity that the Firefly can survive in, so it finally just lets go and leaves and dissipates. I know this is all a bit much, but like I said, Doc can explain it better and more thoroughly. Okay?"

Kirk nodded.

"Some other basics," Moms said. "We don't do ranks here, but I'm your team leader and Nada is the team sergeant. Go to him before you come to me. That's not because I'm big on chain of command, but because he can usually solve more things than I can. He has more time on the team than anyone. His focus is you, the team. My focus is Ms. Jones and the mission. Got it?"

Kirk nodded.

"But, as they say, my door is always open, except sometimes it's not. If that sucker," she nodded toward the big steel door, "is shut, there's a reason for it. We do not want to be disturbed."

"Unless it's a Zevon," Nada added.

"Unless it's a Zevon," Moms confirmed. "You're going to be the team commo man," Moms said. "*My* commo man. Which means you can hear everything I hear if you choose. I ask you not to listen in when you give me a channel to Ms. Jones. If I want the team to hear Ms. Jones, I'll put it on the team net. Clear?"

"Clear."

"I ask you to keep to yourself anything else you hear that isn't on the team net. If I want the team to hear it, I'll put it on the net. Clear?"

"Clear."

She reached into a drawer and pulled out a device that looked like an iPhone except it was attached to a wristband. "You've used the PRT before?"

"I trained on it, but they weren't issued."

"I know. Ms. Jones set that training up." Moms tossed it to him. Kirk caught the state-of-the-art device. The screen was active. He strapped it on. "Now you've been issued one. Our commo goes through you and that for security reasons."

Moms reached into a pocket on her fatigues and pulled out an acetated pad similar to what Nada was thumbing through. "This is the team Protocol. We don't call them SOPs here. We call them Protocols."

"More scientific," Nada threw in. "Makes the Acme geeks feel better."

Moms opened it to the first page. "Ms. Jones gave you her spiel. I just want to highlight a few things from my team leader Protocol for you."

For once, Nada remained silent.

Moms began reading, but it was obvious she had the words memorized. "*The most basic tenet of teamwork is honesty.*" She paused and glanced at Nada. He raised an eyebrow but didn't say anything. "Except when you have to lie to someone outside the team to accomplish a mission," Moms finished her first rule.

"*Everyone on the team is a leader*. Except when I make a decision.

"*We do everything as a team*. Except when I tell you to do something alone.

"*Don't get in a pissing contest with someone on a balcony. You just end up pissed on and smelly*. If you have a problem with someone, especially one of the Acme Assets, let me know and I'll deal with it. Which reminds me." Moms reached into her drawer and pulled out a badge case and tossed it to Kirk. "You're now a senior field agent of the FBI. Your photo ID will be here within an hour or so. That badge and ID will be enough to keep pretty much anyone you have to deal with who is on the outside off your ass. Someone thinks they outrank that badge, you send them to me."

She looked back down at her Protocol. "*Keep a positive attitude*. Except when something has to be wet. Then you get nasty." Kirk opened his mouth to ask, but she was quicker to the answer. "We've got three levels of missions here as determined by Ms. Jones. Dry, damp, and wet. Dry is something to be contained and further studied. So we want whatever it is intact.

"Damp is it's to be contained, and if you can't contain it intact, then you can break it.

"Wet is it's to be contained by being utterly destroyed. Fireflies and Rifts are always wet."

She had said the last without looking down. She glanced at the page once more to find her place. "*Discipline and accountability stays inside the Nightstalkers*. We are ultimately accountable only to the survival of the human race."

Kirk blinked.

Moms looked him in the eye. "That's no bullshit, okay?"

Kirk nodded.

"*Be on time*." She frowned. "I need to reorder those two."

"I told you that last time—" Nada began, but she waved him silent.

"*Keep your mouth shut about the team when outside the team. Or Roland will pay you a visit.*"

"And it will be a wet experience," Nada added.

"*Follow Protocols*," Moms said. "Even the smallest ones. And I, actually Nada, will be ripping Mac a new one for sneaking two extra beers while we're technically on call." Moms smiled. "And last but not least, keep your sense of humor. You're going to need it." She closed the book and raised her eyebrows. "Any questions or concerns?"

"No, Moms."

Moms sat back in her seat and gestured for Nada to begin.

The team sergeant got up and picked up the top binder. "Nuclear Protocol, including facilities, materials, weapons, etcetera." He tossed it to Kirk, who caught it. Nada picked up the second binder. "Biological Protocol. There are some nasty bugs out there, and hard as it is to believe, there are people in labs trying to make nastier ones. It's not like Mother Nature can't be quite the motherfucker by herself." He tossed the second binder. Third binder: "Chemical. Really, you do need to read all this stuff, 'cause Doc or an Acme might not be by your side. Pretend you're in graduate school for things that can kill. Learn which ones kill quickest and fastest." He paused. "You know your three Bs, right?"

"Breathing, bleeding, broken," Kirk said, listing the priorities for triage.

Nada nodded. "For us it's the three Cs. Containment is the first priority. Nothing else matters if whatever shit we're trying to deal with spreads. Then concealment." He noted Kirk's surprised look. "Panic can kill as much as the actual problem. Word of some of the things we've had to squash gets out, people will go bonkers. The people out there in the world got twenty-four-hour news channels. They're hungry for bad shit, like the way weathermen pray for hurricanes to hit so they can stand on that pier with the wind howling around them. The news would eat up the stuff we deal with and the public would panic. *War of the Worlds*–type shit. The third C is control. That one is regulated by Ms. Jones's directive whether it's dry, damp, or wet. Got it?"

"Containment, concealment, control."

"Good."

Nada picked up a stack of three more binders. "This is just a bunch of stuff. And some of it is pretty weird. They list every single mission the Nightstalkers have been on since it was founded in 1948. Makes for great late-night reading."

Moms cut in for the first time. "Don't concern yourself so much with the problems, because some of them won't happen again, but look at the way the team dealt with it and consider possibilities."

Nada dumped the three binders on top of the ones already in Kirk's lap.

He grabbed the thickest one off the desk. "This is the one I call the Dumb Shit Scientist Protocol, but don't ever let Doc hear that. This lists all the incredibly dumb things scientists have done that damn near wiped out the human race." Nada's eyes shifted to the wall between the CP and Ms. Jones's office, as if she could hear through two feet of steel-reinforced concrete. "Pretty high up on that list is what happened at Chernobyl."

Last, Nada tossed a pocket-sized team Protocol. "That's your first priority reading. You've got forty-eight hours, then anyone can ask you anything in it and you'd better know it and your place in whatever it is.

"There's a locker with your gear on it. Check it, but don't move anything around. I assume in the Rangers you had standard operating procedure for the way everyone rigged their gear, right? So you can grab anyone's vest or ruck and know exactly what's in it and where it is? We do the same."

Kirk nodded, remembering pulling blood-and-viscera-drenched magazines out of a dead squad mate's vest during a particularly nasty firefight.

Nada sat back behind his desk and pulled out his own team Protocol. "Moms's Protocol is page one. Mine is page two." He hummed something as he scanned the list. "Let me give you some of the more important ones." His finger slid down the page. "*Nothing is impossible to the man who doesn't have to do it.*" He looked up. "Ms. Jones usually keeps the politicians and the press and the various government agencies off our backs during a mission. But every once in a while someone sticks their beak in. Gotta ignore 'em or they'll get you killed." He looked back down.

"*Smith and Wesson beats four aces.*"

Kirk smiled, having heard Uncle Ray say the same thing.

Nada wasn't smiling. "We go in packing heat and we've got heavy stuff on call. We can bring hell down if we need to. Don't hesitate. Err on the side of containment rather than collateral damage. You ever see those movies where that couple manages to escape those nasty government agents trying to contain a government screw-up because they're so fucking special?"

Kirk nodded.

"They ain't special. If we're containing something, there's a reason. We kill those people if we have to. No one gets out alive. Got it?"

Kirk nodded.

"We've never had to nuke anything to contain it," Moms added.

"Yet," Nada said.

"It's a miracle we've made it this far without another nuke having to be used, one way or the other," Moms said. "But we can call in a nuke strike if the problem warrants it and Ms. Jones concurs with her superiors." She nodded at Nada. "Please continue."

"*The latest information hasn't been put out yet.* What I mean by that is we rarely get a chance to plan a mission like most Spec Ops do. ST-6 ran rehearsals for the Bin Laden hit for months before going in. Neato and nifty keen if you can. But when we get Zevoned, it's wheels up in thirty minutes and then it's Moms on the sat link with Ms. Jones and we develop the plan en route. We almost always HAHO or HALO"—he paused, glanced at the badge on Kirk's fatigue shirt, and nodded—"a recon man in first. Because even with the best intel, we usually have no clue what we're dealing with until we get eyes on the target and then boots on the ground. So you've got to be prepared to adapt quickly or die."

He read on. "*There are two types of scientists: the steely-eyed killer and the beady-eyed minion and it's hard to tell them apart. The latter can get you killed. I don't think I'm paranoid*"—it was Moms's turn to snort—"but keep as close an eye on any Acme Asset as you do the problem. Sometimes they can dick it up even worse than it is.

"We love Doc as one of us," Nada said, "but even his brain starts thinking of the wonders of science sometimes before he faces the reality of the danger. He got snakebit in the shoulder on our last op and didn't even notice until we told him." Nada raised an eyebrow. "The snake had a Firefly in it."

Nada slid his finger down the page, reluctantly skipping some of the ones he'd accrued over the years for sake of expediency and focus. "*They give these people guns?* Besides the scientists, sometimes you got locals on scene. Their guns don't know the good guy from the bad guy. We parachute in and then come in on the Snake—you'll meet the Snake later, it's pretty cool—we scare the shit out of people. We've been shot at by supposed friendlies. So no one is friendly except another member of the team until we have containment."

Nada snapped the Protocol shut with a snap and put it back in his pocket. He looked Kirk in the eyes. "This last one is key. No matter what Doc or an Acme says, my bottom line is this: *Just tell me how to kill it.*" Nada smiled and stood, along with Moms. "Well, I think that's a pretty good introduction, don't you?"

Kirk staggered to his feet, burdened with binders. "Uh, yeah. I'll get to work—"

He was cut off as the phone on Moms's desk starting playing a tune: "Lawyers, Guns and Money."

"That's a Zevon," Nada said as he ran toward the door, his phone also now playing the tune and the PRT chiming in a second later.

Despite the very slight time delay, they were all in sync.

CHAPTER 7

The rusted sign pointing toward the old corrugated barn had a dozen old bullet holes in it and one could barely make out the faded lettering in the dark: *SEE ALL THE POISINUS SNAKES 75cents.* Eagle was driving the blacked-out Humvee using night-vision goggles, because Eagle always drove, and Roland was singing "Lawyers, Guns and Money" while manning the fifty-caliber machine gun in the roof turret because Roland always sang that when they headed to the Barn holding the Snake and he always manned the fifty. Whom Roland hoped he could shoot out here in the middle of the Ranch was something that wasn't even worth asking. One never knew, but someone had to stand in the hole because it was pretty crowded inside the Humvee. Moms was in the passenger seat, head hunched over, speaking on a secure line to Ms. Jones.

Roland got to his favorite, slightly altered lines—"*Send lawyers, guns and money, Moms, get me out of this*"—as Nada flashed his security badge at the two guards who popped up out of hide holes, automatic weapons at the ready, night-vision goggles on, and red lasers aiming dots on Eagle and Moms. Those dots also designated a target for a Hellfire missile remotely mounted somewhere out there in the darkness. If the guards pulled their triggers or their monitors went dead, the Humvee would be a smoking hole in the ground.

The two contractors had seen the team more than enough times to know who they were, but Protocol was somewhere between cleanliness and godliness for Nada, so they peered at the badge, then leaned into the Humvee and flashed the retina scanner at the team jammed inside, Eagle lifting his goggles momentarily for the check.

"What if one of us isn't who we think we are?" Eagle asked, because Eagle always asked questions like that. He received no answer as the guards waved them through.

Eagle gassed—technically dieseled—the Humvee and they raced toward the Barn doors, which looked like they were ready to fall off, but were actually two-inch-thick reinforced concrete and steel and could take a direct hit from an RPG and pretty much ignore it—pretty much like the team ignored most of Eagle's observations about the universe.

The sensor above the door picked up the transmitter in the Humvee and the doors ponderously swung open. Red nightlights flickered on inside, preserving the night vision of those not wearing goggles and keeping Eagle's and Roland's NVGs from overloading. Eagle didn't slow and they slipped through the still-opening doors with less than an inch to spare on either side, and not one of the others—except Kirk, who'd never been with Eagle on a drive—had a moment's worry that Eagle would crash them.

Eagle slammed the brakes and spun the wheel, skidding the Humvee around to the side of the Snake. Moms was still on the link to Ms. Jones, occasionally nodding or asking a question. As Nada carefully watched, the team loaded the craft with a quick, well-honed routine, Kirk bumbling along as best he could, mostly trying not to get in the way.

Except nothing was routine for Nada, so he had taken out his acetated Nightstalker Protocol, checking off the twenty-three items in the pre-op load Protocol. He'd erase the checks when they got back, in order to be ready for the next mission.

If they got back.

Moms signaled with her free hand to Nada, still listening to Ms. Jones on the sat phone.

"We've got a Courier gone black near Salt Lake City."

"Package?" Nada asked.

Moms shook her head. "Don't know yet."

Roland pointed Kirk toward his area. It was packed and ready to move, and he grabbed the rucksack containing the portable satellite radio, along with a freshly generated set of codes that were spilling out of a printer next to the ruck.

Then he helped Mac carry the heavy plastic demolitions case into the cargo bay and secure it next to the larger team box that stayed in the Snake at all times. That box held a wide variety of gear, from climbing ropes to arctic clothing to chemical/biological protection suits, parachutes, dry suits, spare radio batteries, two million in gold coins for barter, etc. etc.; someone with an extremely paranoid and inventive mind had packed it.

Nada was always bitching it was missing a lot of stuff they were gonna need.

Doc, med kit in hand, slid out of the way by getting into the aircraft and taking a seat.

Roland easily carried an M-240 machine gun in one hand and a Barrett fifty-caliber sniper rifle in the other while his ruck bulged with ammunition for both along with other deadly goodies. Roland slapped the M-240 into a mount that could extend when the back ramp went down, while Eagle was doing preflight, even though a Support mechanic did a preflight on the Snake every day.

At Nada's order, Roland removed the left side gun mount and bolted the rescue/lift hoist in its place, connecting the power cable. Just in case. Mac, having secured the demo, loaded the ramp-mounted M-240, making sure the belt would run free and clear. Roland slid the Barrett upright into a sheath along the forward bulkhead, then checked his MP-5 submachine gun, while Kirk dialed up the proper frequency, linked his PRT with the radio, and did a Satcom check, locating the nearest MILSTAR satellite to bounce a signal off of. Then he found two backups. Just in case. He updated the current set of codes.

Since this was a Courier op, Mac and Roland then prepared a sling load rig in the belly of the Snake and made sure the attaching points were ready.

When Eagle settled down in the pilot's seat and the dual engines began to whine with power, and the other team members fastened their seat belts in the cargo bay with all gear stowed, Nada went over to one of the numerous dirty glass cases set on tables along one side of the shed. A sign warned *Danger: Extremely Poisinus*. Nada reached in and hit the open button.

The top of the Barn split apart, propelled by powerful hydraulic arms. As it was doing so, Eagle was rotating the wings to vertical. Nada hopped into the crew chief's seat directly behind Moms—who was in the copilot's—and put on his headset just in time to hear Roland finish Warren Zevon's song:

"*I'm a desperate man. Send lawyers, guns and money. The shit has hit the fan.*"

"Technically," Eagle observed, as he always did when Roland finished, "Moms is coming with the Nightstalkers, guns and money."

"We don't need no stinking lawyers," Mac drawled.

"Roger that, brother," Roland said, checking the load in his MK-23 Mod 0 offensive handgun. His blood was up and he always got excited when Zevoned. "Yo, Eagle. Got a round in the chamber?"

The Snake lifted off the ground and Eagle shot them straight up, the tips of the wings clearing the open doors with a generous two inches on either side. Next to him, Moms sighed and reached over. Since a Snake pilot must always have one hand on the cyclic and the other on the collective, Moms unsnapped Eagle's holster and pulled out the modified gun designed specifically for Special Operations Forces. She pulled back slightly on the slide, saw there was indeed no round in the chamber, and pulled the slide all the way back, letting it slam forward, chambering a round for the pilot. For everyone else on the team, the mantra, as it was in Delta Force and other elite units, was that their finger was their safety. But Eagle needed the lever pushed to safe, which Moms made sure of. She slid the gun back into the holster.

Chagrined, Eagle glanced at her and mouthed *thanks*.

In the cargo bay, Nada was checking his watch, having timed the team from alert to liftoff. He didn't seem pleased, but he never seemed pleased, and was writing something in his Protocol, apparently having figured out a way to shave a few seconds off.

"Mission," Moms said in a tone that brought to a halt any further chatter. "One of the Couriers went off the grid at a truck stop on I-15, about one hundred and twenty miles from here."

Everyone swayed as Eagle banked the hybrid aircraft hard and accelerated as the wings rotated from vertical to horizontal. Once they snapped into place he kicked in the afterburners. The dim glow from the night-mode instrument panel was the only light on the aircraft. No running lights, no searchlight. Eagle had the night-vision goggles down over his helmet visor. On the interior of the visor was a heads-up display giving him pertinent flight data, most especially whether the forward-looking radar picked up any obstructions. They were flying less than thirty feet above the desert floor and crossed Nevada Route 375 as he curved them to the north and east. The exterior of the Snake was painted flat black with no markings.

If any of the UFO enthusiasts lurking at the infamous mailbox that led to the gate to Area 51 looked up at the muted roar of the engines, they'd just gotten the bonus of seeing something that was whispered about but had never been photographed.

"Package?" Nada asked.

"A variation of the H5N1 virus," Moms relayed. "The pickup was a biochem lab at the University of Colorado."

"Fuck," Roland muttered. "Bugs. I hate bugs."

"It's a virus, not a bug," Doc corrected. "The original has a sixty-percent kill rate but could be contained."

"His truck isn't off the grid," Moms continued, "his monitor is. Truck GPS says it's been sitting at the truck stop for over an hour. We've gotten nothing on the local cop chatter so the site is quiet."

"So the Package might still be inside," Nada said. The glum way he said it indicated he thought not. But then again, he'd been nicknamed Nada because he always figured not only was the glass half empty, but whatever was left in it could kill you. He'd gotten his nickname within thirty seconds of leaving Ms. Jones's office, a record. Unfortunately, every person who'd been there for that ceremony was no longer on the team and several were no longer breathing.

"Monitor down isn't good," Doc said, because the Courier's monitor going dead meant he was probably dead. Doc often said obvious things, but he was a scientist and a doctor and he'd learned people often missed the obvious, especially some of the more focused soldiers on the team.

Eagle snorted. "Stupid Courier probably got rolled at the truck stop by some surfers trying to make money to make it to California and it went bad; not someone after a bug. Probably lying in the john after getting his ass kicked, monitor broken."

"Sounds like a tech steal by professionals," Mac said. "They're probably three states away by now." Mac always hoped to be pitted against James Bond in one form or another.

"Or the dipshit Courier knocked loose the monitor wire to the transmitter," Roland noted. "Or went in to take a shower at the stop and forgot to bypass the alert when he unstrapped it."

"Or he got taken down by professionals who want the bug," Mac said.

"Virus," Doc repeated.

Eagle was thinking out loud. "How would professionals have known about the virus, the van, the Courier, and the route? We don't even get that unless we're Zevoned."

"I can guess," Nada said. "Fucking Courier is sitting in a brand-new, white, unmarked van that rides low because of armor plating, and the guy's some dumb-ass ex-grunt, strapped to the gills with guns and not acting like the dumb-ass truck driver he's supposed to pretend to be. My four-year-old niece Zoey would have figured out what he was." Everyone groaned at the mention of Zoey because Nada always referred to any situation caused by stupidity as a Zoey, yet no one knew if she was real or not. *Zoeys led to getting Zevoned*, Roland was known to say. Too often. "I've warned"—he caught himself—"*advised* Ms. Jones about the Couriers."

"Come on," Mac said. "This bug—"

"Virus," Doc muttered.

"—bug is getting transferred and—" But this time Mac was cut off by Moms and no one spoke when Moms cut you off on the team net.

"Tell us about the virus, Doc."

"If it's a variation of H5N1 from a college lab," Doc said, "it appears some scientist has been playing around with what most people call the bird flu. A couple of people at the University of Wisconsin did it a while back and it caused quite an uproar in the community."

"The scientific community," Eagle said with disgust. "I think it's criminal that these people are allowed to play around with lethal experimentation via government grants just to earn a PhD. It's like letting local police departments have nuclear weapons just in case they need them for crowd control."

"Hey," Mac said. "Remember the time the nuke—"

"Quiet, please," Moms said, without rancor. "Support is setting up a Forward Operating Base out on the Bonneville Salt Flats. Nada. Plan?"

"The van is still there," Nada said. "As always, the Package is more important than the Courier. We go in quiet. Send a HAHO jumper in, check the van for the Package. It's there, we lift it out intact and then check the interior at the FOB. Then the HAHO looks for the Courier if he's not with the van."

Mac unbuckled and was opening the team box.

"Who is HAHO?" Moms asked.

Nada hesitated.

"For fuck's sake," Moms said, a slight exasperation sliding in, "I know you go for the guy who's gone the longest without a jump so he can maintain his jump status."

Mac had a parachute rig out and was checking it.

"Last jumps?" Nada asked.

Each man rattled off the last time they'd stepped out of a perfectly good aircraft and done a free-fall parachute jump. Regulations required a jump every three months in order to keep jump pay at free-fall rate: a whopping $225 a month.

Not surprisingly, Eagle was furthest out from his last jump, twelve days away from losing his status.

"Well, that ain't happening unless someone else on the team's gone through flight school while I wasn't watching," Moms said. "Everyone else is pretty tight so let's forget about pay and focus on mission. Roland. You're taking point. Don't kill everyone down there, please. Unless they try to kill you."

"Yes, Moms." The sincerity in his voice belied all his early songs and words. He'd wipe out the entire truck stop if Moms told him to; so with his promise one could assume the safety of dozens of civilians.

"Should I suit up?" Roland asked, looking at Doc.

Moms looked at Doc, indicating it was his call.

"Negative. They seal that stuff tight and it would take a big blast to get into the vault on the van. Such an event would have made the police scanners."

That was good enough for Roland, although most might have had their doubts about jumping right on top of a superbug. Roland unbuckled and crouched next to Mac. The engineer put the parachute on the weapons man's back.

"Left leg," Mac said as he passed the first strap between Roland's legs.

"Left leg," Roland confirmed as he snapped it into place.

Eagle began to gain altitude, because the HA in HAHO stood for high altitude.

"Right leg," Mac said.

"Right leg," Roland echoed.

They went through the routine of rigging, then Mac sat back down. Nada got up and did the JMPI: jump master parachute inspection. Eyes and hands ran over the rig, checking everything. Done, he gave Roland a light slap on the shoulder, indicating he was good to go.

"Wait one!" Moms called out, an unusual display of surprise for her. "Correction. Correction on the Package. Support got the damn Package invoice number wrong but the right pickup location. The Package is not a virus."

Everyone breathed a sigh of relief. Until her next words. "It's the hard drive from the laptop from our Fun Outside Tucson."

"Fuck me to tears," Nada muttered.

CHAPTER 8

Roland stood on the open ramp, fifteen thousand feet above Utah, as calm as if he were waiting in line at Starbucks. Of course, Roland had never waited at a Starbucks, but one gets the idea. They were at fifteen thousand AGL because any higher and everyone inside would have to be on oxygen. As it was, the breathing was hard. Roland was looking down. It was easy to see I-15 running north to south. The glow of Salt Lake City was north of their current location. Eagle had offset a horizontal mile from the Flying H Truckstop where Ms. Jones told them the van was located. At least where the van's GPS tracker was, Nada reminded everyone. The two might no longer be connected.

"Go," Eagle announced.

Roland stepped off into darkness. He spread his arms and legs, got stable, then pulled the ripcord. The opening shock jerked him upright, and he looked up to make sure he had good canopy while he grabbed the control toggles for the chute.

* * *

Above him, Moms waited until the ramp was shut before issuing her next order. "Eagle, get us to five hundred AGL, into hover mode, and be ready to move in fast if Roland has any problems."

Five hundred was the altitude at which the Snake could hover and not be heard at all by anyone on the ground.

"Don't hit Roland on the way down," Mac added, because Mac always had to add something.

* * *

It didn't even occur to Roland that he might get hit by the Snake dropping altitude. He was focused on the truck stop and the area around it. So far, everything looked normal as he watched an eighteen-wheeler pulling out of the stop and turn onto the ramp for the interstate.

As he passed through eight thousand feet he spotted the van. Parked in the shadows, away from the bright lights of the truck stop and filling station. At least the Courier had done that according to Protocol.

"Eagle, thermals around the van," Roland asked as he adjusted his descent.

"Very slight heat sigs coming from the driver's compartment of the van," Eagle said. "Doc, take a look. The sig isn't right. I'm going lower."

Roland was using a clockwise spiral to descend, checking all directions.

Doc's voice came over the net. "You've got two warm spots in the front of the van."

Two? That wasn't good, Roland thought.

Doc continued. "But, ah, I'd say we have two corpses losing body heat. Not hot enough, even through the roof of the van."

"Any other heat sigs?"

"Closest human is refueling over by the pumps," Eagle said. "Couple of deer in the field to the west about five hundred meters out."

Roland was about to pass through four thousand feet. He took a moment to ready his MP-5 on top of his reserve. The M-240 machine gun was on his side, rigged tight against his body. He reversed his spiral, because Protocol said he was to reverse directions after passing through four thousand feet. Why? He'd never thought to ask.

"Wind?" Roland asked.

"From the north-northwest at twelve knots, gusting to eighteen," Eagle reported. "You're still clear. We're holding at five hundred, to the west, offset three hundred meters. I'm deploying the gun if you need backup."

Roland didn't bother to look in that direction. If Eagle said that's where the Snake was, that's where the Snake was.

When Roland hit two thousand AGL, he started dumping air, accelerating his descent because he was in range of someone firing from the ground and there was no point in taking his time. He made one last curve, had his approach set, and then aimed straight for the van, still dumping air. Roland had perfected the craft of driving a parachute into an art over the course of 1,342 free-fall jumps.

Thirty feet above the van, he flared the chute, breaking his rapid descent so that when he landed on the roof, the only sound was the thud of his boots like a heavy gong, and not the crack of bones breaking. There is a fine line between the two.

From the wind report, Roland knew he had to cut loose the chute or get blown off the top of the van by a gust. He popped the quick releases on his shoulders, then grabbed the MP-5 and did a quick three-sixty.

Nothing close.

Roland aimed the gun down. He knew the specs. The roof was armored. If anyone was alive inside they knew something had come down on top of them. Roland swapped out the MP-5 for the M-240, preferring the heavier firepower.

Roland jumped off the roof, turning in the air, peering in the windshield as he came down, machine gun at the ready.

He landed on the parking lot. "We've got what looks like two KIA in the front of the van. The Courier and some girl who got double-tapped."

"Roger," Moms said. "Inbound."

Roland put his back against the front fender of the van, half-crouched out of sight of the interior just in case one of the apparently dead people wasn't dead—or was perhaps a zombie—and somehow blew out the bulletproof glass and came after him. But he figured the priority was whoever had done the killing, and they were outside somewhere.

He heard the whine of the Snake, muffled by the trucks passing on the interstate. The fast ropes came down and then the rest of the team. The Snake went back out to hover over the wilderness to the west and provide cover.

Moms was on point, appearing out of the surrounding darkness. Nada and Kirk went past and spread out, putting themselves as security between the van and the truck stop, going to a knee, their weapons at the ready. Mac joined Roland along with Nada and Moms.

"Why'd you land on the roof?" Mac asked. "If it's rigged with a motion detonator, you'd have set it off."

Roland shrugged. "I like having the high ground. Guess it isn't rigged with a motion detonator. One less thing for you to check."

Mac didn't need to be told what to do. There was a Protocol for a Courier van. He nodded and the rest of them moved away.

Mac moved quickly but efficiently. Running his hands gently everywhere his eyes went, as coordinated as Nada had been with the JMPI. Mac was also sniffing as he searched, and listening, head slightly cocked. Mac had once defused fourteen IEDs along a single stretch of road in Afghanistan in less than six hours. Like Roland and free-fall parachuting, Mac had taken his craft to an art form. He finished the exterior. Then he put on a headlamp and turned it on. He slid underneath, covering the entire bottom, slithering along the ground. Finally he came out from under the van and turned the lamp off.

"No break-in," he reported. "No triggers. The outside is clean."

Moms signaled and they moved back to the van. Moms gestured and Roland held out his cupped hands as he squatted. Moms stepped into his massive hands and he easily lifted her up so she could look down in the front.

"Two KIA," Moms confirmed. "Open her up, Mac."

"Clear," Mac said.

Roland put Moms back down and they moved back once more, leaving Mac alone. He took out the remotes he'd programmed on the flight in, using the data from the Depot for this van. One by one he turned off the alarms and locks.

He walked over and put his hand on the driver's handle. Mac cracked the door, checking for tripwires. Satisfied, he jerked the door open.

The Courier tumbled out and Mac stepped out of the way, letting the body slam onto the pavement as he went up on the step, weapon at the ready. "She's been double-tapped," he reported.

He stepped back down and checked the Courier. "Knife up through the jaw. He went quick."

Mac went around to the back and opened the two heavy doors. "Bad news. Safe is open. The Package is gone."

Moms and the rest of the team other than the two men on security came up. They all went to the rear first, looking in.

"The van *was* locked and secure, right?" Moms asked.

"Correct," Mac answered.

"Fuck," Nada said. "Inside job."

"Rig it for sling load and let's get it out of here," Moms said, but she was looking about, into the darkness. Because someone out there had done the impossible.

* * *

Five kilometers away, in the foothills of the Wasatch Mountains, Burns was watching through a night-vision scope as the team rigged the van to be hauled away. It had gone down exactly as Burns had experienced numerous times in the past as a member of the Nightstalkers.

According to Protocol.

Nada and his Protocols.

Burns nodded.

CHAPTER 9

THE NEXT DAY

In the middle of the southern part of the Bonneville Salt Flats, out of sight of I-80, a convoy of semis and Humvees had circled up. Much like the Donner Party that had crossed this same desert so many years ago. Except the Donners had gotten lost and had to detour to Pilot Peak way off to the north, losing valuable days, resulting in—months later—getting snowed in high in the Sierras. And eating one another.

Nada was in that kind of mood as the Snake came to a hover over the empty space in the center of the circle. Eagle gingerly descended, depositing the sling-loaded van onto the desert floor. Then he sidled the Snake over and set down, opening the back ramp.

They had a few hours before dawn and Ms. Jones wanted this wrapped and brought back to Area 51 before the sun came over the Rockies to the east. Moms had been on the Satcom with Ms. Jones the entire flight and the team had been unusually quiet, the bodies of the Courier and the girl on the deck in the center of the cargo bay. Her ID meant little: a runaway who'd gotten caught up in some bad shit. There was no doubt she'd been the bait, given the way the Courier's pants had been opened. No one had even made a joke about shrinkage, which indicated the seriousness with which they were viewing this breach of security.

"Best they never know," Mac said suddenly as Eagle cut the engines and they all got to their feet.

Everyone turned to him in surprise, even Moms. Mac pointed at the girl, her face mangled beyond recognition by the two bullets. "Better the family thinks she's still out there somewhere. Alive. Hope is better than knowing for sure what the parents don't want to know for sure. Trust me on that."

Moms nodded. "Ms. Jones says she'll be taken care of."

Mac's face tightened. "I didn't mean taken care of. I meant no cop with a badge shows up at her parents' door, some complete stranger, and tells them their daughter's head has been blown off 'cause some dickhead couldn't keep his pants on and some other dickhead wanted a hard drive. Best they not know. Sometimes hope is all you got."

Mac stomped down the ramp into the desert and out beyond the perimeter into the darkness.

Kirk was surprised, because Moms had kept her mike hot during the last part of what Mac said, and everyone heard Ms. Jones reply on the team net. "I understand, Mister Mac. They will never know." Then Kirk heard the click as the link went back to just Moms and Ms. Jones.

Nada looked down at the bodies as a Support team with two body bags appeared at the bottom of the ramp.

Nada pointed at the Courier: "He forgot why he was here."

CHAPTER 10

Doctor "never call me *Professor*, I earned my degree" Winslow left his lab on the campus of the University of North Carolina into the darkening evening with the hunched shoulders of a man whose day had been less than fulfilling. He occasionally, but not often, wondered if everyone who worked for him in the lab, from the techs to the various levels of graduate students and postdocs aspiring to his own position, ever noticed his bored resignation.

Physics was a young man's game, and now that he was in his forties, it wasn't as though his synapses were going to fire more rapidly and come up with a brilliant new theory. He'd seen it in those older than him. It had been a gentle, almost unnoticed slide from original brilliance to his single decent, well-paying idea—now gently fading into the past—to his eventual harrumphing for or against whatever the topic was depending on who was paying him and how much he stood to lose intellectually. Physics was like acting or novel writing or any other venture where one stepped into it with youthful verve and high expectations, but only a handful became Tom Hanks or Hemingway or Einstein.

Winslow found it amusing that so few understood that blinding ambition was the necessary ingredient of any intelligence or talent. He had the ambition, and as he pushed open the building door into the stifling heat of summer and the almost empty parking lot, he thought it was ironic that Ivar, his most talented student, had no ambition at all. It was the reason so many successful scientists stole the work of their lessers. Someone had to do something with it. A mind was a terrible thing to waste.

He walked to his car, the sweat already ruining another good shirt, and thought of Darwin, who'd read Wallace's letters about evolution; while they shared many theories, Darwin was the one who ran with the big one. How many people knew who Wallace was? Darwin had had the ambition while Wallace had been content to merely be mentioned by the greater man.

Winslow's wife, Lilith, had a Serbian grandmother who'd filled her head with tales of Tesla and how Edison had screwed him over, and how even Einstein's wife, well-educated in her own right and ahead of her time, had lost out on her contributions to her husband. Winslow wasn't sure he bought into the latter part, but the fact that Lilith was raised with the concept that stealing was an integral part of science made them a good pair in the ambition area. She just didn't realize he wasn't Tesla. Poor Tesla, whose better concept for alternating current had been relegated to the electric chair instead of home lighting, due to the manipulations of Edison, who had some of his assistants "accidently" kill animals with AC current to show its "danger" and secretly lobbied to get AC in the electric chair. It wasn't surprising that no one wanted to turn on a light that shared the same current that Sing Sing used to turn off someone's lights.

Winslow smiled. He had to remember that for the dinner party. He pulled his cell phone out and hit the record button so he wouldn't forget: "No one wants to turn on a light that shares the same current that Sing Sing uses to turn out someone's lights."

Talking into the phone was why he didn't hear the footsteps behind him. It was only as he clicked the record app off that he heard the voice right behind him and almost jumped out of his shoes.

"I've been everywhere but the electric chair and seen everything but the wind."

Winslow spun about, the phone held out as if there were some app that could protect you from a stranger sneaking up on you in the dark.

"Who are you? What are you talking about?"

The man wore a hat, his face in darkness. There was an implied threat in the way he stood, in just the way he breathed. "Something from my old life. It's a Nada Yada."

"A what?"

The man gestured with his hand and there was clearly something metallic in it. "Just unlock all the doors and get in the car, Doctor Winslow."

Winslow hesitated, considering his options. Swing his briefcase? Run? Scream?

He pressed the unlock button on his car key as he looked anxiously about at the tall smokestacks poking up above all the lab buildings so they could vent the by-products of various procedures. A distant blue light indicated where you could press an alert for campus police. Very distant. Too distant. Maybe this stranger only wanted the car?

"Get in the driver's seat."

Winslow slid into the leather seat as the man got in the back, behind him.

"Hot out, isn't it?" the man said, as if this were the most normal of occurrences for him. "You'd think there'd be Fireflies out, it's so hot." He laughed to himself, a private joke apparently. There was a slightly manic edge to his laughter.

"What did you say?" Winslow felt his fear lessen slightly at the odd comment.

"Fireflies," the man repeated. "You have to wonder where they are. And relax your grip on your briefcase, Doctor, because if you swing that at me, it will only result in severe damage to that arm."

Winslow tensed once more. "That's an odd thing to say during a robbery—fireflies."

"Who says I'm robbing you, Doctor Winslow? Maybe I want to sell you something?"

Winslow swallowed, feeling a wave of excitement greater than his fear sweep through his body. "So you have the fireflies?" he whispered, playing along on the sneaky spy stuff, figuring it was some code word.

"You don't even know what a Firefly is, do you? But you do know what a Rift is, correct? You did get that e-mail from your former student. He didn't know what Fireflies were either. None of you really know what you're doing. What would you be willing to pay me if I said I have what you need? Does the name Craegan ring a bell?"

Winslow had to bite back the instant answer that formed on his tongue: *Anything*. He thought for a moment. "Fifty thousand."

"Move the decimal place."

Winslow wanted to turn and shout that was robbery, but he knew it actually wasn't. Winslow glanced up at the rearview mirror. The man was sitting back, hat still keeping his face in the dark. Winslow reached for the light switch.

"Don't." The man laughed, the manic edge sharper. "The Fireflies got to me."

"What are you talking—"

The man tossed something over into the passenger seat.

Winslow saw the hard drive with the ASU control number on the side. "I'll need time to get the money," Winslow said. "A week?"

"What are you going to do?" the man asked. "Take out a fourth mortgage on your house?"

Winslow started in surprise.

"I wouldn't be here trying to make a deal if I didn't do my homework," the man said. "I know you don't have the money. But there is someone who does have the money who actually lives rather close to you." Burns tossed a slip of paper over the seat. "Tell him it's an investment. He's the sort of man who would be interested in that. But I wouldn't cross him."

Winslow picked up the paper. He read the name. "But—"

"Trust me on this," Burns said. "He can loan you five hundred thousand. It's nothing to him. Unless you don't pay him back."

Five hundred thousand was nothing to what he could reap if he made this work, Winslow thought. "All right. Five hundred thousand."

"Smart man." The man shifted in the seat.

Winslow resisted the urge to grab the hard drive and race back inside and start right away.

"Something you need to know," the man said, "if you want to not get caught and stay alive. Unlike Mister Craegen."

But Winslow's mind was racing ahead, hearing the applause from the audience in Geneva. Forming the words to the speech that was now inevitable. "Yes?" he muttered, his mind on other things.

"You need to shield it so there are no emissions once it activates," the man warned. "Especially muons."

"Muons?"

"That's how they can find you," the man said.

"Who?"

"The Nightstalkers."

"Uh-huh." Winslow wondered how much the Nobel medal weighed. How it would feel on his chest.

The man held a hand between the seats. "Give it to me."

As Winslow reluctantly handed the hard drive back he saw the scars on the back of the man's hand. The drive disappeared and then the man extended a small slip of paper. "Once I see the five hundred thousand in that account, I'll call you. Set up a dead drop so you can get the drive. You know what a dead drop is?"

Winslow tensed at the term.

The man laughed again, sounding a bit insane, but Winslow wasn't listening. "Of course you don't. Tradecraft. Not required learning for physicists. Put simply, I'll call you and tell you where you can find it. It's now on you, Doctor."

The man abruptly got out of the car, slamming the door shut. Winslow powered down his window. "How soon—"

"As soon as you deposit the money." The man was gone into the darkness.

As Winslow put the car into drive to race home, he began to hear the applause once more.

* * *

Moms and Nada sat in the CP still discussing various ways they could catch Burns. Arriving back at the Ranch just before dawn, most of the day had been spent standing down from the Courier operation and doing the After Action Report. Now payback was on their minds.

In the Den they were discussing various ways to kill him.

Given the state of the van, it had to have been, as Nada had immediately surmised, an inside job. Someone who knew the Protocol, knew the vans, knew the Couriers, knew it all.

It only took till early afternoon for Ms. Jones's long arm to discover that Burns was off the grid.

"'How often have I said to you that when you have eliminated the impossible, whatever remains, however improbable, must be the truth,'" Eagle quoted.

"About twenty times in the past year," Mac said. "Why don't you come up with something original?"

"I never liked Burns," Roland said. He was throwing a hatchet at the three-foot-high stump of a tree. How the stump of a tree had found its way out here to the desert and down into the Den was a mystery, but it had quickly become the magnet of all matters of throwing devices: hatchets, knives, spears. Bored men needed some release. Bored killers liked to throw killing devices.

Mac snorted. "Moms named him after Major Burns from *M*A*S*H* for some reason. Moms never likes naming anyone and she was surprised when Ms. Jones chose it. I don't know what they picked up in him. He didn't like the name either."

Eagle went over and grabbed the handle of the hatchet. He grunted with effort, trying to pull it out after Roland's throw. It came on the second jerk. He walked to the other end of the team table and prepared to throw.

"Duck!" Mac yelled as Eagle let loose.

Kirk took it seriously and dove under the table—just in time, as the top of the weapon hit the stump and it recoiled back, skidding across the table and then clanking to the floor.

"Dude, we have a rule!" Mac said as he picked up the hatchet. "You don't get to throw."

Eagle frowned. "I'll get it eventually."

"You'll get one of us eventually," Mac said, holding the hatchet out to Kirk. "Let's see how our new man does."

Kirk remembered the woodpile, the one Pads had forced him to make that summer after finding him hiding in the hollow of the old tree down by the creek. Pads had ordered him to cut the old tree down and stood there pulling from the bottle as Kirk, then known as Winthrop Carter, did it. Then Pads had given him a quota of wood to be cut every day from the dead tree, until there was nothing left of that tree but kindling. No more hide spot, and every log tossed on the fire that winter was a reminder that you couldn't hide from Pads.

Kirk threw, and the hatchet flashed across the room, hitting the trunk with a solid thud, the blade burying deep into the wood.

"Damn," Mac said. "*You* can throw."

From the corner of the room, Doc said a single word. "Rifts."

All activity ceased as Doc continued. "While you gentlemen have been concerned all day with Burns and his betrayal, I believe we need to further educate Kirk on Rifts, since we might well be facing one sooner than anticipated."

Mac and Roland sat down at the team table. Kirk grabbed the seat closest to Doc, who was in the armchair that had been in the CP for the in-briefing with Nada and Moms.

"Let's start with what we don't know," Doc said. "We don't know what Rifts are, nor do we know what the Fireflies are. Not exactly. But skipping all the scientific jargon and theories, let's construct a framework from which you can conduct operational tactics."

Kirk said nothing, beginning to understand Nada's warnings about the scientists.

"My best guess is that Rifts are tears to the multiverse. To either a world parallel to ours or another world entirely. And the

Fireflies are probes. Some think the Fireflies are living entities who have crossed over, but the way they inhabit objects and creatures indicates a level of programming and not innate intelligence to me. Some of the choices the Fireflies make aren't exactly the best—the cactus in the Fun Outside Tucson, for example."

"Tell that to Burns," Roland said. "And that rabbit didn't seem a smart choice, but if Nada had been a shade slower, it would have torn your neck open and you wouldn't be here. And the rattler *did* get you."

Doc flushed; whether in embarrassment or anger, it was impossible to tell. "Yes, yes."

"Doc," Roland said, "as even you said: he don't need theories." Roland put his heavy hands flat on the table. "We're the Nightstalkers. We, the Shooters, kill Fireflies, and Doc there, the Scientist, he shuts the Rift. That's it. Moms and Nada told you how we kill the Fireflies. If it's living, I usually ending up flaming it until there's nothing but ash. Other stuff, Mac and I and the rest of the team blast and flame until there's nothing left. Then this little gold thing floats up out of whatever it was in and—poof—no more Firefly."

"But how did this start?" Kirk asked.

"When the first Rift was opened," Doc said.

"Who did that?" Kirk asked.

"A German scientist here at Area 51," Doc said. "Near the end and after World War II we brought a bunch of their scientists over here to work on—"

"Fucking Nazis," Mac said.

"—various projects under the auspices of Operation Paperclip. We fought the Russians for the brain trust left from the Third Reich. It made Guantanamo look like a joke. Most people know about the ones we used in the space program, but we took whoever we could grab, and there were several theoretical physicists who had really produced nothing of practical use for the Germans, but were let loose in the labs in Area 51 to experiment—"

"Fuck around," Mac said.

"—and one of them developed a way to open a Rift in 1948," Doc said. "You can read about it in the binders that Nada gave you. It turned out to be a mess, since no one had encountered the Fireflies before and it took them a while—"

"And a lot of good men," Mac interjected.

"—before they were able to figure it out, shut the Rift, and destroy the Fireflies. The first version of the Nightstalkers was formed under the supervision of a committee called Majestic 12 and originally headquartered at Area 51. Their primary mission was to find and destroy Fireflies and close the Rift they came out of. Since 1948 there have been twenty-seven recorded openings of Rifts."

"All in the US?" Kirk asked.

"Most," Doc said. "The theory behind them is the key, and ever since 1948, it's been like the Holy Grail of physicists to create a controlled Rift and figure out what's on the other side. No one has even been able to control one and no one has ever figured out what's on the other side."

"They've all dropped the Grail," Eagle said. "They can open them and Doc here can shut them, but they can't be controlled. Pretty much everyone who has opened one gets sucked through. To where, we have no idea, but such is the price of stupidity."

"What about Rifts outside the US?" Kirk asked.

"The Russians have a team like us," Doc said, "and between us we cover the world. We've done five missions overseas."

"Not fun," Roland noted.

"The problem," Doc said, "is that science has the potential—"

"To screw things up," Moms said from the door of the CP. Kirk reacted without thinking, hopping to his feet and popping to attention like he was back in the Ranger Bat.

Moms smiled. "I like this. It's like the real army."

"Don't get used to it," Nada said from behind her.

"Chill, dude," Mac said.

Kirk sheepishly sat back down, the habits of the Rangers hard to let go of.

"In my opinion, the real birth of the Nightstalkers," Moms said, "was not 1948, but on the sixteenth of June, 1945, not too far from here in the desert outside Alamogordo Air Force Base."

"A Rift?" Kirk asked.

"No. Worse." Moms came over to the team table and took a seat. Nada also grabbed a chair. "On that day, at five thirty in the morning, the first atomic weapon was detonated. You have to understand the context. They were trying something unknown. There were no computer projections. Those guys were using slide rulers. Some of the smartest people out there in that desert, people who had helped build the bomb, were convinced they were going to start an atomic chain reaction that would consume the entire world. And they detonated it anyway.

"Oppenheimer looked at the mushroom cloud and thought of a Hindu saying: *I am become death, the destroyer of worlds.* At that point, man crossed a line that few have really focused on. We became capable of destroying ourselves."

"And we haven't stopped since," Nada said. "Not long ago, at the supercollider near Geneva, they discovered the—what is it, Doc?"

Doc had a defeated look on his face, having been through this discussion before. "The Higgs boson particle."

"Often called the God particle," Eagle threw in.

Nada picked back up. "But when they first turned that thing on, there were some scientists who speculated they might actually cause a black hole and consume the planet," Nada said. "But they turned it on anyway."

"That held an incredibly small possibility," Doc argued.

"But a possibility nonetheless," Nada said.

"The pursuit of knowledge—" Doc began, but Nada cut him off again.

"Us and the Russians, both our teams, we were over there, waiting that day." Nada shrugged. "We weren't sure what we could do, but we were ready to try if anything went wonky. And they actually did—nine days after that thing was turned on it broke."

"Magnet quench," Doc said, as if anyone had an idea what that meant.

"Right. Clusterfuck," Nada clarified. "We'd redeployed back to the States and had to fly back over there. They lost five tons of super-heated helium. Took forever to cool it down. Faulty electrical connection, they said. Took the thing off-line for over a year. And that still didn't stop them. They fired it up again. And again and again. Until now they found one of the things they were looking for. But what if they find something they weren't looking for?"

"Would you have us move back into caves?" Doc asked.

"I'd prefer if we didn't blast ourselves back into caves," Nada argued.

"The Higgs boson could hold the key to figuring out the Rifts and the Fireflies," Doc shot back. "It might make that part of our job unnecessary if we really can control the Rifts."

"I don't want to control the damn things," Nada said, "I want to stop them. Forever. I've lost friends to the Fireflies."

"All right, gentlemen," Moms said, cutting off the growing argument. "Speaking of caves, Doc, show our newest member the Can. The rest of you, grab some sleep."

Doc made a face indicating it was not a task he relished, but he got to his feet. "Come with me, Kirk."

* * *

Doc hated this part of his job, but it was necessary. Every member of the team had to understand the process. The elevator inside Groom Mountain had been descending fast for over ten minutes and suddenly came to a jarring halt next to massive air ducts that poured cold air into the cavern.

"Don't like being underground?" Kirk said as the whine of the elevator wound down.

"Not particularly," Doc said. He didn't want to get into how his mind was calculating how much rock and dirt was above them, automatically figuring out the weight, and what kind of pressure that would exert if it suddenly collapsed. He knew the odds were unlikely, but that knowledge was scant comfort.

They were over two miles below Area 51. This facility, having taken over three years to build and costing over fourteen billion dollars, served one purpose: to detect Rifts as they developed and then locate them.

Doc shoved aside the metal gate to the high-speed elevator and they walked down a corridor carved out of solid rock, over ten feet wide and ten high.

"Ahead is a natural cavern, a void that was discovered early in Area 51's history. No one thought much of it, until it was decided we needed to put in a Super-Kamiokande."

"Right," Kirk said. "The Can."

Doc glanced at him and noticed Kirk had a slight grin.

After two hundred yards, the tunnel opened into the large natural cavern eighty yards deep and eighty wide. They paused in the entrance as Kirk took it all in.

"Most people think there is only one Super-Kamiokande in the world. Over in Japan, deep inside a mine shaft. But we have this one and the Russians also built one, after we figured out that it could detect a Rift in early formation. Sharing data with the Russians and Japanese, we can eventually triangulate the location of a Rift."

A steel grating extended out over the open space, with several workstations.

Doc pointed down. Flat black water reflected the overhead lights. To Kirk it looked like the water in the quarry back home, on a moonless night. Scary, dark, and deep.

"This is a stainless-steel tank holding that water. Sixty meters wide by sixty deep. Along the walls of the tank are over twenty thousand photomultiplier tubes. They are extremely sensitive light sensors that can detect a single photon as it travels through the water and reacts with it. They are all linked together to those displays over there."

A young Asian man was watching the displays Doc indicated, one of two people on the duty shift. The other on-duty person was a young woman five desks away, peering at her screen with a rather bored expression.

"Since we built this, the Can has detected the formation of every Rift in the past seven years: nine altogether. So it is not exactly the most exciting place to work, unless something bad happens."

"Sort of like the Nightstalkers," Kirk said.

Doc raised his voice so the two worker bees could hear. "The Can is critical in getting us on-site as quickly as possible. We even managed to block three Rifts from opening by arriving before the formation was complete." He walked over to the young man. "Anything?"

"Nope. Everything's quiet." He nodded toward a stack of papers. "The latest printouts are there for you, Doc."

"Technically," Doc continued to Kirk, "this is a ring-imaging water Cerenkov detector. Cerenkov light is produced when an electrically charged particle travels through water. The reason this has to be so far underground is to allow the earth and rock above us to block out the photons emitted by man's devices on the surface of the planet. It also helps that we are in the middle of the desert."

"Yeah," the young man said, "but we're underneath Area 51. Some researchers do some strange experiments in that place. Once in a while we pick up some weird readings."

"Yes," Doc said, not wanting to dwell on that. "But most of the Can is focused into the Earth. It covers the entire planet. Since charged particles should not be emitted by the Earth itself, no one thought to use it that way. It was only when, at the most classified levels, information on the Rifts was shared among various governments, that someone checked the data over in Japan and found they'd picked up abnormal readings through the planet when each Rift occurred. So we had the Japanese keep an eye out, and sure enough, for the next Rift, they picked it up, even before it opened. So it became a priority to build one here and in Russia."

"What exactly are you looking for?" Kirk asked, pretending to be interested. He now also appreciated Nada's last Yada: *Just tell me how to kill it.* This place was all about telling them where the "it" to be killed was, and he appreciated that, but still...

The young man answered that. "We're looking for muons."

"Right," Kirk said. "Moo-ons?"

"Seriously," Doc said, "there is a reason Moms makes me take every new team member down here. I know all you are thinking of is *just tell me how to kill it.*" Doc laughed at the surprised look that flashed over Kirk's face. "Yes, every Shooter focuses on that. But you have to understand the Rifts aren't fantasy and the Fireflies aren't magical. It's science. We will figure it out someday."

Doc pointed down at the dark water. "Eighty years ago physicists thought the building blocks of matter were the proton, electron, and the neutron. They also knew about three other particles: the photon, neutrino, and positron. But there was a problem. The protons in the proximity of the nucleus, holding equal charge, should repel each other, but they didn't. It was a Japanese scientist who found the reason, and he was awarded the Nobel for his brilliance.

"He came up with a new force to keep the protons in place, which required a new particle, which he called the meson. He determined that the ratio of the force in this new particle was inversely proportional to its mass. This made the meson two hundred times larger than the electron.

"Once the theory was out there, lots of scientists started looking for mesons. One of the best ways of doing that was to study the sun because it puts out the strongest electromagnetic field in the solar system."

"Sort of the way Eddington proved Einstein's relativity right by studying eclipses," Kirk said, causing Doc to take a couple of intellectual superiority steps backward.

"I had a really good teacher," Kirk explained, seeing Doc's surprise. "Everyone needs at least one really good teacher, even someone from Parthenon, Arkansas. He liked giving us weird information 'cause he knew some of us liked it." Pads didn't, Kirk recalled. He'd learned early on to keep the little nuggets to himself or else Pads probably would have kept him from even going to school. It was only because of the free lunch that Pads allowed any of them to walk the three miles to the small schoolhouse.

"That is true," Doc agreed. "I went into physics because of a high school teacher."

"So we got something in common there," Kirk said.

"We have the team in common," Doc said.

"That too," Kirk allowed.

Doc stared at him for a few moments. "All right. Back to the physics. What they found was that it was more than just the meson. There were two particles: one had the strong charge with little mass: the pion. The other had a lot of mass but little charge: the muon. Both are very unstable and decay rapidly when separated. The muon decays into three particles: an electron, a neutrino, and an antineutrino. Discovering this was the start of particle physics, which opened the doorway to what you just referred to: quantum mechanics and special relativity as well as Einstein's energy-mass relation.

"Which brings us to the Rifts," Doc said. "For some reason, as they form, they start emitting muons. And the muons decay in a weird way. Which is why I came up with my multiverse theory. I believe that this difference means the rules of physics on the other side of the Rifts are different than our rules."

"Can I ask you something?" Kirk said.

"That's why we are here," Doc replied.

"What happens to the Fireflies if the Nightstalkers aren't around to destroy them?"

"They are very destructive, depending on what they occupy. Before the Can, the Nightstalkers had to focus on police reports, news reports, anything that indicated a strange occurrence and then go investigate."

"Maybe we're pissing them off, opening Rifts into *their* world," Kirk noted.

"Maybe," Doc allowed. "But we live on *our* world."

"Not arguing with you, Doc."

"The Can gives us thirty-eight minutes of warning that a Rift is starting. It picks up activity, but we can't locate it for thirty-eight minutes. At that point, there's enough activity that one of the other Cans picks up activity, which starts us in the right direction. Then, after forty-six minutes, we can triangulate and pinpoint the exact location."

"Not much time."

"It's why the Protocol for getting to the Snake, loaded, and airborne is thirty minutes," Doc explained. "And there's something else," Doc added. "Another reason we take this so seriously. Why the Russians might even be more worried about the Rifts than us."

"And that is?"

Doc glanced at the young man at the computer. "Let's head back up. It takes a while." Before he walked away, Doc picked up the thick stack of printouts.

They went back down the tunnel and got on the elevator.

"Tunguska," Doc said.

"And that is?"

"A place in the middle of Russia. Where there appears to have been a nuclear explosion before there were nuclear weapons. In 1908 something went off; most think it was a meteor exploding in the air, just before it hit the surface of the planet. It blew with a thousand times the power of the bomb we dropped on Hiroshima and took out eighty million trees."

"That's a lot of trees," Kirk said as the rock walls surrounding the elevator raced by.

"Yes, it is," Doc said. "The kicker, though, was when the Russian Can went online. They picked up very, very faint traces of the exact same type of weird muonic activity from Rifts still emanating at Tunguska. Right in the center of where that blast occurred."

"That's not good."

"It is not."

"So the Rifts can develop into something very bad," Kirk summarized.

"Ms. Jones believes so. She thinks there is a possibility that a Rift can become a Portal. She thinks that what was forming on our last mission was a case where a Rift was changing, trying to grow. Trying to send something else through. Something that might have come through back in 1908 and caused the Tunguska explosion. Or the explosion might even have been a Portal failing."

They both swayed as the elevator abruptly slowed, then came to a halt. Two Support guards were waiting, one sliding open the gate to the elevator, the other maintaining security. They walked down a hallway, out a door guarded by two more contractors, and then into a massive hangar, burrowed into the side of Groom Mountain. It was quite the contrast as Doc got behind the wheel of the old beat-up Jeep and drove them out to pass by the most advanced aircraft being tested in the world.

As Doc pulled into the growing darkness, Kirk looked over at him. "You know, Doc, in Sniper School, they've got a real problem in their recruitment program."

"What is that?"

"They've got to select individuals who can do two contradictory things. Shoot another human being on nothing but an order. And also *not* shoot on order. Lots of people can do one or the other, but it's a rare man who can do both."

They passed through the Area 51 rear gate, heading toward the Ranch.

"I imagine so," Doc said. He glanced over. "I also imagine there is a reason you bring this up."

"It occurs to me, no offense intended," Kirk said, "that you're just like one of those people we go after who open up Rifts. You want to figure the Rifts out, too. What's causing them, what's on the other side. It's just that you're smarter than those other scientists."

"How so?"

"You're doing it from the inside. All those printouts are important to you. The Can is important to you beyond simply being an early warning device. It's a research device."

A muscle on the side of Doc's face quivered. "I'm not a traitor."

"I wasn't saying you were," Kirk said. "I'm saying you're doing it the smart way. Takes a unique man to do that. Perhaps that's what Ms. Jones saw in you."

CHAPTER 11

THE NEXT DAY

Burns shifted position. Some of his wounds had not quite healed, a terrible itching that just wouldn't stop. He peered through the night-vision scope at the Chapel Hill dog park. It was empty, and a lone flickering light cast long shadows across the hard-packed couple of acres.

The doctor's headlights were like searchlights in the night-vision scope as the car pulled into the empty parking lot a hundred yards away. Burns tracked the doctor as he scurried to the gate. The reticle in the sight had the man's head perfectly framed.

The doctor had a flashlight, which wasn't exactly covert, but Burns didn't have high expectations after meeting him in the parking lot.

Winslow made his way to the trash can and pulled up the lid, wincing at the foul smell from dozens of poop bags. Such was his lust, though, that he reached right in, fingers searching.

That's when Burns got the feeling. It was one many combat vets experienced and the smart ones trusted. It *was* too easy and too dumb. Burns shifted from Doctor Winslow and began to scan the area beyond the parking lot, into the trees.

Through his night scope, Burns caught the faintest glimmer in the trees a quarter mile away and he immediately knew what had caused it: someone breaking the seal on their own night scope and letting the computer-generated light out. It was gone as quickly as it had appeared, but Burns pressed his eye socket tighter into his own rubber seal to prevent the same mistake.

There was a sniper out there covering the doctor making the pickup.

Where the hell did Winslow get a sniper? And Burns knew right away: an investor protecting his investment.

In the dog park, Winslow withdrew the hard drive from the bag with a trembling hand.

From his perch, Burns could have sworn the doctor was doing some kind of jig. A Snoopy happy dance perhaps? As the doctor ran back to his car, Burns focused on the real threat in the trees. He waited, a trait Nada had impressed upon him as essential to survival.

After thirty minutes, the sniper emerged from the trees. Burns tensed as a second person, rifle slung over his shoulder, emerged fifty meters away. A dark van, headlights off, pulled into the parking lot and both got inside.

Two snipers on over-watch.

Burns nodded. This was good. There would be extra protection.

CHAPTER 12

THE NEXT DAY

The Research Triangle at the junction of the towns of Durham, Chapel Hill, and Raleigh, North Carolina, started out using the brains from nearby Duke and the University of North Carolina to do just that: research. Then more businesspeople with financing were bought in, more patents were sold, and a shift from pure research for knowledge and science to research for profit took over the region.

There is a difference.

Southeast of Chapel Hill, and southwest of Durham, near Jordan Lake, is a large gated community set pretty much in the middle of nowhere: Senators Club. In the most exclusive part of the exclusive Senators Club, Doctor Winslow was preparing for a dinner party, the day after having secured his future at the dog park.

He stared at himself in the mirror while the electric toothbrush buzzed in his mouth. He used it three times a day for the full two minutes, just like the instructions said. He was good about instructions and he always read them first, while whatever he bought was still in pieces in the box. He wondered about people who'd buy something and start putting it together like they'd been born just knowing how to assemble a bookshelf. They were the people who left off screws that didn't fit, as if the manufacturer had sent no plans, no instructions, and didn't have a purpose for everything in the box.

Over the buzz inside his head, he could hear the caterers preparing for the party and his wife's excited voice telling them what to do. As if they didn't do this for a living and she wasn't just a nuisance. He supposed such nuisances were part of the perils of their job description. But why hire professionals if you were going to flit around them and tell them how to do the jobs you hired them to do? He had married Lilith even though she rarely read or followed instructions, leaving it dependent on her moods. He glanced at her sink in the bathroom bigger than most people's living rooms. Her toothbrush sat on its charger and it had never run for the full two minutes. He'd timed her on several occasions and she'd never broken one minute. Always moving on to the next thing before the first was properly done.

His vanity was pristine and Lilith's was covered with bottles and brushes and cords to blow-dryers and irons and things whose purposes he couldn't imagine, and he ran a lab that made some of the most sophisticated scientific equipment in the country—in the world, for that matter. But his wife's vanity and its machines were as much a mystery to him as relativity was to her. She wasn't a dumb woman, almost smart, but he'd caught her reading in the huge Jacuzzi tub one time with a lamp clamped to the towel rack above her head to shine down on the pages while the cord stretched across the room to the nearest plug.

She had a doctorate, too, but he never thought of her that way. It was in some arcane field that served no useful function:

interdisciplinary philosophy. Sometimes he resented that they shared the same title of doctor, as if the top of her heap of education somehow equaled his.

He rinsed and walked to the large closet to the right of the bathroom (also bigger than most people's bedrooms) that was all his. His wife left his laundry hanging on the hook outside the door and never invaded this inner sanctum, like a redneck would value his man-cave with his naked-girl racing calendars, old fridge full of beer, and gun rack.

He stopped at the first built-in and admired his six-piece watch winder, rhythmically rocking back and forth, keeping the elegant timepieces inside running. It was his favorite thing in the house. It cost more than most people's watches and its entire purpose was to keep the timepieces running because they weren't on his moving wrist. It was actually the height of indulgence for a man who'd grown up on a dairy farm in Wisconsin, spending his childhood in the barn, wrist always moving over and over, never stopping, in between morning chores and evening chores and going to school and to sleep at night, as if he were the machine he now admired doing the work for him.

He always saved the "choosing of the watch" for after he was dressed, the crowning event in his ritual.

He opened the drawer where his socks were neat little bundles arranged by color and use: dress, casual, and workout, with subdivisions in each. There were times when he knew his wife wouldn't be home when he opened all the drawers and cupboards in the huge closet like some secret cross-dresser on a quiet afternoon and just stared at the perfection of a place for everything, and everything in its place. He loved how the colors of his dress shirts worked from white to light to dark from left to right, matching the suits hanging over them. And the ties on the motorized rack could roll up, rank after rank, like soldiers going to war, also ranked by color.

But he was always drawn back to the socks. His mother had tried to keep up, but the farm had taken too much out of her and she'd drawn the line at sorting socks. Everyone has their limits. She cleaned, she had her own rules, but his socks she dumped in his drawer in one tangled mess. Luckily he was an only child, so he didn't have to sort his out from a sibling's. But the amount of time he spent looking for two that matched? In grad school he'd sat through a boring lecture by writing an algorithm for the hours he'd wasted on what should have been solved before the drawer.

He reached into the drawer and moved aside the neat pile of socks dedicated to matching his various golfing outfits and picked up the laptop. He felt a rush of excitement, like the redneck would if one of those girls on the calendar actually entered his man-cave.

He'd finally broken a rule, but it was going to make him rich. Technically, richer than he'd been once upon a time, but why quibble over some zeros?

His students thought ten million was a lot of money, but he knew it wasn't. Not when you had to fill the watch winder with six timepieces of quality and then support the timepieces with the lifestyle worthy of them and buy a house in Senators Club. And then fill that house with things required of a house in Senators Club.

It was a big house.

He'd been surprised when he'd received that e-mail from Craegen out of the blue.

But sometimes life gives you opportunities and you have to make the best of them.

Craegen had been ambitious; Winslow remembered that much about him. The e-mail was a boast, a slap at a professor who years ago had blown off a young freshman who had been too eager and not paid his dues. Somehow Craegen had gotten a bootleg copy of the original Rift program. And he was going to do it, figure it out, be acknowledged as the genius he was by doing what no one had done before: bring it under control. Winslow's eyes had glazed over as the slaps in the face had come one after another. Near the end Craegen had temptingly written some of the algorithms. Incomplete, but enough to let Winslow know he was for real, which was the staggering blow.

But now he had what had once been Craegen's. It had never occurred to Winslow to ask the strange man how he had gotten the drive or where Craegen was or how he even knew about the e-mail. Such details weren't essential. What was on the drive was the key.

It had all been very cloak-and-dagger yesterday and last night, full of dire warnings, and the garbage can full of dog shit had not been fun, but the prize overwhelmed even the five hundred thousand he'd forked over.

Winslow paused for the first time, a slight ripple of concern slopping through his brain. The money had been surprisingly easy to obtain, but that had been cloak-and-dagger, too. Winslow's mother had warned the children that they should never, ever borrow money. But Winslow's mother had died in the farmhouse, as the auctioneers were selling everything off and Winslow was away on his full scholarship ride. Winslow knew Lilith would not be pleased if she knew whom he had gone to for the loan and the terms he had agreed to. But it wasn't about the money. Even he was aware of that.

Perhaps it was a midlife crisis?

What is a midlife crisis for a physicist? Not a red sports car or dewy-eyed grad students. He'd already been through both those, the latter several times.

But the Nobel?

The ultimate prize for a physicist whose career was on the way down, because they aged like ballerinas, the youngest and the brightest getting all the attention. He'd struggled through enough productions of *Swan Lake* with his wife to see that the leads never had crow's-feet. Not around their eyes anyway. The old physicists tended to stick ever tighter to what they thought they knew, never reaching out for the new for fear of learning that what they'd believed for decades was wrong.

He could admit he was wrong if this turned out right.

He'd arranged the dinner party to empty out the lab this evening except for Ivar, so the student could move the final pieces downstairs at UNC. He trusted Ivar to an extent, because behind his bland expression, Winslow could see the intelligence minus the same hungry ambition eating away at most grad students' chests. The perfect combination to be used. Winslow found it a bit amusing that Ivar had taken the lack of an invitation to the party as a deliberate slight, when it was really an invitation to share greatness. Rather, more to touch it, as there would be no sharing. One did not share with students. One took.

Ivar was willing to work eighty hours a week like the rest of them for no pay so they could get their doctorates, so they could work other kids behind them for eighty-hour weeks while they tried to invent something they could sell to the corporate world they all professed to despise, or, even better, DARPA, the Defense Advanced Research Projects Agency, since everyone knew the government overpaid for everything.

But Ivar was meticulous, so the professor felt reasonably secure knowing the kid was the one in the special lab he'd secretly designed earlier today in a remote corner of the basement of the physics research building for the beginning of this. It was the perfect setup, used years ago for experiments with toxic and radioactive materials and perfectly shielded. More importantly, Winslow needed someone he could trust and who had the smarts to deal with things, since this was the first time he had ever gone off the grid; the first time he hadn't followed the instructions.

The laptop Winslow now held was old, one that had been in the lab forever. Passed beneath the fingers of countless grad students and postdocs. The top was layered with faded stickers of bands long defunct. The key to the laptop was that it was linked to the mainframe that Ivar should have finished moving by now, so its own capabilities weren't important. It was just the originator of the program. The mainframe in the secret lab was going to do the crunching and run the program. Winslow dug deeper in the sock drawer, behind the specially padded ones he'd used during his running phase. He retrieved the hard drive, meticulously labeled by Ivar: *Dr. Winslow*.

Ivar labeled everything that came in and out of the lab and had already fastened the label on the drive during the five minutes Winslow had left the disk in the lab in order for its contents to be copied into the mainframe. Ivar hadn't even asked about the ASU label, his level of curiosity nil.

Winslow dug his thumbnail under the label and peeled it off. He pressed open the slide on the left edge of the laptop and gingerly pressed the hard drive in. He smiled as he watched the computer buzz to life, much like his toothbrush.

He pulled out his cell phone and sent the e-mail he'd saved in draft, with the specific instructions on what Ivar was to do in the secret lab at the same time. Based on the e-mail he'd received from Craegen, and his own examination of the algorithms, it would take weeks for the program to crunch the algorithms and be ready to activate, but they'd be weeks well spent. He put the laptop back in the drawer, making sure the power cord was still connected and leaving the lid open enough so it would stay on. On second thought, he wedged a pair of socks in between the top and the blank spot next to the touch pad, ensuring that it wouldn't accidently close and shut the program down. He covered the laptop with socks. Then he had second thoughts. The laptop might overheat, buried like that, and no one came in here anyway. He cleared the socks off the top.

He put on his suit pants, shirt, tie, and jacket. Then he went back to the sock drawer. He could see the slight glow from the partially open laptop as he did the choosing of the socks. It made him smile. He pulled out his favorite pair.

Then he hovered over the watch winder, mesmerized as it rocked back and forth.

Tonight was a Rolex night.

* * *

Ivar was splitting his attention between watching the mainframe monitor set on a table in the middle of the room, waiting to start a replay of this evening's Duke–UNC alumni charity basketball game, and labeling things. It was after eight and he knew the game was probably over, but he'd studiously avoided accessing any social media on his iPhone or laptop so that he wouldn't accidently find out the score.

Unfortunately, by not checking either, he also hadn't received the e-mail from Doctor Winslow about changing the setting on a critical dampener and shutting down the Internet connection from the mainframe to the old laptop once they both initiated.

For lack of a nail.

It was a saying that would have been lost on the student.

Instead, he was using a label maker. Things had to be organized. This room was below ground level, in the subbasement that was mainly used to store old tables and chairs and desks. Even the building's maintenance people rarely came down here. Why Doctor Winslow had chosen this room off the beaten path, Ivar didn't consider worth pondering. Winslow could have explained to him why he'd chosen this particular room—that the room was shielded and that a single trunk line brought in power and Internet and a landline for a phone—but Winslow didn't believe in explaining to grad students. Besides, Ivar's main concern was that all this gear, new and old, lacked labels. He'd just spent two hours simply hauling the last of it down here from the main lab upstairs.

Ivar glanced over at the monitor. All within parameters. Organized. Doing what it was designed to do, which Ivar knew was something that could be very, very original, although the professor had been rather vague on what the end result should be.

Since he had to miss the game live, he should have been invited to the dinner party, Ivar thought as he labeled a drawer *Label Maker*. It held the extra cartridges to load into the machine. He saw no irony in this.

He checked the clock on the wall. The game had to be over by now. Even if it went to overtime, which would be cool, but fuck those Duke Blue Devils anyway. He'd attended a lecture up there in Durham and one could feel the snobbery slithering off the Duke professor at being made to talk to a bunch of dumb UNC grad students. Everyone had been looking forward to this off-season charity game because it would be played by some of the most famous graduates of both programs.

Okay, Ivar decided. He sat down on the old Naugahyde couch and picked up the remote.

Game time.

Behind him, the first crackle of a golden spark arced around the mainframe.

* * *

Inside Doctor Winslow's sock drawer, the screen of the laptop shimmered out of the darkness and took on the faintest hint of gold.

* * *

Deep under Area 51, it sounded like a hundred angry grasshoppers had been loosed in the cavern holding the Can. Several cycles ago, someone had remembered from an undergraduate physiology class that a clicking sound activated the reticular formation with a higher degree of success than any other form of alarm. They had then taken that to the extreme, just in case both people on duty had fallen hard asleep or into a coma during their duty shift.

Both, however, were awake, and while one turned off the clicking, the other activated the alarm to be transmitted to the Nightstalkers, Japan, and Russia.

* * *

Nada was sharpening his machete, Eagle was reading, Kirk was fiddling with his PRT, Doc was taking pills out of bottles and placing them in various slots on a fishing tackle box (which he had discovered was the perfect way to carry the max array of possible pills efficiently), and Mac was toying with a Claymore mine, modifying the contents.

"Really," Mac said. "They have to print 'front toward enemy' on the front? How stupid are people?"

Nada didn't even look up. "In Afghanistan, one of the Afghan army fellows pulled in his Claymore after an overnight patrol base, just rolling the cord around the body of the mine, and put it in his ruck without removing the fuse. The first time he did a rucksack flop, he blew himself in two and killed three others around him. People are pretty stupid."

Eagle lowered his Kindle. "That doesn't connect directly with Mac's complaint about the printing. It's more in line with the warnings they put on plastic laundry covers: *Don't wrap this around your head: could be bad for you.* I think Darwinism has to get a chance to work. The more we protect stupid people from themselves, the more we ensure the long, slow descent of the human race into idiocracy."

Roland was doing chin-ups on the bar next to his locker. It was either chin-ups or push-ups for Roland most of the time he was in the Den. If he wasn't breaking down a weapon and cleaning it. Moms was in the CP, doing whatever it was Moms did in the CP when she was alone.

Everyone looked up as Nada's cell began playing the tune Kirk had heard once before. Then Doc's, Mac's, Eagle's, and Roland's went off. Barely two seconds later, his PRT began playing "Lawyers, Guns and Money."

Moms came flying out of the CP. "We've got a pre-Rift alert from the Can."

They were already moving toward the exit.

* * *

Downstairs, Doctor Winslow picked at the tiny bit of salad on his plate. It was all strange stuff that he hated, without even knowing what it was called. The farm had its detractions, but normal, hearty food had not been one of them. One had to eat solid food in order to do all those chores. This food was for people who thought pine nuts and cranberries made a salad.

He had a bit of a buzz going from three glasses of champagne he'd gotten down before meeting his wife on the main floor. A quiet celebration all his own. On top of the program initiating at the secret lab, there was the added satisfaction that UNC had won the alumni game handily, and it was fun to rub it in the faces of the Dukies, one of whom was a guest.

The table held fourteen, and he had been able to concoct his favorite mix. Three couples who might be considered his peers, but he secretly knew weren't now, because they didn't know about the laptop upstairs and the program it was running. There were also six grad students. He always invited over a fresh batch each time, because Lilith loved seeing their faces when they had to pick up their passes from the guard at the gate and then pull up in their beat-up little cars and see the huge double staircases and the chandeliers. It was petty, but it kept her happy, and when she was happy she didn't care what he did in his closet. Winslow would never admit to her that he enjoyed seeing their faces, too. He also enjoyed that specified on the gate passes was that they expired at midnight, adding a fairy-tale edge to all of it. Poof and they would return back to their miserable little apartments.

Lilith had called him a sadist when she walked around the table. Mixing the haves with the have-nots. His point, which he knew was a waste of time to explain to her, was that a have-not would not make it to a have if they didn't get to see what they had. There was some pronoun confusion there on his part, but Lilith understood the base drive to cause turmoil. As Gore Vidal had once famously said: "It is not enough to succeed. Others must fail." Winslow had understood the sentiment the minute he heard it, and he always remembered it, not even needing his recorder app to remind him.

Still, the guests seemed happy and his buzz was growing and he was considering a fourth glass of champagne. He had much to celebrate although he could not speak of it. He'd never been much of a drinker, not like Lilith, who could put it away faster than you could pop the cork. Looking down the long table he could see the flush of her cheeks and the liquid glaze in her eye that meant she'd also had more than three while awaiting their first guests.

Winslow sighed. Her drinking could go one of three ways later in the evening, after the last guest departed. From the very low chance of an enthusiastic blow job, to the higher possibility of torrents of tears and recriminations on how he'd destroyed her career, her life, and her one chance of happiness, to the most likely—and optimal—result of her simply passing out on the bed, leaving him free to go back to his closet. He idly wondered—for the first time, perhaps because of his own inebriated state—what that one chance had been? He felt like she'd pretty much let her chances pass her by well before he met her.

Winslow poked at his sliver of purple lettuce and thought of her in a long gown in Sweden sitting at the table as he accepted his award and made a short (but smart) speech that was just about complete on the recorder on his phone. He knew she'd be happy then, because the Nobel, despite high-minded protests to the contrary, was a prize. And when one won a prize, it meant many others had lost. He must have smiled at the thought, because the physicist seated next to him asked:

"What are you so happy about?"

"Ah, a new experiment," Winslow said. The four grad students who worked in his lab and his one physicist competitor from Duke all frowned, wondering what he could be talking about. Winslow abruptly grabbed his full glass of champagne and downed it. "To knowledge!"

Startled, the others at the table awkwardly followed suit.

Feeling emboldened, Winslow gestured for one of the wait people to load his glass once more.

* * *

The Snake lifted out of the Barn and Eagle wasted no time shifting the wings from vertical to horizontal. Eagle took them up to high altitude to fly a waiting racetrack, making sure the cabin was pressurized, because once they got a location for the Rift, the higher they were, the faster they could move. They all knew that on the other side of the world the Russian team was also airborne, but because of the recent theft of the hard drive, odds were the Rift was going to be on this side.

Moms was on the link with Ms. Jones, running through the things they always ran through on a Rift alert. Air Force refuelers were being scrambled at all points of the compass to top off the Snake if the distance to the target was greater than the craft's range. For the moment, the number-one priority of the entire US military and the Support staff at Area 51 was to back up the Nightstalkers. At various military posts around the country and overseas, Quick Reaction Forces were being alerted, with no clue what they might be involved in.

Mac was kicking back in his seat and on the team net. "Hey, Doc. What's the number, given that we got human error already involved courtesy of our stupid Courier?"

"I'd say it's grave, perhaps at four."

Kirk looked across at Mac and raised his eyebrows in question.

"Doc got a Rule of Seven," Mac explained. "We could be in the middle of some heavy shit, bullets flying, Roland flaming things, and Doc will be trying to figure out how bad it could get. He says true disasters, like the *Titanic*, or a plane crashing—"

"Hey!" Eagle yelled from the cockpit. "None of that."

"—require a minimum of seven things to go wrong, one of which is always human error. So far we ain't never hit higher than a five, but that was pretty bad."

"Forget the Rule of Seven and focus on the Rule of One." Nada was writing in his Protocol, having figured out a way to save six seconds during loading. "It don't take seven things to kill you. Once is bad enough."

* * *

The waitstaff came out with dinner, pretending it came from the kitchen, which was a joke because Lilith couldn't boil water without burning a hole in the pan, despite the Viking stove and whatever fridge, some big name, that she absolutely had to have. Lilith was on her feet, chattering, as if she might have to dash to the kitchen to correct something.

Winslow would have laughed, but instead he turned to the cute grad student, Mary, next to him and thought she might be someone who would dash in to tend to something, but not food. Mary was short, toned, and had wavy red hair that attracted lots of attention.

"When are your orals?" Winslow asked Mary.

She blinked.

"They can be right now," the drunker professor to her other side said.

His wife glared from across the table. "Remember, you don't have a prenup, dipshit."

So they all started talking about prenups, which didn't bother Winslow because he knew Lilith would gut him before she'd get a divorce.

"We don't have a prenup, do we, darling?" Lilith said. That silenced the table.

His wife held up her glass and a waiter refilled it.

"I do love my Champers," she said, calling the champagne by a name that generally set Winslow's teeth on edge. She lifted the glass, some spilling over the edge of the Waterford crystal. "If I leave you, I get nothing, correct?" She looked around the table, stopping at the three pretty grad students, each for a moment. "Nothing." She smiled coldly. "Which is why *I* will never leave."

Everyone started asking for their dessert. The haves had seen this before, while the have-nots were appropriately embarrassed.

The professor raised his glass to Lilith, thinking, *I've got to get rid of her*. He glanced at Mary and thought she might make a nice third ex-wife. But his mind kept sliding back to the computer. He put the glass down and went all the way upstairs to take a leak, but really to look at the laptop. He realized he was staggering slightly and there was a slur in his speech, but he didn't care. He paused in the closet and checked the computer. He was surprised to see the golden glow on the screen.

No data. Just the glow.

He knelt in front of the laptop, as if worshipping it, mesmerized by the glow.

He had no idea how long he had been like that when he suddenly shook his head, snapping out of the trance. His wife probably thought he was off with one of the grad students. He hurriedly got to his feet and made his way downstairs, taking the closest staircase this time, making sure he had a firm grip on the handrail.

As soon as he recovered his seat, he indicated for his champagne glass to be topped off once more.

This was going to work!

* * *

Nada was checking the time, and he looked forward, toward Moms. Her head was cocked at that strange angle she had whenever she was on the direct link to Ms. Jones.

Moms slapped Eagle on the shoulder as Russia and Japan triangulated with the Can under Area 51 to get the first rough approximation of the pending Rift. "North or South Carolina."

Eagle hit the thrusters and they were racing east.

* * *

UNC was ahead and only two minutes to go. The DVR cut to commercial and the jerks at the cable company didn't allow fast-forwarding on some things. Ivar picked up his iPhone and checked his texts and e-mails, relayed from the small wireless transmitter he'd hooked up to the Internet line running into the lab.

"Frack!" Ivar exclaimed as he saw Doctor Winslow's e-mail about the dampener. It was time-stamped over three hours ago.

Ivar looked at the computer. There was the slightest of golden haze around the mainframe. Anxiously, he checked the monitor and breathed a sigh of relief. All within parameters.

He went over to the keyboard and began to type in the code that should have been typed in three hours previously.

* * *

Winslow could barely sit back down. He felt drawn to the computer with an urgency he couldn't comprehend. Lilith was still fuming at her end of the table. Winslow tried to remember what had initiated it. Something about prenups?

Lilith fixed him with her gaze. "Stephen here wants to know more about your experiment. Your *new* experiment. You know, the one you haven't told *me* about."

Winslow glared back. Stephen the chemist was an ass. He'd correct you if you called him Steve or even Steven as if you were ignoring his silent syllables. Winslow downed his glass of champagne and thought of the laptop. The golden glow. He noted that his wife's hand was on Stephen's arm. He'd never considered the fourth possible end of the evening—Lilith with someone else.

"I'm afraid you wouldn't understand it, Stephen," Winslow said.

All the grad students were tracking him now, because it was one thing to be left out of the loop concerning what was going on at the lab, but it was another to see him in his cups and his wife provoking him. This would make great social media chat later.

Mary thought she was saving him by jumping in. "Yes, Doctor Winslow. What is this experiment?"

But that was just throwing gas into the fire. Winslow jumped to his feet, startling everyone. "I'll show you."

He took the stairs two at a time, his rage steadying him. The drawer was partly open. He unplugged the laptop and cradled it in his arms as he took it downstairs.

He was tempted to slam it down on the dining room table, but a small part of his brain that was still functioning knew that would be dangerous to the program running inside.

Stephen laughed, fueling Winslow's rage. Stephen, who'd invented a time release for the pills that made overactive children go limp. "I hope your lab equipment is newer than that laptop."

It *was* old. Under the bright light of the chandelier he could see a fading sticker for John Kerry, buried underneath a couple of band stickers. His real guests, not the students who were too young, hadn't voted for Kerry. When a person got into houses like this, no matter what they'd chanted in their youth, most tended to change, as they had too much money. Which was funny because he'd met Lilith at a rally for liberals and he remembered what his own postdoc supervisor had told him at the time: everyone's a liberal until they buy their first sofa. Students and liberals bought couches. For a moment, through the alcohol fog, he tried to tally how many sofas were in his house, but realized it was futile because there were rooms he'd only been in during the Realtor tour.

He heard Lilith give that girlish laugh, which meant she was now more inclined toward oral sex than evisceration and lamenting, but it was directed at Stephen, whose right arm was angled toward Lilith, under the cover of the table, which helped explain the sudden shift. He realized he'd zoned out, caught again by the golden glow.

Lilith was calling his name and he let the counting and memories go. "Yes, dear Lilith?"

"Are you going to show the rest of us?" Lilith was pointing at the laptop, the charm bracelet that she adorned with a new trinket every year, like a soldier accrued battle ribbons, dangling from her wrist.

Winslow turned the computer so that they could all see why he'd be standing on that dais in Stockholm. Everyone stared back blankly.

"Cool screen saver," a less-than-quick grad student complimented.

"I can't believe you got that old screen to be so bright," another noted, as if that was what he was working on. "Did you figure out how to increase the refresh rate?"

"You fucking idiots," Winslow said. "Don't you see? And Lilith, why don't you just blow Stephen right here under the table?"

* * *

The mainframe now glowed. Ivar stared at it, trying to figure out what label he could put on it. He dropped the labeler and hit the enter key for the dampener again and again.

Nothing.

The glow was expanding, covering the entire table.

Even though he had no clue what Doctor Winslow's experiment was, Ivar had a bad feeling about the golden glow. If he screwed this experiment up, Winslow might derail his PhD.

* * *

They'd topped off once from a KC-135 tanker, somewhere over the emptiness of middle Kansas. Eagle had kept the Snake in lockstep with the bigger plane as the boom from the tanker descended in front of them, sucking in the precious fuel.

There was no discussion about who was going to jump first. Roland rigged, as Eagle began a descent when they crossed the

Smoky Mountains, down into breathable air, and started depressurizing.

Moms held up an iPad from the copilot seat as Mac passed leg straps between Roland's massive thighs. "We've got it pinpointed from the Japanese and Russians. Outside Chapel Hill."

Nada took the iPad and passed it back to Roland, who paused in rigging. He checked the Google maps display, searching for landmarks he could reference on the way down. Jordan Lake was a great one for the FRP—far recognition point—that he could spot as soon as he exited the aircraft.

Then he zoomed, searching for an IRP—immediate reference point—to lock down his landing spot. Roland frowned. It looked like the target was inside a compound. "What kind of place is this?" Roland asked. "Some sort of secure research facility?"

"It's a gated community," Moms said.

"A what?" Roland asked.

"Bunch of houses surrounded by a fence, with a guard at the gate," Moms said. "Sort of like Fort Bragg, except it doesn't have the soldiers or the training areas."

"It will have a golf course," Eagle said.

Roland ran his finger over the screen. "It does have a golf course. You could land an entire stick of jumpers from a 141 on it."

"I want everyone to rig," Moms said. "We're all going in via drop, even you, Doc. Mac, set his automatic opening device at one thousand AGL just in case. But please pull earlier, Doc, like you were trained, and follow us down. Eagle, you're going to Wall the community's perimeter. Put in probes to block any Firefly from getting out of that place." She checked the time. "It's going to be tight, but we can contain this and we have to go in quiet for concealment. Roland, right on the house, top-down, go in fast. HALO," she added, meaning he would free-fall for most of the drop, then pull at the last minute to keep from crashing through the roof. "The rest of us are going out HAHO, right after you. So you don't have much time on your recon before we land, because gravity rules."

"Roger that, Moms." Roland squatted and cinched his leg straps tight. A loose leg strap on opening shock would be literally ball-busting. Ready, he scooted out of the way as Moms climbed between the seats—careful not to hit any of Eagle's controls—to join the rest in rigging and then inspecting each other. There were elbows, knees, parachutes, and weapons all over the place, but every member of the team had done in-flight rigging—not approved for amateurs—many times.

Doc looked very unhappy, having been forced to go through parachute training when he became a Nightstalker, but never liking it. Moms never had him jump if she could help it, but this was the exception that made the rule for the training. And it was the price he was willing to pay to be on the inside.

By the time the Snake crossed over the Uwharrie National Forest where several of them had conducted their Robin Sage graduation exercise for the Special Forces Qualification Course, the Nightstalkers were rigged, passing the iPad around, memorizing this unique target.

* * *

Winslow wiped the Champers off his face. His guests were making their excuses, scurrying to the door, eager to get away from the coming debacle. He pressed his special card into Mary's hand and leaned close. "Call my private number in a bit."

Mary blinked, glanced over her shoulder at his wife, and let the card drop to the floor.

Winslow was impressed. Smarter than she'd appeared. "Winslow."

Doctor Winslow turned. A colleague, albeit from Duke. "Yes?"

"That isn't right, is it?" And with that, the colleague was gone with the rest of them.

At first Winslow thought it was about his wife and the Champers and his telling her to go blow Stephen in front of everyone, but then he saw it. The screen of the laptop was going crazy. The gold field was writhing; that was the only way he could describe it.

Well, of course it was, he realized just as quickly.

It was working.

But why weren't the dampeners kicking in?

* * *

"Opening ramp," Eagle announced.

Roland walked forward, carrying parachute and reserve, a machine gun, a flamer, body armor, ammunition, and a bunch of other gear that added over 160 pounds to his body weight.

"I'm going to give green directly above the LZ," Eagle said. "So if you don't pull, you'll go through the roof, but be on target."

"Funny guy," Roland said.

Mac started humming and the team joined in, and then, surprisingly, it was Moms who began chanting: "*Roland was a warrior from the land of the Midnight Sun.*"

A couple of those in the know joined in.

"*With a Thompson gun for hire.*"

The ramp cracked open and air swirled in. The rest of the team joined in for the next line.

"*Fighting to be done.*"

The ramp locked in place. Roland looked over his shoulder at the team and Moms, a big grin on his face. He gave a thumbs-up.

The green light went on and he stepped off into darkness.

Moms fell silent and so did the team.

Moms stepped forward and took Roland's place on the ramp. In the lead.

* * *

Winslow ignored everyone and grabbed his cell phone. What the hell was that landline number he'd installed in the secret lab? He scrolled through his contacts list and found it, under Nobel. He pressed.

It rang. And rang.

Finally a hurried voice answered. "Yes?"

"Ivar! The dampeners?"

"I'm trying."

Winslow gripped the phone so hard it creaked, close to cracking. "They're not in already?"

"No." There was a pause. "Uh, it's glowing."

"The mainframe?"

"And it's all around the table. It's getting bigger!"

The professor looked at the laptop screen. It too was glowing. Pulsing. Outward. Not possible. But it was happening.

It worked.

Nobel, here I come, bitch, Winslow thought.

"What's the particle reading?" he demanded.

"Negative twelve point six."

"Negative? It can't be a negative."

* * *

Ivar had no clue what was going on, as Doctor Winslow hadn't told him.

He typed so hard the keyboard almost broke, but it was no use. The dampeners Doctor Winslow had developed, something no one had understood, were simply not engaging.

* * *

Roland was at terminal velocity as he dropped through four thousand feet. He was alternating between watching the terrain and houses below and his altimeter.

* * *

"Ivar? Ivar?"

There was a burst of static so strong that Winslow pushed the phone away from his ear. Lilith was in front of him, in 100 percent anger/regret mode. Stephen had smartly scurried out the door with all the others.

"Ivar?"

Just static, then it went silent.

Winslow looked at the screen of the laptop.

A golden pulse surged from the screen, hitting the professor. Smoke rose from the singed spot on his shirt.

"Shut it down!" Lilith was pounding on his back.

Winslow leaned over and his fingers flew over the keys to no avail.

No Nobel?

He punched the small button on the left side to eject the hard drive.

To no avail.

He slammed the laptop shut, but the glow was bigger than the machine and nothing happened. He opened it back up to work the keyboard with one hand while his fingers on the other were still pressing to eject. His hand on the keyboard began to quiver. He tried to stop it, but watched helplessly as that hand tapped the return key and he saw the screen begin to shimmer with lights, brighter than the gold behind them, and these tiny lights started to move toward him out of the screen like when he was a kid and holding a mason jar for the fireflies.

They flew out of the screen as he saw his hand being sucked into it. He had a moment of feeling good, feeling superior, because he actually thought of Ivar and that meant he wasn't completely selfish.

* * *

Roland pulled at eight hundred feet AGL. He had pinpointed the target house, noting several cars moving away.

He touched down on the peak of the roof as gentle as Santa delivering goods to a child who'd been nice—even though the one in this house was almost certainly naughty.

* * *

Winslow saw the gold sparks flash by. The last thing he saw was Lilith's face, screaming something and swatting futilely as the six sparks circled her briefly then raced out the front door.

Then Winslow's arm went into the screen.

Followed by the rest of him.

The big platinum Rolex fell with a thud onto the keyboard.

* * *

Roland popped the quick releases, letting his chute slide onto the roof as he readied the M-240 machine gun. He was scanning, quickly doing a three-sixty, when he saw them come out of the walls of the house and scatter in different directions.

"I count six Fireflies leaving the target," Roland announced. "We've got Rift."

* * *

Lilith collapsed in shock. The hired help had left after serving dessert, the guests scattered at the confrontation, so there was no one left in the house as the Fireflies left.

CHAPTER 13

Moms dumped air, the rest of the team following. "Mac, you take the front yard. Nada, back. Doc, safest place for you is to follow Nada. Eagle, how's the Wall going?"

Eagle had the Snake at sixty feet AGL and was flying the outer fence of Senators Club. Every quarter mile, he fired a probe into the ground. The probes linked to each other, transmitting a field that would contain the Fireflies inside of them.

"It's a big damn compound," Eagle said. "Forty-four percent contained."

"Faster," Moms ordered. "Roland, we're coming in."

* * *

Roland had heard the screaming, which had abruptly stopped, but he was more focused on the immediate area. The Fireflies were out and who knew what they would get into? He grabbed his deflated parachute and wound some of the material around one of the pipes that protruded from the roof, using it as a make-shift rope. He climbed down to a balcony on the second floor. He busted through a large set of glass French doors.

Roland moved swiftly along the second-floor hallway, kicking doors, clearing the top floor.

There were a lot of doors.

* * *

Moms landed in the front yard, dumped her chute, and readied her MP-5. The area was well lit with streetlights and all she needed was someone working the graveyard shift to spot her. Then again, the only people here who might work a late shift were ER doctors. Support was on its way to help secure the community, but while Eagle was working on containment, she had to maintain concealment. She dragged her chute and stuffed it behind a clump of bushes in front of the house, then went to the wide-open front door.

She slid in the door, back against the wall, quartering the room, muzzle of the weapon following her eyes. The foyer was overwhelming, double staircases wrapping down to an entrance bigger than the house in Kansas where she'd spent many dark years.

She edged around to the open doorway.

There was a Rift. It appeared stable.

A woman lay in front of it.

Moms knelt next to the woman. Reaching into her vest, she pulled out an amyl nitrate capsule and cracked it under Lilith's nose. She stirred, eyes blinking, disoriented.

"How many golden sparks came out of the computer?" Moms asked.

Lilith frowned. "Six. I think six."

"Anything else?"

"No. It got my husband." She giggled drunkenly. "No prenup, but a great insurance policy."

Moms already had a syringe in her hand and jabbed it into Lilith's arm, knocking her out.

Roland's voice came over the net. "I'm coming down the stairs. Uh, the set to the, uh, east."

"Doc, I've got the Rift in—" She looked about. "I guess the dining room. Front of the house, to the right as you enter; the front left coming from the rear."

Doc was breathing hard—he was always breathing hard after he jumped. "On my way."

"I saw six Fireflies leave the house," Roland reported, walking up next to Moms. He took up a position just behind her, covering her blind spot.

"Eagle?" Moms asked over the radio.

Eagle reported in. "Eighty-two percent secure."

"We've got six Fireflies, people," Moms announced on the net. "Let's secure this house as a base of operations and get a Wall around it."

* * *

Eagle shot the last probe into the ground and checked his display. A continuous flashing red light surrounded Senators Club: a Wall that the Fireflies could not breach. They never ventured that far from their entry point anyway, the record being just short of two miles, but the Wall was an extra measure, and the Nightstalkers excelled at extra measures.

* * *

Nada was peering out a front window, hidden by luxurious curtains. All the lights in the house had been turned off and Doc was at work with his laptop and transmitter, the FireWire having been preconnected this time. This Rift was stable so far, but he worked with an appropriate sense of urgency.

Mac had the rear of the house covered and Roland was still clearing the first floor, with Kirk's assistance.

It was a damn big house.

There was no sign of anything possessed by a Firefly, but sometimes the little bastards were on the down low, waiting for the exact right moment to attack.

"No one else in here," Roland finally reported.

Moms switched freqs to talk to Ms. Jones.

"We have containment. The community is Walled. One witness here with us. One scientist through the Rift. Six Fireflies out."

"Support is six minutes out from a Forward Operating Base," Ms. Jones replied. "They will take over the civilian security for Senators Club. Six hundred and forty-four people live in there. Six forty-three now. Let's keep this quiet. Support will keep things looking normal."

"I've got it," Doc announced.

Moms looked over as the golden glow from the Rift snapped out of existence. Doc went to the laptop and shut the lid, wrapping it in a thermal blanket.

"Rift is closed," she reported to Ms. Jones, thankful they weren't having a repeat of the Fun Outside Tucson.

"Good luck and good hunting," Ms. Jones said, then clicked off the net.

Moms joined Nada by the front window. "What do you think?"

"Clusterfuck," Nada said. "There're eyes everywhere in a place like this. Eagle or I walk down the street, they'd call security on us. We don't fit in."

"You think the rest of us fit in?" Moms indicated her camos, body armor, combat vest, and weapon.

"You got a point." Nada frowned. He looked over his shoulder at Doc securing the Rift computer. "Even Doc don't fit in here. We could use an Asset who understands a place like this."

"I'll ask Ms. Jones. This will be our base of operations for the duration. Have Doc Wall it off so we don't have to worry about a Firefly coming in."

"Unless one stayed," Nada warned.

"That might be the case," Moms said, "but I feel better with a Wall up. And Roland said he saw six going out of the house. Doc?"

"I'll have it up in two minutes."

"Good."

Nada looked around. "I don't like this house."

The room was a mess from the dinner party. Moms took a whiff and wrinkled her nose. "We're going to have to clean this up."

She noticed that Nada was glancing around with more disgust than she would have preferred.

"It's just a house, people," Moms announced over the net. "I don't care if there's a baby grand by the front door or two grand staircases. It's another close and burn. Just like the others. We've already accomplished the close."

Nada shook his head slightly, indicating he thought otherwise, but he didn't say anything.

There were indeed two huge staircases that twisted down and around into the foyer like parentheses and Nada didn't understand the redundancy. They both got you to roughly the same place on the same floor. It just made either floor a bit harder to defend if the other floor were breached. In fact, the whole place was going to be a nightmare to secure against infiltration, although they would have the Wall in place to protect against the Fireflies.

"I don't think the architect was thinking urban defense or room clearing when he drew up the plans," Moms said, seeing him look about.

The huge, open windows made Nada nervous as he always envisioned a sniper was out there, tracking his every movement. Before they turned them off, the bulbs in the table lamps had been so dim they made tiny circles of feeble lights under their heavy shades while the overhead recessed lighting had been so bright that any sniper within a mile could have seen them scratch their asses.

Moms cocked her head, which meant Ms. Jones's voice was in her ear. She was nodding, receiving new instructions.

While she was listening, Doc announced: "I've placed four probes on the corners. We've got a Wall extending five meters square from the house."

As he was speaking, Doc walked over to the computer and pulled out his small set of instruments, much like a thief had lock picks.

After a minute, Moms turned on the team net. "Support has the Forward Operating Base being set up around ten miles from here in a secure location. They've got civilian vehicles for us and we can offload our gear from the Snake. Roland and Kirk and Doc will stay here and clean the place up and keep the house secure. Mac, Nada, and I will STABO out to the FOB and drive back in with the gear. Questions?"

There were none. There rarely were.

"Eagle?" Moms asked. "Time to pick up?"

"I'm en route. Be on the roof, please. Three mikes out."

"Here," Doc said, holding out the hard drive. "Ms. Jones would want that."

Moms stuffed it in one of the pockets on her combat vest.

Moms, Nada, and Mac took the stairs two at a time. Mac pulled on the rope leading to the attic, and the trap door opened and a set of wooden stairs unfolded. They went into the dark, hot space, night-vision goggles active. Mac searched about, then led them over to a window that looked over the backyard. He opened and leaned out. He reached into his butt pack and retrieved a short length of rope.

Moms and Nada checked the snap links on the front of their combat vests, because Protocol said they should check their snap links before a STABO. Mac looped the rope over a cornice on the roof and scooted out. He quickly climbed the rope to the roof.

"Two mikes," Eagle reported over the net.

Moms followed, then Nada brought up the rear. They gathered on the top of the roof.

"Check your snap link, Mac," Nada reminded.

Mac pressed the gate, made sure it was looped through the proper part of his vest and not a part that would tear off. "Roger."

"One mike," Eagle reported.

Nada was looking about. Huge houses in all directions, otherwise quiet. He could see quite a ways up here, two stories up plus being on top of the steeply peaked roof. He saw the rolling greens of the golf course not far away. Excellent fields of fire there. But overall: "This is gonna suck."

"Yep," Moms said.

"Gonna be hard to keep concealment."

"We will," Moms said.

"Yeah." But Nada didn't sound very confident. Then again, he never sounded very confident.

"Thirty seconds, from the east," Eagle informed them.

They turned in that direction. In their goggles they spotted the bulk of the Snake coming toward them, wings vertical. A single hundred-foot-long rope dangled from the belly of the beast. The rope had a series of small loops in it, each fifteen feet apart. Eagle brought the Snake to a hover overhead and the rope slid along the roof. Mac clipped in first to the third attachment point from the end. Moms went farther along the rope and clipped to the second attachment point. Nada was last on the final attachment point. As his snap link closed he radioed Eagle.

"We're on."

The Snake lifted straight up.

Mac was drawn up from the roof, followed by Moms, then Nada.

Looking down, Nada was startled. He could swear there was someone on the roof of the garage attached to the house across the street from their new base of operations. But then he was airborne, twisting and turning at the end of the rope as Eagle banked the Snake to head to the FOB, the three figures dangling below the craft.

Looking back, Nada could no longer see that roof.

* * *

Deep in her room, Ms. Jones watched the half-dozen computer displays on the ceiling above her hospital bed. The proximity of Fort Bragg to this latest incident was a fortunate thing. Only sixty miles away and the home of Special Operations, she was able to mass a superb Support Force of active duty personnel, which she preferred over contractors.

They already had an FOB set up, and more personnel and matériel were moving north in convoys and via helicopters and sling loads.

It was nice to have such high-caliber Support, but in the end it would just be the Nightstalkers versus the Fireflies.

It always was.

* * *

Eagle brought the Snake down slowly, allowing Nada to get boots on the ground first, then Moms and Mac. Once they were clear, he deployed the landing gear and settled down right on top of the blinking infrared strobe only visible through his night-vision goggles. The small clearing was set deep in a forest, over two miles from the closest house.

A cluster of Humvees, trucks, and two black SUVs were parked just inside the trees. Troops came out of the woods with camouflage nets and poles and set to work covering the Snake even before Eagle got the back ramp down.

Nada took charge, as Moms was once again listening to Ms. Jones. With Mac and Eagle's assistance they broke the large team box down into smaller loads. The two SUVs were backed up and the cargo compartments loaded to the gills with the items Nada thought would be needed in their new Area of Operations.

Satisfied, Nada turned to Moms and waited.

She had her head cocked for another thirty seconds, then switched off. "Nothing new," she reported. "Let's go."

A soldier came running up with something. Two stickers. For Senators Club. They applied them in the proper spot on the windshields. He also handed them a transmitter, one for each car.

"What's this for?" Nada asked, seeing no buttons on it.

The soldier shrugged. "No idea. I was just told you'd need it."

Mac got in one SUV with Eagle, and Nada took the wheel in the other while Moms took the passenger seat.

"Crap," Nada said as they pulled out of the FOB, through a narrow dirt track in the woods, lit by chem lights set up by Support.

"What?" Moms asked.

"Civvies. We're gonna need civvies to move around in that place."

"We can forage. I'm sure there are a ton of clothes in the closets upstairs."

Nada gave her a doubtful look but said nothing further. They came out of the forest and turned onto a paved, double-lane state road.

"Besides," Moms said, "our personal civvies are as bad as wearing uniforms there. We need civvies that fit in."

Nada repeated his dubious look.

They came to the sign indicating the turn into Senators Club, just as the GPS informed them to make the correct choice and turn. They left the state road onto a road flanked by well-manicured brick walls. There was no guard on the first gate. In fact there was no gate, just a massive, ornate sign. Another, less ornate sign informed them they were now in Senators Village. Behind the trees on either side they could see rows of townhouses.

"Is this where the help lives?" Nada asked.

"No," Moms said. "They probably live in that trailer park we passed about a mile back. This is where the younger people who aspire to move farther in live."

Another brick wall and a slightly better sign indicated they were now entering Senators Park. The single-family houses were close together, a smattering of trees giving a moderate sense of privacy. They were mostly one story and small. The next level was Senators Forest, where there were more trees and the houses were larger and held claim to bigger lots. The whole place was like a canal with locks and dams, and you could only enter if you could rise to the level.

"At least they make the class structure formal here," Nada said.

Moms shrugged. "We got a pass to the inner sanctum and we have a job to do."

They went through a two-hundred-yard belt of trees, the outer buffer for the inner sanctum of Senators Club. The guard on the gate waved them through, only focused on the sticker and not able to see the occupants through the tinted windshield. "Ms. Jones will have Support take over the security," Moms added.

"Just have to make sure they don't get curious and poke into our mission."

"Ms. Jones will ensure that."

"Won't the locals notice they got new security?" Nada wondered.

"People who live in places like this don't focus much on the hired help," Moms said, "even the ones with guns."

Despite the fact they were now in Senators Club proper, it turned out Doctor Winslow had purchased a house that required another passage. A metal gate blocked the way and there was no guard to wave them through, just a sign that said Senators Ridge. Nada slowed down, trying to figure this out, when the transmitter they'd been given beeped and the thing swung ponderously open.

"They got more gates here than Bragg," Nada said.

There were twenty-four houses along the ridge in four rows of six. It was the highest point around, allowing the occupants to look down on all the others who were scrambling to try and reach this status. The houses also had great views of the surrounding forests and artificial lakes dotted here and there, and the golf course.

"Who lives there?" Nada asked as he drove through, nodding toward a large structure in the middle of a field surrounded by a white fence that stretched for half a mile.

"Horses," Moms said, spying one of the beasts. "It's a stable."

"Geez," Nada muttered. "The horses live better than the people in Senators Village."

Thus Nada and Moms and Mac returned, with Eagle, to Senators Club in the late hours of the night, the time when people skipping out on the mortgage usually drove off in the opposite direction. The SUVs screamed government anywhere else, but not here, where SUVs were the vehicle of choice, the bigger the better. Except these vehicles weren't carrying soccer balls or traveling baseball bags and a half-dozen screaming kids.

The smug voice of the GPS wound them through a warren of curving streets. Each one looked almost exactly the same: hulking houses with square footage in five figures.

"Didn't the architect of this place know how to draw a straight line?" Eagle wondered over the team net. "And what's with the lights pointed in, not out?"

The amount of brick and stone and stucco and wood and granite and slate was staggering, and Eagle was correct: exterior lights, unlike at a firebase pointing out to highlight the enemy, were all pointed inward to display each house in case someone was blind and could miss the monstrosities.

"Landscaping is all too close to the houses," Nada observed. "Good cover for anyone trying to break in."

"They all have security systems," Moms said.

Mac snorted. "The cheapest rent-a-cops you can buy and the cheapest system, I bet."

"They did put a lot of money into the gates and fence," Nada admitted.

As they pulled up into the driveway of the Winslow place, two of the four garage doors opened, indicating Roland was on his game, as expected. As they stopped, the doors slid down behind them.

Roland was standing in the doorway leading to the house.

Everyone got out and opened the cargo doors on the SUVs. Mac, Eagle, and Roland started unloading. Kirk was upstairs providing over-watch.

"There's stuff in the kitchen," Roland was saying, "that I don't even know what they're for."

"They're called appliances," Moms said.

"There's drawers with wires and weird machines," Roland continued, giving his account like he would after having pulled recon on a high-priority high-tech target he needed an Acme to decipher for him.

"Dishwashers, warming ovens, trash compactors, and stuff like that," Moms said as she started helping the others as Nada stood on top of the stairs leading into the mudroom, taking over-watch just in case they got attacked by a weed whacker. "Might be a good place to stash some weapons. Just don't push any buttons," Moms warned.

"I didn't see any buttons," Roland said.

"Just stay away from them then," Moms said. The last thing they needed was for their weapons to get a rinse and hold.

They trooped inside carrying a bunch of gear they might need sooner rather than later. Mac went off to check the security system and Roland went back upstairs to pull over-watch with

Kirk. A few minutes later they heard a crash of something and Roland cursing. He came over the net.

"There's a room full of just dolls and clowns and dollhouses and stuff like that. It's freaking me out."

Moms and Nada exchanged a glance. Roland never got freaked out on a mission. But this was different. The house represented something so foreign to her team that she could see dismissal was turning to intimidation, and that wasn't too far from uneasiness. And, ultimately, fear, although she couldn't see anyone on this team going there. But then again, Burns had lost it in the Fun Outside Tucson because of a cactus. Everyone had something buried deep from some childhood trauma that could get to them, a reality Moms knew very well. For Roland, apparently it was dolls and clowns.

Moms spoke over the net. "It's just a house. A very big house full of lots of stuff. Most of it is for looks. Like the baby grand near the front door."

It was on big brass wheels and Nada immediately turned it from decoration to usefulness by rolling it over to the large front double doors and shoving it against them, then locking the wheels.

Moms nodded approvingly. "See? Nada blocked the front door with the piano. We use what we need for our mission. Improvise, people. It's what we're good at."

"What's the point of having stuff just to look at?" Roland wondered from upstairs, staring at who knows what. Moms knew he could see the point of looking at naked women dancing on some tables: that made sense. A piano? Vases as tall as the cactus from Tucson? Clowns and dollhouses? No.

"Mac?"

"Yo."

"The house security system. Bypass the code so we can run it."

"Already working on it."

"And then set up your own cameras to give us a three-sixty view and put the displays in the room overlooking the front yard. That will be over-watch central. And then tie in to the Senators Club system so you can see everything their cameras see."

"Roger."

"Kirk?"

"Yes?"

"Hook your satellite retransmitter to the dish on the roof. I saw one when we STABO'd off. I want to ensure our com-link is secure. Then steal into Senators Club wireless so Mac can bootleg their video and all other commo. And I want us to monitor that even after Support takes over."

"Roger."

Nada tapped her on the arm. "It'll be dawn in a bit. I'm going to do a perimeter search inside the Wall. Make sure we didn't trap anything inside that's trying to get out."

Moms nodded, but pointed at his MP-5 and his MK-23. "Suppressors." She hit the net. "Everyone, go suppressed."

With a sigh, Nada quickly screwed on the bulky suppressors for both weapons. His sigh was because the suppressors required special rounds, which were less effective than normal bullets. He pulled the magazines in both guns, ejected the rounds in the chambers, then removed magazines marked with a piece of red tape from the specific ammo pouch on his combat vest where everyone on the team carried their subsonic ammunition.

The bulky tubes were not silencers. Anyone who was anyone who used weapons knew silencers only existed in movies. A gun makes a lot of noise in a lot of different ways. The moving parts make noise. The gunpowder going off and blowing out the end of the barrel makes a rather large noise. The crack of a round going through the sound barrier makes a supersonic crack. The best one could do was keep the gun well lubed to reduce the first noise; have a suppressor on the end of barrel to eat up the expanded gases from the gunpowder explosion to reduce that sound to a minimum; and prepare special bullets that were subsonic to avoid the last.

Ready, Nada slipped out the back door and was startled as the floodlights above his head automatically came on. Motion detector. Cursing, Nada went back in the house and turned off all the switches next to the door. He exited and this time, no lights.

There was a pool, almost big enough to take in the Snake. There were enough permanent security lights all over the place that his night-vision goggles weren't needed.

Nada moved around the pool to the back fence. There were woods behind the house, so at least they had a way to move in and out. The neighbors on either side were about fifty meters away in their own hulking McMansions.

He looked for dead zones, places where they could operate unobserved. There was a pool house—he guessed that's what it was called, because it was on the other side of the pool. It had a bar with the biggest built-in grill that Nada had ever seen. It was outside the range of the Wall around the home. He went over to it, opened the metal grate door, and looked around inside. There were steel shutters that could be cranked down. He pondered what their purpose was for a moment: hurricane protection? It was too far inland for a hurricane. Then he realized it was to secure the grill and the other stuff inside. He looked about and spotted a switch. Flipping it, the shutters slid down with a rattle, leaving only the door as an access—or egress—point.

This could be useful.

Nada left the pool house. As he stealthily made a circuit of the perimeter of the Winslow mansion, he noticed something doing a perimeter of its own. A small dog was shadowing him, about ten meters away, just outside the range of the Wall. It was a dog that obviously absorbed lots of bathing and trimming.

Nada went around the front of the house, then pressed his back against the wall, drawing his machete.

He waited, something he was very good at.

But the dog wasn't coming.

Smart dog, Nada thought. Too smart.

He risked peeking around the edge. The dog was motionless, waiting for him outside the Wall.

"I got a possible," Nada whispered on the team net. "Small dog, east side of house."

"Roland," Moms's voice came over the radio. "Back up Nada."

The dog was staring at Nada with unblinking eyes and he was shifting his evaluation from possible to probable. Of course, he'd met some crazy dogs.

He heard a door open and a light went on down the street. A woman called out in a half whisper, half yell: "Skippy! Skippy!"

Nada checked out the dog. It was focused on him.

"Skippy!" The woman's voice was an octave higher. "Treat! Treat!"

"I've got the dog in sight," Roland reported.

"Roland. See the pool house?" Nada asked.

"The what?"

"The thing on the other side of the pool with the steel shutters that are closed."

"Roger. Understand." Roland might not know pool houses and he might be nervous around dolls, but he was quick with tactics.

Nada extended the stock of the MP-5, then tucked it tight into his firing shoulder. He stepped around the corner of the house, pulling the trigger fast, semiautomatic. The suppressor made low chugging sounds as rounds left the barrel. The clicking sound of the gun's mechanisms was like music to Nada's ears.

Every round hit the dog, knocking it back.

It did not die.

Nada kept shooting. The dog darted right, growling and snapping its teeth.

The bolt on the MP-5 locked open, but Nada had been counting his trigger pulls and was pushing the eject button for the mag as it did so. He slammed home another mag of subsonic without missing a beat.

But the dog was faster. Nada got three rounds from the second mag into the dog, aiming for the head, before it launched.

It hit the Wall just six inches from Nada's face and bounced back.

Stupid Firefly.

Nada flipped the switch and fired the rest of the mag on automatic at the stunned thing on the ground just in front of him, ripping shreds out of it.

Moving out of the darkness to the right, Roland was walking steadily forward, firing his MP-5 one-handed, adding to the carnage. In his other hand he held a recycle bin. The Flamer was on his back, the pistol grip secure in its asbestos sheath.

The dog rolled, trying to get to its feet, except Nada had severed both front legs with that automatic burst.

Nada reloaded one more time, fired half the mag into what remained of the dog, then dropped the weapon to the end of its sling while drawing his machete. The dog's head was still moving, teeth snapping, and the rear legs scrambling. Nada slammed the point of the machete down through the dog's chest and flipped it right into the recycle bin.

Roland slammed the lid shut on the bin.

They could hear the dog scrabbling around inside. Teeth ripped at plastic and a hole appeared.

Nada and Roland ran for the pool house. The hole grew bigger as Skippy shredded plastic. Roland skidded to a halt in the doorway of the pool house and threw the bin in. Nada fired over Roland's left shoulder, riddling the bin and Skippy inside.

Roland pulled the pistol grip and fired the flamer.

The steel shutters contained the flame, and the dog was ashes in seconds.

The Firefly rose, hovered, and then dissipated.

"One down," Nada reported. He looked at the pile of ash. "Sorry, Skippy. You might have even been a good dog."

He tapped Roland on the shoulder. "Good job. Go back in and take over watch. I'm going to finish my perimeter sweep, then I'll be in."

Roland nodded.

Nada went back to the front of the house, then moved around, staying inside of the jungle of plantings that blanketed the front. He was almost to the front doors when he froze as he noted a glow to his right and up. He saw a teenage girl seated on the sloping roof on top of the garage of the house across the street, smoking a cigarette, an open window behind her. The room behind the window was dark. She was looking straight back at him, even though he knew she couldn't see him in the shadows and without night-vision goggles.

She gave a little wave.

"We're being observed," Nada reported. "Front, across the street, on the garage roof."

Inside the house everyone stopped what they were doing, grabbed weapons, and crawled to windows, except for Eagle, who maintained security to the rear.

"How many?" Moms asked.

"One."

The girl looked to be around sixteen or seventeen. Nada saw three red dots fix the girl: laser-aiming beams. Moms, Mac, and Kirk.

"She's a girl," Nada said.

The dots didn't move.

The girl did, taking one last deep drag on the cigarette, then did something Nada had only seen on army posts. She field-stripped the cigarette. She blew the shredded butt off her hand into the air where it dissipated much like the Firefly had just done.

"It's just some kid smoking," Kirk said, and one of the dots disappeared. "You said they can't get into people, right?" The other two dots also disappeared.

"Not just some kid," Nada muttered. "A smart kid." He wondered for a moment if Skippy had been her dog, but it had been an older woman's voice calling out for the dog, not a girl's. Still.

The girl stood and disappeared into the window just as the light in the hallway to the left of that window came on. The girl slid shut her window and the room stayed dark for a moment, then there was a faint glow in her room: the doorway opening and someone checking on her.

Nada finished his perimeter sweep without further incident and came inside via the back door. Moms was seated at the kitchen bar, her MP-5 on the granite top, her head cocked, meaning she was talking to Ms. Jones, laptop open in front of her. Kirk was at one of the front windows, peering out with his goggles. Doc was checking the old laptop, performing mechanical surgery with small instruments.

Moms cut the connection with Ms. Jones. "Support is moving more Assets in."

"I think we might have an Asset in this enemy village," Nada said.

"The kid?" Doc asked without looking up. "She probably still wears a retainer at night."

Moms nodded and spoke over the net so everyone could hear. "Ms. Jones gave me some info on places like this from someone she talked to. This whole community is full of what are called helicopter parents with nothing to do but follow daily schedules full of ballet classes and violin practices for their kids."

"I like the violin," Doc said. "I used to play as a kid."

Moms ignored him.

"What do you mean, helicopter?" Eagle asked from rear security upstairs.

"They hover over their kids and keep watch all the time when they're not working."

"The girl across the street didn't get observed by the helicopter," Nada noted. "I get the feeling privacy around here is as rare as an old clunker on cinder blocks." He walked over and looked at the dark window. He suspected she was still there, standing back away from the window, the way an experienced sniper would keep the muzzle of his weapon well inside the room. Only idiots in movies poked the gun out so it could be spotted.

"Fifty percent security," Moms ordered. "The rest, get some sleep."

Nada quickly broke the team down into guard shifts that would get them through the next few hours until dawn. "Remember, there's five Fireflies out there and a lot of civilians. We'd like to keep most of them alive."

Eagle spoke up in a falsetto, because Eagle liked to leave things on a high note: "*I can't think about that right now. If I do, I'll go crazy. I'll think about that tomorrow.*"

"Shut up!" Roland and Mac and Kirk shouted over the net in unison.

* * *

Outside the gate to Senators Club—across the road, hidden in the forest—Burns had watched the Snake fly by earlier, three figures dangling below. Then the two SUVs came not much later, which meant the FOB was close by.

Protocol as always.

He pulled out his cell phone and dialed a number.

The person who answered wasn't happy about being woken up so late.

He was even less happy at Burns's words: "You need to get out. The Feds are moving into Winslow's house."

The voice on the other end cursed in Russian, then asked a question.

"I'll tell you about your investment soon," Burns said. "I'll call you. Stay in the local area."

He flipped the phone shut. His skin itched where he'd been flayed and punctured.

He forced himself to wait and was rewarded when two large Chevy Blazers raced out of Senators Club, tinted windows hiding the occupants.

Another piece that could be used when needed.

CHAPTER 14

THE NEXT DAY

Despite the quality of the accommodations, the team spent a restless couple of hours waiting for sunlight. As those off duty rose just before dawn for Stand-To, a military tradition as old as the military, they explored the house.

"There are more toilets in here than in my entire town," Eagle reported over the net as he took care of his morning business.

Moms had taken over the master bedroom as her new CP. "They got two in the same bathroom up here."

Eagle and Mac then got into an earnest discussion of the Freudian implications of that many toilets and Moms simply told them to shut up and stop clogging the net. She came downstairs where the rest of the team was gathered and brought a deafening silence when they saw her.

"We got to blend in here," Moms said. "There are plenty of clothes upstairs. Improvise, gentlemen."

She was wearing a tennis skirt and some top that made her look much more attractive than she wanted. They were all staring at her long, toned legs. No one really noticed the tennis bag slung over one shoulder.

"Everything else in the closet was impractical," Moms defended with little conviction. "This is athletic and allows me to move around and not be noticed."

Nada shook his head. "Give it up, Moms." They all knew the outfit stripped her of the appearance of competency, but ultimately everything a person wears is some sort of uniform. They knew it had cost her a lot to take off her cammies and put on those little socks with the pink fur ball above the ankle.

"Actually, there *is* a practical aspect to this," Moms said. She dropped the tennis bag on one of the sofas and unzipped it. Her MP-5, suppressor screwed on, lay inside along with extra magazines, grenades, her suppressed MK-23, a knife, and other goodies.

"Smart move," Nada acknowledged. "About the only way you'll be able to move around here armed and concealed."

"Think golf clothes, gentlemen," Moms said, with a nod toward one of the staircases. "Then think golf club bags."

"And golf cart," Eagle said. "There's one parked in this little garage next to the big garage."

"We can modify it," Mac said. "We can probably get the extra flamer and Roland's M-240 rigged on one. Laser designator. I saw an ATV in there, too. I can merge them." Mac was getting excited at the thought of playing with these toys.

As Moms picked her MP-5 up, the team trudged upstairs to even the score. Winslow had apparently been a pretty fit guy, but none of his golf clothes would fit Roland. The weapons man had to search for the largest pair of sweatpants he could find along with a hoodie with a yacht club logo. Mac and Eagle looked like mismatched golfers, in shorts and loose shirts, which allowed them to strap their MK-23s underneath them. Doc, not having dedicated his life like the others to staying fit and trim, had to do a bit of searching to find a shirt that would fit. Nada saw Eagle reaching for a pair of black silk socks and simply said: "No."

"How many feet did this guy have?" Mac asked, noting the socks in their neat bundles and the rows of shoes that lined one entire wall.

"Check this out." Roland had opened another one of the unending supply of doors and a small room with a wine fridge and microwave sat next to a small copper sink. "You could live in here."

"How many wrists did this guy have?" Mac asked, looking at the watch winder.

The team trooped back down the stairs closest to the bedroom and Moms couldn't help herself. She burst out laughing seeing her team of Nightstalkers trying to blend in, while she was tugging on the skirt to get it lower.

"Not fair," Nada said. "We didn't laugh at you."

Moms sighed, looking at Roland. "You were right, Nada. I'll call Support and have them bring us some appropriate clothes that fit."

Nada pointed, and Mac and Doc went upstairs to pull overwatch security on the street and backyard.

Then the doorbell rang and they all scrambled for weapons. Nada went over and peered out a side window and saw the girl from the garage roof earlier in the morning. He unlocked the wheels and rolled the baby grand he'd put as a barricade out of the way and opened the door, while the rest of the team—except for Moms—was diving for cover to face this new "threat."

The girl's hair was short and blue with a couple of barrettes hanging at angles. "I'm selling Girl Scout cookies."

From behind the big vase, Eagles muttered over the net: "I like the ones that are minty."

The girl strode in with the confidence of someone used to interrupting and said: "Just kidding," as she slammed the door shut behind her.

Moms stepped up. "Excuse me. Who are you?"

She ignored Moms, which made Roland take a step forward from his hide spot in a closet. That finally paused her for a moment as she took in the large man dressed in a hoodie and sweatpants that were strained to the breaking point.

"You know, you all look cray-cray."

"What?" Moms said.

The girl scratched at an old mosquito bite on her arm. "Crazy."

"We don't fit in?" Moms asked, and the girl rolled her eyes.

"Hello. The whole place is crawling with new faces this morning. New guy on the gate, new guy delivering the paper, even new guy raking the sand trap."

Moms had their cover story ready. "I don't know about that. We're a group of postdocs from the University of Colorado, and Doctor Winslow is letting us stay here so we can coordinate our research with his staff while he and his wife are on vacation."

The girl pulled up the piano bench. "Yeah. Tell me another."

"Excuse me, young girl—" Moms began, but the girl pointed.

"Your legs are hairy. You haven't had a wax in a looooong time, if ever."

Nada looked over at Moms's legs, professionally this time, and the girl was right. Standing by the window he could see the light layer of hair that cancelled out the tennis skirt. *Smart kid*, he thought. He watched her dig at the bite on her arm and noted her fingernails were painted bright green. She chewed her nails and cuticles but she took time to personalize her nails.

"What do *you* think we're doing?" Nada asked.

She looked up with the surprised expression of someone who was seldom asked her opinion. "Well. You're in Doctor Cray-Cray's house—"

"Doctor Winslow."

"I meant the wife, Lilith. She's a doctor, too. And you killed Skippy and—"

"That wasn't your dog, was it?" Nada almost seemed concerned, which caused a surprised look to cross Moms's face.

"Do you think I'd have a dog named Skippy? Hellooooo?" She shook her head. "Listen, I know this place sucks, but it's my place and I don't like weirdoes dropping in—like literally dropping in—and killing dogs, even dogs who are cray-cray and—"

"Could you please stop saying that?" Moms implored.

"I love your lip gloss."

Moms looked stunned for a moment.

"Just kidding," the girl said.

Eagle was laughing now over the net, the concept of Moms wearing lip gloss tickling his warped sense of humor.

Moms forgot they were on the net. "What's so funny?"

And Nada shocked everyone with his answer. "You're too good-looking to be wearing lip gloss or worrying about waxing your legs."

Moms flushed, everyone one beat off by the presence of the girl. Roland was hoping a Firefly in something really cool, like a six-hundred-pound bull, would come crashing through the front door right now because all this attention toward Moms was making him fidgety and killing things calmed him down. Except they did have the Wall up. Still, a man could hope.

"So we're really not blending in?" Nada asked, to cover his gaffe.

"Yeah. And you killed a dog, so that's like seven sore thumbs."

"Seven?" Moms asked.

"I can count," the girl replied.

"We saw you last night," Nada said.

"'Cause I wanted you to, helloooo?" she said, and Nada looked helplessly at Moms. "I'm just guessing here," the girl said, "but I think you're a bunch of government dudes—and dudette," she added, nodding at Moms, "and something really cray"—she caught herself— "odd is going on around here. Those people left here in a hurry last night and there was some screaming."

"How old are you?" Moms asked.

"Sixteen. How old are you?"

Moms didn't reply.

"So you're thirty-five."

Mom's cheeks flushed and that's how the team learned that Moms was thirty-five. They all owed Doc ten bucks.

"What do you think is going on?" Nada repeated.

The girl stopped scratching at her arm and started gnawing at a cuticle and Moms knocked her hand away. "Don't do that."

"No touching, bitch, I ain't cutting myself."

Everyone tensed and the girl noted. "Cool. So you're in charge. Love that." She leaned forward and parted her blue hair a bit. "My curling iron did that to me this morning."

They could all see the angry-looking burn hiding in the blue. Then she held up her hand, the one she'd been chewing, and said: "And Skippy bit me. He's, was, a mean dog, but he never bit me before." There was an angry gash, half-concealed with an inadequate Band-Aid.

"Doc," Nada said into the throat mike. "Down here with your kit. Eagle, take upper rear over-watch."

The girl continued. "Granted, Skippy was a ditz of a dog, but I've always been good with dogs and he nipped me last night." She swooshed the wound with her little green-painted fingers.

Other than Eagle leaving, no one was moving and she looked about. "Helloooo?"

Doc came in with his med kit. "Let me take a look at that."

The girl stared at him dubiously for a moment. "You really a doctor? I mean a doctor who, like, treats people rather than makes things in a lab? 'Cause we got lots of doctors around here who wouldn't know the right end of a scalpel."

"I'm a real doctor," Doc said, and everyone on the team was surprised he didn't add in the usual about his four PhDs on top of his MD.

"What about your curling iron?" Moms asked.

"It isn't my curling iron anymore. Am I getting warm?"

Moms nodded and Roland reached behind him and pulled out his golf bag of weapons and began strapping up.

"Whoa," the girl said as Nada and Moms pulled guns from under their shirts and chambered rounds. "Liftoff." She smiled. "Just kidding."

"Where are your parents?" Moms asked as Doc worked on her burn and bite.

"At work. Helloooo? The mortgage is ten grand a month. Where do you think they'd be?"

"Why aren't you in school?" Nada asked.

"Spring break?"

"Seriously," Nada said. "Is it spring break?"

"Yeah, you're a bunch of grad students for sure. It's summer. Fourth of July soon?"

Nada sighed. "So there are a bunch of kids home without parents around?"

The girl laughed. It was the youngest thing about her, the laugh. "Helloooo. Swim practice, Bible camp, violin, piano, dressage, traveling soccer and baseball and dance team? Nobody here but me. All the mommies and daddies are at work to pay for all the nannies driving everyone everywhere all the time."

"Why aren't you practicing something?" Moms asked while Nada was on the net, telling Eagle and Mac to come down and prep for a Firefly swat.

The girl did a remarkable series of three backflips across the marble floor, ending up in front of the piano. She leaned over and started to play. It wasn't perfect, but the message was clear: don't have to practice when you can do. Her green-tipped fingers were flying across the ivory as Eagle and Mac came down, golf bags on their shoulders, weapons in hand. Roland had his flamer on his back and machine gun in hand.

"Can you play the violin?" Doc asked.

"Can you?" she asked him, not missing a stroke on the keys.

Nada started to laugh and the team turned toward him because Nada never laughed.

"She's our Asset," Nada said. "Our Scout."

"Oh," the girl said. "I love love love that movie."

"What movie?" Mac asked as he checked the fuses he was putting in the pockets of his golf shorts.

"Really?" the girl said. "Scout and Boo Radley and just nothing?"

"And Atticus," Eagle threw in.

"We get it," Moms said, trying to get the derailed team back on track. "The curling iron."

"You want me to get it?"

"NO!" Everyone said it at the same time, causing the girl to actually pause in her playing.

"So, we all cross the Rubicon?" the girl asked.

Nada looked at Moms. "I like her."

Moms gave him a look.

"I mean, she's young," Nada said, "but she knows the area and is quick and—"

Scout slammed the lid over the keys and sang at the top of her lungs: "*Love it, love it, love it, the lady is in charge. The boys have to ask.*" She turned toward the front door. "Let's go to my house." She looked over her shoulder at the group, loaded with weapons, explosives, and flamer. "Might not want to walk across the street like that."

The team scrambled to jam everything back into the golf bags, tennis racket bag, and shopping bags (eco-friendly, they boasted) that Eagle had uncovered in the garage. When they were done the team stood in the foyer and Scout shook her head. "Better, but not going to fly. You look like a bunch of government people hiding your weapons in a tennis racket bag, golf bags, and supermarket bags."

"What do you suggest?" Nada asked, earning him a hard look from Moms.

"I go over there with one of you to protect me from my curling iron—I cannot believe I just said that last part—and I open the garage, and the rest of you drive from here to there in your big black gas-guzzlers. It's not far. I think you can make it without getting lost."

Moms sighed. "All right, Roland, you escort—"

As soon as Roland stepped forward, Scout was shaking her head. "No, no, no, and no." She wrapped her arm around Nada's bicep. "I prefer this gentleman."

Roland frowned, Moms sighed once more, and Eagle laughed again.

"He ain't no gentleman," Mac said.

"He's been nicer than any of you," Scout said, the seriousness of her tone causing everyone to shut up for a little bit and feel the truth.

"I don't fit in here," Nada said.

"We meet anyone, I'll take care of it," Scout promised.

"Tell them I'm the new gardener?" Nada asked.

Scout laughed. "I can do better than that." She tugged on his arm. "Come on, before that curling iron burns down my house."

Moms opened her mouth to say something, but Scout already had Nada out the door, the heavy wood slamming shut behind them.

"Well," Moms said.

"I'll get the SUVs ready," Eagle said, heading for the garage.

"I'll load the gear," Roland said, gesturing for Mac to help.

"I'll help load, too," Kirk said.

Moms was left standing alone in the foyer, staring at the closed front door.

* * *

Nada walked across the street next to Scout. He noticed that while her house was on scale with most of the others—ridiculously large—the one to the right of hers was on a scale all its own, at least twice the size. Looking more closely, he also noted a lot of things that troubled him. A small security camera was tracking them. As if on cue, the sprinklers came on. All of them, surrounding the house in a wall of water.

"Yeah," Scout said, "that's been the real problem until you people arrived. Bluebeard's house."

They reached the porch.

"Wait there," she said, pointing at a swing. Before Nada could say anything, she disappeared inside the house, returning a few seconds later with a garage door opener. She sat down next to Nada.

"I watched them build that thing." She pointed at the mansion, more a fortress. "I could sit in my room in the day and on the roof at night and watch. And a lot of stuff was done on it at night. Stuff Bluebeard didn't want anyone to know about."

"Who is Bluebeard?"

"The cray-cray who built it and lives in it. But he's gone a lot. He's gone now. He took off with his friends in two SUVs just after you guys arrived, so that was also weird."

The garage door opened across the street. As the black SUVs rolled down the driveway, Scout opened her own garage doors. In ten seconds the team was across the street and in the safety of another garage. Scout hit the remote and the doors rolled down.

Nada stood.

"Where are you going?" Scout asked.

"To join my team," Nada said.

"They can't handle a curling iron?"

Nada considered that. Sometimes the Fireflies went into the deadliest creatures or things and sometimes it was like they'd simply bounced into something and gotten stuck. A curling iron didn't strike him as a particularly deadly event, although the burn on Scout's head was not to be discounted. She was lucky the Firefly hadn't shot enough juice through her to kill her.

The earpiece crackled on the team net.

"Nada?" Moms asked.

"I'm keeping front security," Nada said. "We've got four more Fireflies free, don't forget."

"I don't forget." Moms's voice was a bit harsher than normal.

"Tell me about Bluebeard and the house," Nada asked Scout.

"I've rarely seen him," Scout said. "Just his SUVs, with tinted windows, right into the garage and out. Like you guys. He doesn't have a mailbox, which is kind of weird, too. I told my parents and they told me to mind my own biz. I even told the dummy who runs the security thing and he told me Bluebeard paid his fees just like everyone else, more in fact, so pretty much the same. When they were building it, I saw them put in, at night, a safe room deep in the basement, except I don't think it's a safe room. And I also saw them unload a couple of really big safes, which is just plain weird."

"Safes?" Nada stared at the dormer windows along the second floor and could swear he saw the silhouettes of gun mounts inside. He scanned the yard and noted small mounds around several struggling trees that didn't seem to be getting much attention. The landscaping was very different from all the other houses on the street. Switching from considering a house in a gated community to a firebase inside a larger defensive complex, Nada could swear those mounds were laid out with a perfect firing pattern for a series of Claymore mines. If they went off, anything on that lawn would be sprayed with hundreds of small steel ball bearings. A perfect kill zone.

"Did you see who put in the bushes?" Nada asked.

"The shrubbery?" Scout said. "Nope. People here make some weird demands, but who plants shrubbery in the middle of the night or when no one is around?"

Scout pulled a crumpled pack of smokes out of her pants and lit up, just before Nada yanked it away.

"You're too young to smoke."

"When is old enough?" Scout shot back. "It hasn't been ten hours since you killed my neighbor's dog. And you're looking at a minefield over there, aren't you? I saw the people he hired to put in the shrubbery."

"Why did you lie to me?"

"Because no one ever believes me." Scout said it simply. "They were the ones you hire off the corner at the gas station, not landscapers. And they did a lousy job, but they put in those bushes—"

"Shrubbery," Nada interrupted, and she laughed before continuing.

"In the middle of the day in the exact spots where he had little stakes with red flags on them. I've lived here long enough that the placement made no sense from an aesthetic point of view. So I watched that night, and old Bluebeard crept out in the dark and he buried things in each of the mounds at the base of each."

"Claymore mines most likely," Nada said.

"You really think he put mines in?" Scout was surprised. "Even I started doubting me. 'Cause that's real cray-cray."

"Why do you call him Bluebeard?"

"Why not? Not like we've ever been formally introduced."

Nada pulled two bent cigarettes from the pack and lit both, handing one to Scout.

"For Chrissakes, Nada." Moms stood in the doorway.

"Did you get it?" Scout asked.

"We got it."

"Did you destroy my bathroom?"

Moms grimaced. "There was some damage, but we'll have Support here in less than an hour to fix it just like new."

Scout smiled once more, transforming her into someone almost charming. "*Why ask for the moon when we have the stars.*"

That brought the hint of a smile to Moms's face. "All right. If she knows this place as well as she knows her movies, she's an Asset."

"What's the movie?" Nada asked.

"Don't worry about it," Moms said.

"*Now, Voyager*," Eagle announced over the net, because Eagle always had to fill the information void.

Moms tugged on the skirt once more.

"The skirt's not too short," Scout said. "You're too tall for it. Doctor Cray-Cray was like five-six."

"Got an extra cigarette?" Moms asked, sitting on the other side of Scout on the bench. "Kirk got himself a little burned, but nothing bad. New guys always screw something up on their first Firefly mission."

Nada shook one almost bent in two out of the pack. He carefully rolled it between callused palms, lit it, then handed it to Moms.

"Two down. Four to go," Moms said. Then she took a deep drag as the garage door opened and the team shot across the street and disappeared into the other house.

"Do I get paid?" Scout asked. "'Cause I really, really need a job, 'cause I figure I have to buy a new curling iron, you know? I'm so tired of babysitting."

"People let you watch their kids?" Moms asked.

Nada took a last puff on the cig and then field-stripped it. "I'd let her watch my kids."

"You don't have kids," Moms said.

"I'd let her watch Zoey," Nada said.

"From what you've said of Zoey, she and Scout would get along just fine," Moms said.

"Do I get a gun?" Scout asked, and Nada and Moms said in stereo: "No!"

CHAPTER 15

Ivar was suspended in the golden glow emanating from the mainframe computer. He had no idea how long he'd been like this, but he'd already peed in his pants. Except that had happened when the golden glow initially pulsed out and wrapped around him. He was facing the steel door, because he'd been running for it as the glow expanded.

Thus he saw the door slowly swing open. The silhouette of a man was in the dark hallway outside. He had a gun in his hand, a very big gun.

The man stepped into the room and Ivar saw his face.

That was bad.

The man looked past Ivar, toward the mainframe. He stepped forward. Ivar wanted to yell, warn him not to, but he couldn't speak.

The man stepped into the golden glow, but instead of being frozen in place like Ivar was, his body shivered, as if getting a jolt of energy. The man opened his mouth, wide, very wide, and inhaled. Ivar could swear that he was sucking in the golden glow.

CHAPTER 16

Ms. Jones's desk was getting disturbingly cluttered as Pitr placed objects on it in order. She knew the Nightstalkers thought her some sort of obsessive-compulsive about having a clean desk. Some thought she wasn't even real, and they were correct in a way, since sometimes she really wasn't in that chair in the office when they thought she was. None knew about Pitr, who entered and left through her private chambers behind the steel behind her desk, hidden in the shadows and never when the team was in the Den. She spent most of her time in the bed when she wasn't talking to Moms and/or Nada or in-briefing a new member in her chambers. Even sitting was exhausting. On the really bad days she just used the holographic projector.

But she was real and she had a very specific reason for everything she did.

Right now Pitr had laid out the objects in the correct order in which she had to consider their connections:

The hard drive from the Fun Outside Tucson and the "fun" happening in North Carolina, delivered to Pitr by Support just minutes ago. It had initially been programmed by:

Henry Craegan's file, including the taunting e-mail from him to:

Doctor Winslow's file. How had:

Burns found out about the e-mail and the connection? His file lay there, too, along with:

The situation report via Moms from Senators Club, which was getting thicker with each secure e-mail and Satphone conversation transcription.

Ms. Jones immediately made one connection. "Burns learned of Winslow by accessing Craegan's e-mail records on the hard drive."

Pitr nodded.

"Still no word where Burns is?"

Pitr shook his head. "No. Support is on it."

"What about the report from the University of Colorado Acme Asset?" Ms. Jones asked.

Pitr's American accent was much better than hers, with barely a trace of his Russian roots. This was because he actually went out into the world and interacted with people away from the Ranch and Area 51. He was slightly younger than Ms. Jones, handsome in a rugged way with gray hair just starting to tinge his temples. His most distinguishing feature was his smile, revealing perfectly aligned white teeth and making him appear to be a person without a trouble in the world. Ms. Jones often believed it was that smile that had caused her to make the decision that changed everything back on April 26, 1986.

"The report was inconclusive," Pitr said. "Worse, the Acme has disappeared. It might be a rather unsettling coincidence, except, of course, we don't believe in coincidences."

"No, we don't."

"But we had no record of a Rift there."

"Perhaps Mister Burns had something to do with that disappearance to accelerate the movement of the hard drive back to

Area 51," Ms. Jones said. "It had been scheduled for pickup a week later, so there was a shuffle in assignments. That's why we got the initial Package report wrong and a rookie Courier ended up getting assigned a priority-one Package."

"That's likely."

"Have Support follow up there," Ms. Jones said. "Find out what happened to the Acme. Start with the student who signed the drive over to the Courier."

Pitr leaned over her and adjusted the drip in one of the three IVs that fed into a shunt in her chest.

"The good news," Pitr said, because Pitr always focused on good news—someone had to, "is that the Nightstalkers have finished off a third of the Fireflies and the Rift didn't act abnormal as it did in Tucson."

"That in itself is cause for concern," Ms. Jones said. "First that it was different in Tucson and then it wasn't different in North Carolina. Is it not the same program?"

"I don't believe so," Pitr said. "Doctor Winslow had time to work on it. He's older, so we might assume he went the old way."

Ms. Jones looked at her desk. "There's five things there."

"Ah," Pitr shook his head. "You aren't a believer in Doc's Rule of Seven, are you?"

"He has a valid point," Ms. Jones said. "I have often deconstructed the events which brought you and I together and changed our lives and they more than fit his theory." Ms. Jones closed her eyes. "I must constantly remind myself of things, Pitr. Both good and bad. The Nightstalkers think I make speeches to remind them, but it's as much to remind myself." She lifted a hand, staring at the red scars and then pointing at Pitr. "You were so gallant when you flew your helicopter in to Chernobyl that early morning after the reactor blew."

Pitr grimaced, not liking it when her mind went back to that time, because it would lead only one way. "You did all you could."

"I did not and that is why we are here." She sighed. "I worry about Nada and his Protocols. They followed Protocol that night."

"They followed Protocol after already having made many mistakes," Pitr corrected her. "It was the mistakes that caused the Protocol to go wrong. You were the only engineer there who kept telling them to stop. Who pointed out the mistakes they didn't want to acknowledge."

"They were worried about their bonuses," Ms. Jones allowed. "And no one wanted to call Moscow."

"You made that call."

"Too late."

"You saved my life," Pitr said.

"And many others died."

"You did all you could," Pitr repeated. "You are the way you are now because you went in that bunker and pulled out the man who made mistake number seven, as Doc would label it."

"He died in my arms," Ms. Jones said.

Pitr shrugged. "I never understood that."

That surprised Ms. Jones. "That he died?"

"That you went in and got him," Pitr said. "All these years, it is not consistent with your speeches, even the speech you gave me that day. I was young and only thinking of medals and duty and honor. Of flying above and dropping my concrete on the tower. And you stopped me. You told me there was no honor dying for a mistake."

"Ah, Pitr," Ms. Jones said, "you misremember. I told you that mistakes happen, that is part of life and death, but once you know it's a mistake and you let people die for it in ignorance, that is murder. Your commanders knew everyone they sent over that tower would die, and yet they said nothing. That is indeed murder. I knew many in Pripyat would die if not evacuated immediately, yet did not force that issue. I live with that every day."

"You were a junior engineer, not a general."

"I should have contacted Kiev and given them a warning. This was a case where concealment, the second of our Cs that Moms lectures the team about, was criminal. It is why I talk to her constantly to make sure we are not having another Pripyat or Kiev. We will always have more Chernobyls." She pointed weakly at the material on the desk. "I fear things are accelerating with this incident. There are times when things are not as they appear."

"But going back to my point," Pitr said, "you ran into that room and pulled out the man who started the disaster. But you saved my life and stopped me. The two are not consistent."

Ms. Jones smiled weakly. "But that *is* the point, my dear Pitr. Today, I would not run into that room to save a man already dying. Today I would let you fly over that tower, but first I would make sure you knew exactly what flying over that tower meant. That it was a death sentence. Then you would have a choice. Today I would scream to Pripyat and Kiev in every way I could about what was coming. They had time, but the people in charge at Chernobyl and then in the Kremlin did not want to admit a mistake."

"There was collateral damage," Pitr said. "There almost always is."

"There's no such thing as collateral damage," Ms. Jones said. "The definition of collateral is being an accessory. Being part of. That's where the *co* comes from. People who are ignorant cannot be collateral. They are victims. People have to know and make choices. That's why that door is the way it is." She nodded at the exit to the Den. "Why everyone on the team hears everything and knows everything. When a Nightstalker dies, it is a terrible thing but it is not a tragedy, because they know the dangers and they know why they are dying. Everyone on the team is expendable, which sounds harsh, but it is realistic. Someone has to be."

"You take too much responsibility," Pitr said.

Ms. Jones laughed her cough. "Still, you don't understand. Telling people the truth relieves one of responsibility. It is then their decision what they do, not yours. It is only when you lie or deceive them that you continue to hold responsibility."

Pitr rubbed a hand across his chin, a bit unnerved. "What is wrong?"

"We have done well so far," Ms. Jones said. "We have stopped a half-dozen incidents that would have been the equivalent of a Chernobyl or worse over the years. But we have never had something like Burns in the history of the Nightstalkers. Someone from the inside going outside. Going rogue. Bringing one incident," she pointed at the hard drive, "to another incident. That worries me."

"And there are times you're not worried?" Pitr asked.

Ms. Jones reached a hand up. Pitr took it in hers.

"You are a comfort to a crazy old lady, my dear Pitr."

CHAPTER 17

The team came trooping into their new base of operations, dropping their gear. Roland was gathering MP-5s, as Roland always cleaned the team's weapons after every mission, whether they were fired or not. It was not only Protocol, it was Roland's passion. Otherwise he'd be doing chin-ups or push-ups.

Nada, Moms, and Scout came in the front door. Nada rolled the baby grand back against the doors and locked the wheels. Mac did a quick recon of the house to make sure no one had come in the back while they were across the street.

"You should put on some pants," Scout suggested to Moms, who had Kirk switching freqs to call Ms. Jones. The commo man had a large white bandage on his left hand. "You keep tugging on it and everyone's going to know you aren't from here. Plus, the hair."

"Support will be bringing us clothes soon." Moms frowned. "There was a room in your house that looked like its only purpose is to wrap gifts."

"It is," Scout said.

"Your parents give a lot of gifts?"

"No. But the room makes my mom feel better with all the ribbon and boxes and cards."

"Why would anyone want to be from around here?" Moms wondered.

Scout giggled and Nada gave her a playful thump on the head, which actually hurt because he'd forgotten about the burn from the Firefly curling iron. "Ouch!"

"Sorry, but don't giggle," Nada said. "It's only cute in babies."

Scout rubbed her head gingerly. "Don't hit girls. It's never cute."

Nada started to reply, but Moms cut in. "For Pete's sake, Nada. Could you remember you're on a mission here?"

"What mission is that, exactly?" Scout asked. "What are Fireflies and how do they make a curling iron attack me and a dog go cray-cray?"

"You don't have a need to know," Moms said.

"So you don't know what they are either," Scout said triumphantly.

"We know how to kill them," Roland said, looking up from the bolt of an MP-5 that he was running a darkened toothbrush over, removing specks of dirt that actually weren't there but he suspected were.

"Excuuuuse me," Scout said. "But this is my turf and you guys are pretty clueless around here, tennis skirt and all. I don't care how many guns you have."

Roland frowned in irritation. "How does she know how many guns we have?"

"See?" Scout said, looking at Nada and Moms.

"I've got to call it in," Moms said and she headed upstairs. Every team member watched her as she ascended, tennis skirt swaying. "On task, gentlemen," Moms called out. "On task. Nada, let me know when my civvie pants arrive."

Moms looked around the master bedroom. There was a king-sized bed with a massive headboard carved from what she assumed was some expensive wood. There was also a little alcove off to one side. She went to it and stopped, stunned by the simple beauty of a window seat covered with a pretty blue cushion.

"Oh!" Moms exclaimed, but she had enough sense of control to keep it off the team net. She reached into her pocket and pulled out her Federal ID, ranking her in the "do not fuck with me unless you're the president and even then…" echelon of government. Behind the computerized ID card was a page cut out from an old magazine. Moms carefully unfolded the aging paper. The picture was almost the spitting image of this little corner. Moms's mother had ripped the picture out of an old magazine when Moms was five and used a magnet advertising the local feed store to hold it to the front of the fridge. It had epitomized everything their shotgun shack on the Kansas high plains wasn't and represented some sort of vague hope her mother had held on to that one day there would be better days.

Sometimes hope is not a good thing.

Moms ran her hands along the cushion. She gasped as she lifted the seat and there were pillows and comforters stored in it. Moms stared down at those objects for a long moment.

Moms took a deep breath, shook her head, then pulled some pillows out and arranged them on the seat so she could lean back against one side. She also fluffed a comforter and tossed it over her bare legs. Then she settled in to talk to Ms. Jones about the mission.

"So far you seem to be having a little difficulty in rolling this up," Ms. Jones said.

"We've only got two Fireflies so far," Moms said.

"I have an Asset en route who lived in that community for several years," Ms. Jones said. "He was on the Acme list and is now a professor at Georgetown. He should be there later today."

Moms hesitated. "We have an Asset."

"A local recruit," Ms. Jones said approvingly.

"You could say that."

"You sound skeptical."

"Nada recruited her," Moms said. "She's just a kid. Sixteen."

"Ah! Children are often the most observant. A good choice on Mister Nada's part."

* * *

Downstairs the team was doing the things it usually did on an op when it wasn't killing or sleeping. Maintenance. Roland was cleaning weapons. Mac was separating out and molding charges, adapting them to their current environment, which meant shaped charges that made less bang but were just as effective since they were more directional. Kirk was on over-watch after having ensured Moms had a secure Satcom link through the TV dish on the roof of the house, and also linking the wireless in the house to a National Security Agency scrambler so no one could intercept or break the scrambling. Kirk could look out the front window, but he also had a half-dozen 27-inch Mac monitors surrounding him that not only had the entire perimeter of the house covered, but were also flashing ten-second feeds from the security cameras—there were a lot—spread around Senators Club. It would be confusing, but Nada had shown Kirk the Protocol for this setup, which had been designed by one of the Acme scientists who was an expert in physiological psychology and how quickly and often the brain could input visual data from a variety of displays and still cognitively process it.

So far, Kirk had a headache but spotted nothing out of the ordinary that indicated a Firefly possessing a creature or object. His hand throbbed, but he'd refused any sort of painkiller offered by Doc, because they were on a mission and he needed to stay sharp.

Doc was also upstairs doing something. Eagle was in the minigarage continuing the work Mac had started on the hybrid ATV/golf cart. The usual stuff in unusual ways. Adapting.

Nada was seated at the kitchen bar, on the laptop, doing recon by Google. Scout was sitting on a bar stool next to him, her legs dangling, telling him he was doing it all wrong by just putting in keywords.

"Ask questions," Scout said. "Google works a lot better that way because then you're looking for answers."

"Yeah, yeah," Nada muttered. He had just accessed the home page for Senators Club. He figured the more he knew about the place, the better he could figure out how to attack whatever the four remaining Fireflies had gotten into. They'd been lucky so far with just a dog and a curling iron. He had a feeling the rest weren't going to be so easy.

He spoke into his throat mike. "Kirk, is Moms still on with Ms. Jones?"

"She just clicked off," Kirk responded.

"I'm here," Moms said over the net. "What's up?"

"I'm doing an Area Study of Senators Club," Nada said. An Area Study was part of the Bible of Special Operations. Anywhere in the world they went, they spent as much time as possible studying the locale. For the Nightstalkers, often an Area Study wasn't feasible as they dropped in guns blazing, like with the Fun Outside Tucson. The first Special Forces teams into Afghanistan had had three weeks to do their Area Studies, mission planning, and briefbacks. Nada had a few minutes at the kitchen counter in Senators Club, which was a luxury for the Nightstalkers.

Nada glanced at Scout. "Correct me if any of this is wrong."

"Okay."

Nada read over the net: "*Senators Club is the Research Triangle's only gated community. It is regarded internationally as one of, if not the most desirable place to live in the southeastern United States.*"

"Subtle," Eagle commented.

"I like Texas better," Mac said.

Scout chimed in. "*It's twenty-four hundred acres of the most finely tended golf courses, hiking trails, lakes, and tennis courts designed for exceptional living, all at a price for the discerning buyer.*"

"You sound like a brochure," Eagle said.

"Twenty-four hundred acres?" Kirk wondered over the radio. "Why are some of the houses on top of each other?"

"It is in the brochure and right there on that website," Scout said. "Plus how can you compare yourself to the Joneses if you can't see them? And how can you tell when undesirables like you show up if you can't see your neighbor?"

"Hey!" Roland paused in cleaning his pistol. "We're the last line of defense protecting these people from the things that go bump in the night!"

"You just killed a curling iron," Scout said. "Do you get a medal for that?"

Mac laughed. "Old Kirk could probably put in for a Purple Heart: got burned grabbing for a curling iron. That would look real good."

Roland started running the toothbrush across the pistol's lower receiver so hard, it was surprising sparks weren't flying. "I don't like this kid. She's a smart-ass. Why do we need her?"

Scout spun about on her bar stool and jumped off, going into a handstand. She spoke, upside down. "I know where every security camera is, all the blind spots, and where every motion sensor in the place is. All the trails off the beaten path. All the ways to sneak around twenty-four hundred acres without being spotted." She pushed up with her arms and landed on her feet. "You guys couldn't even kill a dog without having some dumb girl see you. That is not part of the exceptional living experience offered by Senators Club."

Nada spoke in a low voice. "You were lucky that dog didn't rip you to shreds. Things taken over by Fireflies are pretty nasty."

"Well, that's a good question," Scout said, returning to her stool. "Why *didn't* Skippy rip me to shreds?"

Nada opened his mouth to answer, then realized there was no answer. He looked from the kitchen to the living room, where Roland had stopped trying to file down the lower receiver with the toothbrush and Mac placed a shaped charge that could burn through two inches of steel on Lilith's expensive coffee table. The door from the garage opened and Eagle walked in carrying a bag of clothes Support had just dropped off, using a FedEx truck as cover. Moms came down the stairs, still in the tennis outfit.

"Why *didn't* the curling iron fry her?" Eagle asked. "Damn near fried Kirk when he secured it, before Mac blew it into a thousand pieces."

"My curling iron is in a thousand pieces?" Scout actually seemed horrified. "My mother is so going to be all over me about the mess."

"Support is cleaning your house up, remember?" Moms said, looking through the bag and pulling out a pair of pants with her name safety-pinned to them. "It will be just like it was."

"Did you get me another curling iron?" Scout asked.

Moms looked at Nada.

Nada spoke on the net. "Kirk, get me Support."

"Roger," Kirk replied. There was a click over the net.

"Support, did you replace the curling iron?"

There was a pause, then a new voice came on, like Mac's but southern, not Texan, there is a difference. "Why sure, Nada. Exact same model. House is clean as a whistle. Them gate transmitters work for the final gate, old friend?"

"Sure did, Cleaner," Nada said, having recognized the voice. "Thanks." He clicked that freq off the team net.

"Cleaner?" Scout asked.

"He's the guy who comes behind us and cleans up," Nada said.

"I bet he earns *his* pay," Scout said.

"We all do," Roland said.

"On task, people," Moms said, and Roland's scars flushed red, although whether from embarrassment or anger, it wasn't clear. She pulled out a pair of khaki pants and a sport shirt and tossed them to Roland. "Those will fit better."

Nada looked at the computer screen. "Feel free to interpret," he said to Scout. "*The exclusive life experience bestowed by Senators Club being the fact that it is situated on the highest elevation in the region—*"

"I like the high ground," Roland muttered.

"*—which features spectacular three-hundred-and-sixty-degree views of the surrounding countryside for miles in every direction.*"

"So they can look down on the peons," Eagle said, which earned a roll of the eyes from Scout.

"*The houses built here match the uniqueness of the terrain, meeting stringent standards for beauty, functionality, landscaping, and friendliness to the environment. Senators Club's priority has always been to coexist in harmony with nature.*"

"That harmony ain't gonna last long," Mac said, "if it attacks us."

Nada pressed on. "*This has brought together over nine hundred special, committed, and engaged families from all over the world to our community. We have residents from twelve countries and thirty-two states who have chosen us as their ultimate destination for living.*

"*Our private oasis of understated beauty and elegance—*" Even Nada had to pause as Eagle laughed, Mac snorted in disgust, and Kirk just said: "What the hell?"

Nada cleared his throat. "Uh. Where was I?...*understated beauty and elegance situated in the intellectual capital of the South, the Research Triangle—*"

"Hah!" Mac said. "That's like saying you're the tallest contestant in a midget beauty contest."

"All right," Moms said. "We know what we've jumped into. The Fireflies are our mission. We get them, obliterate them, and get out. Clear?"

"Clear," everyone on the team responded.

Roland was pulling off the way-too-tight sweatshirt, and Scout's eyes bulged as she saw his torso, whether it was because of the toned muscles or the puckered scars that three bullets had made on his upper right chest. Roland didn't notice as he pulled on the sport shirt.

"Change the pants in another room," Moms said to him.

"You never told me if I get paid," Scout said.

"Don't you have to be home sometime?" Moms asked, because once more the team was off balance.

Scout hopped off the stool and did three cartwheels toward the front door.

"You're going to have to keep both feet on the ground," Moms said, "because you're giving me a headache."

"It's the Ritalin," Scout said. "I'm hyperactive."

"It ain't working," Roland groused.

Doc looked up from his tackle box full of goodies. "How about a little Valium?"

Scout's eyes grew wide. "You have some?"

"No, he does *not*," Moms said.

Behind her back, Doc nodded.

Scout smiled at Moms. "I must be off."

"Where are you going?"

"You just asked if I had to be home, duh." Scout stopped at the grand piano blocking the doors. "Uh, pleeeze."

"You're going home?" Moms tried to confirm as Nada hopped off the stool and moved the piano.

"Yaaah. Sort of. I do connect with the world," Scout said. She checked her watch and made a face. "You guys really suck. Not enough time to ride my horse. I've got to get the dinner out of the fridge and into the oven so when my overlords finally arrive home, they can dine."

"You have a horse?" Eagle asked.

"Duh. I live in Senators Ridge inside Senators Club. I do take advantage of some of the things offered me."

Moms opened the door. "Be careful. There are Fireflies out there."

"They already went after me twice," Scout said. "What are the odds?"

"Shh!" Nada warned.

"You guys take care of yourselves." And then Scout was gone.

CHAPTER 18

In the basement of the physics building, Ivar, no longer held by the golden glow, read the list of equipment the man had just handed him. The man had typed something into the keyboard and the golden glow had subsided to a pulsing ball about two feet in diameter just above the computer.

Ivar looked up at the man, about to protest that all this was going to be difficult to get, then saw the eyes, pulsing with the same gold as the ball, and decided not to. Then he realized this was his chance to escape, to get away from whatever the hell was going on in here.

The man still held the gun in one hand, but it wasn't pointed at Ivar, as if he could sense that Ivar was not a threat.

"What's your name?" the man asked.

"Ivar."

The man smiled, and that made some of the scabs covering the scars on his face crack, as if he hadn't smiled since the wounds had been inflicted. "I'm Burns. That's what they called me. But I'm more than Burns now. Do you understand?"

"No."

"Good," Burns said. "You don't have to. You're thinking of running away." He reached into a pocket and pulled out a gold chain with a large black stone on it. He snapped the gold neck-lace around Ivar's neck. "Think of this like a dog collar, except the stone also transmits everything you say or hear. I will be listening to you. Every second. Tell no one about what happened or what's going on in here or about me. The gold is lined with a very high grade of explosive. You try to tell someone about what's happening in here, I'll blow your head off. You try to take the collar off, it explodes. And your head goes pop. So don't make your head go pop, clear? It's really messy. You'll be back here in two hours or I'll blow your head from your shoulders. Got it?"

Ivar could only nod.

Burns put a comforting hand on Ivar's shoulder. "Trust me. I work for the government."

CHAPTER 19

As darkness loomed in the east, Moms, with some trepidation, sent the team out to patrol Senators Club to track down the remaining Fireflies. Nada had laid out the entire facility in a grid pattern and assigned sectors to each element.

She sent Eagle out in the modified golf cart to patrol the golf course, which seemed logical, except instead of clubs in the bags strapped to the rear, he had a variety of weapons, and the cart was actually the shell of a cart layered over the ATV frame and engine.

Mac got to ride on a Segway dressed in a security uniform, and Moms warned him not to take it apart to see how it worked until the mission was over.

Kirk didn't get to go. His bandaged hand might raise questions, so he got to pull over-watch. He sat amidst the computer monitors and monitored, the grid pattern taped to the bottom of one of them so he knew where each element was going and could track them.

Nada took one of the SUVs to drive about the place and carry some bigger weapons and special gear in case one of the recon personnel made contact. Doc wasn't exactly the recon sort, plus he told Moms he had work to do.

Moms went with Roland and walked out the front door, because Moms believed the best recon was boots on the ground, even if in this case it was her tennis shoes and Roland's boots. As the golf cart, Segway, and SUV scattered, they had barely made it to the sidewalk before Scout appeared.

"Well, hey there, Moms and Hulk."

"That's not my name," Roland said.

"Shouldn't you be doing homework or something?" Moms asked.

"Summer," Scout once again reminded her. "The overlords have had their repast and are now safely ensconced in their room after their daily quota of wine."

"You shouldn't talk about your parents that way," Roland said.

"Who said they were my parents?" Scout asked. "I never called them my parents. My parents died when I was two in a plane crash and I've been passed through six foster homes since then."

Roland flushed. "I'm sorry."

Scout laughed. "Got you."

Roland took a step forward but Moms put an arm across his chest. Not that her arm could physically stop Roland, but her pinky could stop him in gesture. He halted but glared at Scout.

"Do you always do that to people?" Moms asked. "Pull their leg?"

Scout shrugged. "Never."

Moms shook her head and was about to say something when a big BMW slowed and a window slid down with a rush of cold air floating out.

"Hey, Doctor Carruthers," Scout said.

"Hey, Greer." He looked past her at Moms and his eyes settled on Roland. "You all right?"

"Sure." Scout reached out and took Roland's meaty paw in her tiny hand. "This is my uncle George from Wichita."

Carruthers's eyes immediately glazed over at the mention of a place he'd never been and had no desire to see.

"Uh, hello, sir," Roland managed to say, resisting the urge to tighten down on Scout's hand.

"And?" Carruthers asked, shifting his gaze back to Moms and running his eyes up and down her body in its civilian clothes, which caused Roland to take a half step forward while Scout hung on with all her might, a pretty useless attempt, but it was the attempt that brought sanity back to Roland.

"This is my aunt Betty."

"Hello, Aunt Betty," Carruthers said. "So you and George are married?"

"No!" both Moms and Roland said at the same time.

"You see," Scout said, sliding into the exchange smoothly, "Betty is George's sister. They run a big farm outside of Wichita."

"A farm." The way Carruthers said it, you'd think they were running a prison.

"Nice to meet you," Moms said. "We just love this place. It's so big and wonderful and so, so," she searched for more adjectives, "green."

"You really are from Wichita," Carruthers said. "Take care." And with that he powered up the window and drove away, keeping to fifteen miles an hour to take the speed bumps.

"Greer?" Moms asked.

"Everyone here a doctor?" Roland asked.

"Enough are," Scout said, ignoring Moms's question, "that I just call everyone doctor. It's better to err on the side of caution."

"Like the Acmes," Roland observed, for the first time agreeing with Scout.

"Isn't your world full of titles and rank?" Scout asked as Moms started walking down the sidewalk, Roland on one side, Scout on the other.

"The big part is," Roland said. "The army and the other agencies, but not us."

"Why not?"

Moms answered. "It's not good for cohesiveness and team building and trust."

Scout laughed. "Who sounds like a brochure now? But aren't you in charge?"

"Of the team," Moms said as they passed under a streetlamp that flickered on, activated by the dwindling daylight.

"And who is in charge of you?"

"Too many questions," Moms said as she paused on the corner and looked about. "This way," she said.

* * *

Upstairs, Kirk watched Moms, Roland, and Scout talk off the guy in the BMW. Then he walked down the hall to the master bedroom. He'd heard someone go by a little while ago. The bedroom was empty, but he heard someone in the closet, the one with the watch winder.

Kirk walked in and saw Doc sitting cross-legged on the floor, a pile of papers spread out in front of him along with a cell phone.

"What's that?"

Doc was startled. "Winslow's notes. And his phone. The phone is locked, but I bet Mac could break the code."

Kirk just nodded.

"I'm on your side," Doc said. "The more we know, the better equipped we'll be to battle the Fireflies and the Rifts. I want to figure out what Winslow was doing. Compare it with the data from the Can. Maybe we can learn something."

"I didn't say nothing," Kirk said. "And you're over-explaining. I've got to get back to over-watch." He paused. "How about sending that stuff to Support? Let Ms. Jones take a look at it. Especially the phone."

Doc stared back at him, then began gathering it all together.

* * *

It was a beautiful sunset to the west. Eagle wasn't distracted by it. He drove the cart on the path that wound along the golf course, scanning left and right.

"Hey!" A florid-faced man was waving his golf club. "Hey, you!"

Eagle turned and rolled up to the foursome gathered around the sixteenth hole. "Yes, sir?"

"What the hell is that back there?" the man jerked a thumb over his shoulder.

"To what are you referring?" Eagle asked, looking in that direction and seeing nothing but a long fairway.

"You need to get that fixed," the man said. "You people charge an arm and a leg for membership and I expect better than this."

"Yes, sir."

Eagle saw another golf cart coming from the other direction, driven by an attractive young woman with blonde hair tucked back underneath her pink golfing cap. She pulled up right next to the hole, short of the most distant ball. "Good evening, gentlemen," she drawled. "Might I interest y'all in some cocktails?"

Eagle, and whatever was wrong with the course behind them, was immediately forgotten as the four went over to get their drinks and chat up the woman, who was a lot sharper than her fake drawl, as she was watching Eagle and not the men, wondering who he was and what he was doing here.

Support hadn't taken over every job in Senators Club. The number of people required to keep these people in the lifestyle they were accustomed to strained even the resources of Fort Bragg. Apparently the blonde golf-cart bar-girl wasn't one Ms. Jones had considered needing replacement.

Eagle got back in his cart, resisting the temptation to flame the golfers with the rig that had replaced the headlight.

He ignored the path and went down the fairway, as this foursome was the last of the day and no one was coming up behind them. The cause of the complaint quickly became apparent as he spotted a dark line cutting across the fairway.

Eagle stopped the cart next to it, but he didn't have to get out to know what it was—any soldier who'd spent time around either the armor or mechanized infantry recognized the pattern in the torn-up grass: a tracked vehicle had cut across the golf course. A big one.

Eagle looked right. A half-built house was on the edge of the fairway. The bright red netting that was supposed to separate construction from golf course was torn to shreds.

"What happened here?" Golf-cart bar-girl said, pulling up to Eagle. She had lost her accent. "And who are you?"

Now that she was closer, Eagle could see she wasn't a girl, but a woman, with lines around her eyes and a weariness that said she had not planned on selling drinks to rich good ole boys on a golf course her entire life, but dreams didn't always come true.

Eagle prepared to launch into his usual "We're the government" spiel, but decided, *Fuck it*. "Something bad. Very bad. You don't want to be around for this."

"You're government, aren't you?" she asked, stealing his spiel. Eagle nodded.

"Yeah. Lots of new faces, especially in security. Can always tell a soldier. My husband was a Marine."

"What's he do now?" Eagle asked as he looked in the other direction, toward where the tracks disappeared into the forest.

"He's holding down the fort in Section 60 in Arlington. Fallujah."

Eagle turned from the path of destruction. "I'm sorry. I've got quite a few friends there."

The woman looked at the scars on the side of his face. "I can tell." She nodded toward the track. "Need any help?"

Eagle shook his head. "I'll be bringing some friends here to take care of this. Best you stay far away."

The woman stuck out her hand. "I'm Emily." She gave a weak smile. "Just call service at the Golf Center if you or your friends need anything."

He shook her hand. "Eagle."

Her smile deepened. "For real?"

Eagle shrugged. "We gave up our names when we took this job."

"Then it must be an important job." Emily headed back to her cart, but paused and looked over her shoulder. "Don't lose any more of your friends, okay? I'll be praying for you."

"Thank you."

She drove off toward the clubhouse.

Eagle got back in his cart and headed toward the trees. He paralleled the tracks. According to his handheld GPS, there was nothing this way but forest and the fence surrounding Senators Club. As he passed into the trees, he could hear the sound of a large diesel engine running. He stopped as visibility was halved going into the woods. Since the cart's headlight didn't work, having been replaced by a flamer, Eagle reached into one of the bags and pulled out his night-vision goggles and put them on. He proceeded forward with more caution.

Eagle spoke over the team net as he slowed down further, having to drive the cart in one of the ruts to avoid uprooted and splintered trees. He was glad Mac had left the ATV's suspension in place. "I've got a very strong possible. Sixteenth fairway, going southwest into the trees. I'm following."

Moms replied immediately. "We're scrambling. What's the Firefly in?"

"Wait one." Eagle moved forward at a crawl.

Kirk's voice came over the net. "One of the Wall probes just went dead." There was a moment of silence. "Eagle, the one that went out is directly in front of you, fifty meters away."

"That's not good," Doc said over the net.

Eagle swallowed hard. He hit the brake and halted the cart as he saw the perpetrator. "It's in a backhoe. A big one. Tracked. Long articulated arm with a large shovel on the end. Already torn up the fence and the shovel is reaching out and digging up the ground outside in a trench. It's moving left to right slowly. Probably searching for the next probe. Tell Mac to load up."

"We lose four probes," Doc said, "we lose containment. But how does it know about the probes?"

"We're on the way," Moms said.

* * *

They all switched to night-vision goggles as the sun's last rays faded in the west. The two SUVs were parked behind them, and despite actually being on the golf course, they'd left the shirts and shorts behind in favor of camouflage and body armor. They were parked right where the backhoe had plowed into the woods. Eagle's golf cart was on the trail of destruction heading into the woods.

They'd left Scout on her front porch with firm orders not to leave the house this night. Not for any reason.

For once she got their seriousness and promised.

Roland had his backpack flamer, and everyone had their personnel weapons, with Nada now carrying the M-203 in addition to his MP-5. Given the suspected target, though, Mac was the key man. He'd had one of the SUVs loaded with shaped charges, AT-4 antitank missiles, and an FGM-148 Javelin fire-and-forget missile system. He took a laser designator and handed it to Roland as he transferred other gear over to the golf cart.

"A complete ATV would be better," he complained as he loaded the cart.

"We use what we have," Moms said. "You're the one who modified it in the first place."

"Yeah," Mac said, grinning, and Moms realized he'd set her up. "I didn't have enough time to do it as well as I'd like, especially the suspension, but..."

"Yeah, yeah," Nada said. "We get it."

"How far to the target?" Mac asked.

Eagle checked his GPS. "Two hundred and twelve meters from where I last saw it. It's moving pretty slow, because it's tearing up the fence and a trench along the outside, searching for the probes."

"I don't like that," Doc said.

"And it's going east?" Mac asked, focusing on the kill, not the problem.

"Yes."

Mac turned to Moms. "Do you have Excalibur on call?"

"They airlifted in one gun." Moms nodded and help up a finger. "Kirk, get me our Eighteenth Field Artillery Support."

Kirk dialed up the correct frequency on the PRT, then held it in front of Moms so she could read the correct call signs on the backlit screen.

"Lion Six, this is Nightstalker Six, over."

The reply was immediate. "This is Lion Six, over."

"We need Excalibur prepared for a fire mission. Let me know when it's ready. We will send you the code for our designator. Over."

"Excalibur is already loaded, and we will sync as soon as you give us the authorization code. Over."

"Do you have our location? Over."

"Roger. Over."

"It will be danger close to us when we call it in. Understand? Over."

"Danger close. Roger, we'll put it on the dime. Over."

"Stand by. Out."

Moms nodded at Kirk and he sent the authorization code.

* * *

On the edge of the small open field that was the FOB, a single M777, 155-millimeter howitzer had its barrel aimed toward Senators Club. It had been sling-loaded in by a CH-47 Chinook as part of the Support package Ms. Jones had specified. It had a gun crew of five, and if any of them wondered why they had their big gun loaded in the middle of North Carolina, none of them were talking about it to their battery commander.

It beat being in Afghanistan on a firebase.

The round in the howitzer was the M982 Excalibur, a GPS-guided munitions that could take the location of a lased target and blow the hell out of it. The howitzer had a range of twenty-five miles, so Senators Club was easily in range, along with most of Chapel Hill, Durham, and some of Raleigh. This particular gun crew, during one fire mission supporting a Ranger patrol that had been ambushed in Afghanistan by a much superior Taliban force, had fired twenty-five Excalibur rounds at the targets lased by the Rangers. The targets were eighteen miles away on the other side of a range of mountains. All twenty-five rounds landed within ten meters of the designated targets and over sixty insurgents were killed and the patrol broke the ambush.

In layman's terms, that meant the Excalibur was a very effective long-range killer and the 155-millimeter round packed a lot of punch.

* * *

"Let's go," Moms said.

They moved into the woods, Moms in the lead, as always. Behind her, Mac drove the cart with the Javelin, missiles, laser designator, and other tools of the trade. Nada and Eagle were on the right of the wedge, while Kirk and Roland were on the left. Doc was in the center.

They reached where the fence had been. A pile of mangled iron was all that remained of a twenty-meter section. Moms pointed at a hole. "The probe was there. Doc?"

Doc moved forward, Roland and Kirk providing cover, and pulled a probe out of his backpack. He slammed it into the ground and activated it. Kirk checked his PRT. "It's live, but this thing has taken two more out that way."

He didn't need to point as everyone could see the path the tracks had torn along the fence line. The backhoe was dragging its shovel along the ground, taking out a foot of soil, easily uprooting the probes that had been fired into the ground by Eagle from the Snake.

"They ain't never been this smart before," Nada said.

"How do they even know about the probe and the Wall?" Doc asked.

Nada paused. "The dog. Skippy. It jumped into the Wall around the house. I thought it was trying to attack me, but maybe it was checking out the Wall?"

"But then how could *this* Firefly know?" Doc asked. "You flamed that Firefly."

"Enough speculating," Moms said. "Mac, prep the Javelin."

Mac opened up the tripod for the Javelin and set up the weapon system. Not as powerful as the Excalibur in the howitzer miles away, it was an immediate fire-and-forget solution to put some hurt on the opposition if needed. Mac had the control for firing it wired into a remote system strapped to his wrist.

Once the Javelin was ready, they moved along the fence and could hear the engine up ahead and the screech of metal getting mangled. They went down into a stream gulley and climbed out, the earth torn up from the treads of the metal beast that had gone ahead of them easily visible. Everyone froze when the backhoe went silent.

"Wait," Moms said.

They stood still for several minutes. One of the hardest things for a soldier in a combat situation to do is to wait on the enemy to make a move, for the enemy to make a mistake, even if, as in this case, the enemy was several tons of machinery.

After ten minutes, there was still no indication of movement ahead. Reluctantly, Moms waved the team forward and they moved down the swath of debris, Mac maneuvering the golf cart.

Kirk suddenly paused. "Hold on. Something's not—"

Headlights sprung alive, close and to the right, blinding them by overloading their night-vision goggles. As they ripped them off, they could hear the roar of the engine powering up as the shovel on the arm came slamming down, narrowly missing Mac, but severing the cart in two. The backhoe was large, over twelve feet high with a thirty-foot articulating arm, terminating with an ugly-looking clawed shovel. Mac rolled to the left as the arm lifted and thudded down into the ground, so close it caught the sling on his MP-5, pinning him in place. The rest of the team began firing, but the rounds ricocheted off the metal, going in all directions, tracers arcing every which way.

"Cease fire! Cease fire!" Moms screamed over the radio, realizing they were more likely to kill each other with the ricochets than damage the machine.

The arm lifted for another attempt at killing Mac, but he anticipated it, leaving his MP-5 behind and running to the rear half of the cart, Kirk joining him as they grabbed AT-4s. The arm swung, knocking the cart and Kirk twenty feet in a tumble, Mac ducking and just barely getting grazed, which still sent him flying ten feet.

Now that they were farther away, Roland began firing his machine gun, the rounds ricocheting off the metal. Nada fired a forty-millimeter grenade and it exploded in the cabin of the thing, ripping it to shreds, but not slowing the machine in the slightest.

This was no curling iron.

Mac knelt and raised an AT-4 to firing position on his shoulder. "Backblast clear!" he yelled, waited two seconds even as the clawed bucket rose up over his head, then fired, aiming for one of the treads. Flame blossomed behind Mac as the 84-millimeter HEAT (high-explosive antitank) round hit the backhoe's left tread and blew it apart. Mac dumped the empty tube and dove out of the way as the shovel crushed the rear of the golf cart.

"Back up! Back up!" Moms ordered, seeing what Mac had done.

Mac grabbed Kirk, who'd had several ribs broken from the blow that had knocked him flying, dragging him back, and Kirk kept a firm grip on the AT-4 he'd retrieved.

The machine kept coming forward. It pulled along the tread until reaching the break, and then the road wheels continued pushing it off. The backhoe slewed to the left as the intact tread still had traction.

The machine halted for a moment, as if the Firefly were considering the situation.

Mac let go of Kirk and grabbed his AT-4. He fired, breaking the other tread.

"All right," Moms said. "We've got a stationary—" She paused as the arm reached forward, extending to the end of its length, dug down into the ground, and then pulled back, lurching the rest of the backhoe forward toward the team.

"They never go easy," Nada muttered.

"Javelin," Moms ordered.

Mac aimed the designator and pressed the fire button. Behind them, the Javelin roared to life, shot up into the air, arced over their heads, and came straight down into the engine of the backhoe. The explosion reverberated the team back with a shock wave.

For several seconds there was an echoing silence. Doc ran over to Kirk, who was trying to stand up, but unable, the pain from his broken ribs excruciating.

"Shit," Nada muttered as the backhoe's arm began to move, eerily silent, no engine power, but the Firefly somehow providing power to the machine the same way it kept animals that were dead moving.

Roland slammed home another hundred-round belt of ammunition into his machine gun and Nada kept pumping out forty-millimeter rounds, taking bits and pieces off the edges, but doing little real damage.

"Nada," Mac said. "The hydraulic lines to the bucket, along the arm."

"Got it," Nada said, understanding what Mac wanted.

Lowering the M-203 and tucking his MP-5 to his shoulder, Nada fired single round after single round with the precision of a surgeon. The nine-millimeter bullets cut into the lines, hydraulic fluid spraying out. Without the pressure, the arm began to slow down and then fell to the ground with a heavy thud.

Another short pause in the battle.

Then the road wheels that supported the track spun furiously, and even without track, they moved the vehicle forward. And even without hydraulic fluid, the arm lifted up in the air and poised to do more smashing.

The backhoe slithered down the trail toward the team and Moms realized it would be on them faster than they could retreat.

"Lion Six. Fire for effect on laser! Danger close. Danger close."

Mac leveled the laser designator at the backhoe.

The voice of Lion Six came over the net. "Shot over!"

"Shot out," Moms said as everyone scrambled back for cover, Roland helping Doc haul Kirk back.

"Splash over," Lion Six warned, indicating Excalibur was five seconds from impact.

"Splash out!" Moms screamed.

Everyone dove, eating dirt.

The Excalibur round hit the center of mass of the backhoe. The blast lifted everyone a few inches off the ground and slammed them back down. Pieces of backhoe and metal shrapnel whistled by. Through it all, Moms was watching. As the smoke cleared, out of the pile of rubble that had been the backhoe, a small golden Firefly arose, and then dissipated.

"Everyone all right?" Moms asked as she got to her feet.

"Kirk's got a couple of broken ribs," Doc reported from where he was checking the wounded man's chest, "but otherwise he's okay." He pushed a syringe into Kirk's arm. "That will help with the pain."

"Got an itsy bit of shrapnel," Mac said. "Only hurts when I frown, so I'll keep smiling."

Moms and Nada ran over to him, kneeling at his side. Mac was seated with his back against an uprooted tree.

"Doc!"

Doc raced over. A piece of backhoe had slashed through Mac's body armor and cut a furrow along his left side. Blood was freely flowing.

Doc reached into one of the front pockets on his combat vest and pulled out what appeared to be a shaving can painted blood red. It had two nozzles side by side. He pointed it at the wound and sprayed, the two streams meshing just before reaching the gash. One stream was fibrinogen and the other thrombin, forming an instant bandage with 85 percent more efficient blood-clotting abilities than any other coagulant. Ms. Jones made sure the Nightstalkers got the latest gear, especially stuff that would keep them alive.

Moms ran over to Kirk. "Get me the Support freq."

Kirk was ahead of her, no longer feeling any pain, focused on the mission.

"Support Six, this is Nightstalker Six. I need a priority one medevac. Over."

"Shucks," Mac said on the team net, "this is just a scratch. No need for a priority one."

"Medevac en route. ETA six minutes. Over."

"We'll mark the LZ with IR strobe. It's on the edge of the golf course. Out."

The team was gathered around Mac.

"We *can* move him?" she asked Doc.

His hands were crimson. "Yes. It's mostly controlled. But we need to move fast. He's lost a lot of blood."

Moms was about to issue an order when Roland simply reached down, lifted Mac gently in his arms, and then began running back toward the golf course.

"Nada, you secure this until Cleaner arrives." She shook her head. "Call him in, okay?"

Nada was steady as a rock. "I got it."

Moms ran after Roland and Mac.

* * *

"This is a bit more than a girl's bathroom and a cleaning iron," Cleaner said, surveying the damage.

"Yeah, I know," Nada said.

Cleaner walked forward on his carbon-fiber prostheses. He'd lost both legs just below the knees on a Nightstalker mission years ago.

"How's Mac?"

"They got him to Womack at Bragg," Nada said. "He's going to be fine. Probably just have a nice scar."

"We all have nice scars," Cleaner said as he walked around the crumpled remains of the backhoe. "All right. I'll bring in some heavy equipment, get the trees cleared out, plow down the damage. Announce we're renovating this part of the golf course. It's weak, but what are they gonna do? Sue us?"

CHAPTER 20

THE NEXT DAY

Back in the house, Doc was tending to the minor scrapes and bruises everyone had accumulated during the Fun on the Golf Course. Eagle had over-watch. Roland was at the dining room table, cleaning the stack of weapons from the previous night's activities. It turned out that sometime during the battle, a huge chunk of the machine had landed on Roland's foot, but his steel-toed boot combined with the churned-up dirt had saved him from any significant damage. So, of course, Doc was giving him a lecture on foot fungus, which he'd discovered while checking it. It seemed Roland had fungus in abundance.

"That would be two Purple Hearts," Doc said to Kirk. "You keep it up, you're going to get one posthumously."

"Technically, according to regs," Nada said, "since we're on the same op, it would still be one Purple Heart."

"We don't do medals," Moms said, wiping sweat and dirt off her forehead with a formerly pristine white towel in the bathroom off the kitchen, then wrapping it around her neck to absorb the sweat that was still flowing despite the air conditioning. She slumped down in an armchair, promptly staining it with forest, golf course, and backhoe detritus. Nada walked over and knelt next to her. "You all right?"

"We almost lost containment," Moms said. "If it had taken out several more probes, the Wall would have been breached."

"It didn't."

"We definitely lost concealment," Moms said. "No way can Cleaner fix that golf course in time for the first foursome in the morning."

"He's on top of it," Nada said, explaining Cleaner's plan.

"What about all the explosions?" Moms asked. "We made a heck of a racket."

"Yeah," Nada acknowledged. "Support says they logged eighty-six calls complaining about it so far."

"And?" Moms said.

"Fourth of July," Kirk said.

Moms and Nada looked at him questionably.

"Today's the second," Kirk said. "Announce to the inhabitants of Senators Club that the gala Fourth of July fireworks display won't quite come off as planned as the contractors who were setting it up had a slight"—he paused—"large accident on the golf course."

Nada smiled. "Good. Call that in to Cleaner and Support."

There was a knock on the front door and Nada peered out the side window, then moved the piano out of the way. "Aren't kids supposed to sleep in?" he asked as Scout blew into the house, full of energy, the polar opposite of the exhausted team.

"Golf course renovation?" Scout said.

"And a mishap for the planned Fourth of July celebration," Kirk added.

Scout sat at the kitchen bar and swung her legs back and forth. "The last one people might buy, but you're hitting close to the heart around here with the first."

"Cleaner has just closed one of the holes," Moms said. "They can, what do you call it, play around it?"

"Don't know," Scout said. "I've never played golf. Seems terribly boring. Hitting a little ball into a tiny hole over long distances. Of course, basketball seems just as dumb, throwing a big ball through a big hole over shorter distances and slanted toward tall people. How fair is that? And don't get me started on baseball. A no-hitter? So nothing happens and everyone gets excited? I don't get it."

"Hockey?" Nada asked.

As if taking that as some weird cue, Roland announced: "I'm hungry."

They all grabbed meals out of their rucksacks and "retired" to the library, where there was a large table they could all gather around.

"Can they even see the puck from the stands?" Scout asked, following them and going back to hockey.

"Any sport you do like?" Nada asked.

"Cross-country equestrian," Scout said. "Not dressage. Never dressage."

"Don't like either," Roland said as he ripped open a meal.

"You don't know what either are," Nada said. "And I don't either."

"Where's the cute guy, Mac?" Scout asked.

Moms sighed and quickly updated Scout on the Fun on the Golf Course. She related it just like she had to Ms. Jones as soon as they got back.

Scout became still as Moms explained the battle. She concluded with the medevac by an MH-60 Black Hawk from the golf course.

"Is Mac going to be all right?" Scout asked.

"He'll be fine," Doc replied.

"That's wild. Killing a machine. Terminator-like."

"*I'll be back*," Roland said, another strange synapse in his brain firing. "This is a weird room," he also noted.

All the shelves were covered with individual glass doors. You had to lift one up to get at a book. Doc was walking around the room, checking out titles, while everyone else, except Scout and Nada, his meal unopened, was chowing down.

"That don't make sense," Roland said, indicating the glass.

Moms had a laptop open next to her meal and was typing up the AAR in between bites, because despite the verbal one to Ms. Jones, she always had to file a written one that would eventually end up in the binder for future Nightstalkers to read and aid them the next time a Firefly backhoe had to be taken down. "That's to keep dust out," she said.

"Yeah," Scout said. "Miss Lilith was a big fan of easy cleaning."

"She did her own cleaning?" Moms asked.

"Nope, but it's hard to hover over everyone on the cleaning team and make sure they do it exactly the way you want," Scout said.

Doc tapped one of the glass cases. "I think she was more a fan of keeping things behind glass. Did you notice her wedding dress on that mannequin upstairs in the closet in the big glass case?"

"Almost shot it when I was clearing the place," Roland noted.

They all nodded, because each of them had also almost shot it when first walking into Lilith's huge closet. It just wasn't what they were used to, and they were really beginning to want to be back at the Ranch where things made sense and were practical. The library was fancy, but they preferred the Den and the stump of a tree they threw sharp objects at.

Scout was eyeballing Doc. "What do you mean about keeping things behind glass?"

Doc sat down at the end of the table and steepled his fingers, which everyone on the team knew meant another great theory was coming from the great doctor. At least Roland didn't groan, but only because he was busy eating Nada's ration, which the team sergeant had simply handed over when Roland finished his own and looked about, still hungry.

"Well," Doc said, "it's obvious she likes stuff. She likes it because it's *her* stuff. But she doesn't like other people touching it."

Moms looked up from the laptop. "Actually, looks like she doesn't even want to touch it herself."

Doc nodded. "True."

"What's the point of having it then?" Scout asked. She grabbed Nada's CamelBak and was taking a slurp out of it, which was rather outstanding that Nada let her take it, never mind let her drink from it, but she must have figured if Nada would give Roland his food, he wouldn't mind. It appeared he didn't.

"It's part of OCPD," Doc said.

"Huh?" Roland said with a mouthful.

"Obsessive-compulsive personality disorder," Doc explained. "Not like flicking light switches on and off, but rather having to control everything around her."

"Sounds like Miss Lilith," Scout said. "By the way, what happened to Miss Lilith?"

Moms exchanged a glance with Nada. "She had a bit of a breakdown and is being looked after in a secure and very nice place."

"Huh." Scout handed the CamelBak back to Nada and went over to one of the racks. She lifted the glass cover and tugged on a book about bird watching in Bolivia and the whole shelf of books moved easily forward. "These aren't even real books!"

"They don't have to be real to others," Doc said. "But they're real to her."

"A nutter," Roland said.

"Just like my mom," Scout said.

"The one who died in the plane crash?" Roland said, feeling like he'd scored a good one.

Scout ignored him.

"What about your mother?" Nada asked.

"Oh," Scout said, "she's in rehab. A different kind from Miss Lilith apparently."

"For real?" Nada asked.

"For real." Scout noted the concern in his voice. "Oh, not like a place for drugs or anything. She just doesn't like to eat, so every few months she goes in and they stick some tubes in her to keep her running."

"That's terrible," Moms said. "I'm so sorry."

Scout shrugged. "It's pretty normal around here. The only sin is to be fat." She brightened. "My mom does have real books with no glass, so that's good, right?"

"It is," Nada said, trying to sound positive, which was stretching his limits.

"This place is fucked up," Roland said.

"When did you notice?" Scout asked.

"You have any friends?" Moms asked.

"I got you guys," Scout said.

Everyone glanced at each other nervously.

Scout shrugged. "I'm what you call antisocial."

"You're not antisocial," Doc said. "You wouldn't have come to the door that first day if you were."

"My shrink says I am," Scout said with a laugh.

"He wouldn't if you weren't conning him," Doc said.

Scout gave an evil little grin. "Isn't that what antisocial is?"

"Antisocial is when you con yourself," Doc said.

Moms closed the computer lid and tossed the damp towel from around her neck onto the mahogany table.

Scout snatched up the towel. "Miss Lilith would have a fit."

"See," Doc said triumphantly, pointing with steepled fingers. "You have empathy for Miss Lilith's table. Not antisocial. You're smart and conscientious and trying to survive in what is an alien environment for your personality."

"More alien than ever," Scout said as she folded the towel.

Eagle came into the library, his tour on over-watch coming to an end.

"And you're resilient and can function under stress," Doc added.

"Well, don't tell anyone," Scout said. "I got a rep and I got to live here long after you guys are gone."

For a long moment everyone got quiet because there were no words to erase what to them was a brutal truth.

"Roland, over-watch," Nada finally said, because no matter how tired, how fried from action the team was, someone always had to provide security, and Roland would be good for several hours before he came down off the firefight high.

Roland tossed the M-240 over one shoulder as if it were a broomstick and went up one of the two staircases. Which prompted Doc to start arguing with Eagle about which staircase actually was the most efficient to get upstairs to over-watch. Eagle won that one easily by pointing out it would be the one Roland hadn't taken.

CHAPTER 21

Debbie Simmons woke to the sound of someone pounding on her door.

She found a short terry cloth wrap she used for the complex pool and put it on. The last time she felt this bad it had involved tequila and a bachelorette party. She'd sworn off both after that night: tequila and brides, but unfortunately not vodka. She went to the door and peered through the peephole.

Black suits, dark sunglasses, blank faces. Government, no doubt. Her stomach tightened.

She opened the door, worried and feeling naked and realized that she practically was because the wrap usually covered at least a bikini and it was almost transparent. She couldn't tell where the men were looking because of the sunglasses, but one of them brushed past her, grabbed an afghan off the back of a chair, and draped it over her shoulders.

So they were looking, but they were gentlemen.

"Debbie Simmons?" one of them asked, as if they might have come to the wrong apartment, but they had an air about them that indicated they didn't make such mistakes.

"Yes?"

The man who'd asked flipped open a leather wallet briefly showing her a badge, then flipped it shut faster than she could read the ID card below it. "We're with the government."

"Is it about the grant?" Simmons asked. A girl had to try.

"No."

"Is it about that guy who picked up the hard drive?" A girl had to give up in the face of the inevitable.

"Yes."

Holding the afghan tight around her, Simmons flopped down in a chair and pointed at the narrow couch. The two men sat in unison. They removed their sunglasses also in perfect unison, as if they practiced it. Simmons blinked, not sure she was seeing what she was seeing. The one who'd done the talking and flashed the badge had a solid black left eye, the socket surrounded by scar tissue. He must have been used to the surprise because he reached across his body with his right hand and tapped his left arm, making a metallic sound. "I got a deal on the prosthetics. Black was all they had in stock for the discounted eyes in the package deal."

Was that supposed to be funny? Simmons wondered.

"So, Ms. Simmons—" Black Eye began, but she interrupted, trying to level the playing field.

"Doctor Simmons." She usually wasn't a stickler on that, and technically it hadn't gotten final approval from the board, but she was half-naked and had just woken up and had a wicked hangover. A person had to hold on to something because she knew this was going to get bad.

Black Eye leaned forward, placing his hands, real and fake, on his knees. *Shrink*, Simmons thought. That was the universal empathy pose they used. He probably wasn't even aware he was giving himself away with the movement. Simmons crossed her legs and tucked them underneath her in the chair, then crossed her arms, the universal *I don't want to talk about what you want to hear* pose. She stared at him across a wilting hibiscus on the table. He seemed to read her as easily as she'd read him and leaned back on the couch. "Doctor Simmons, my name is Frasier, and good luck on final approval from the board. About the other day with the Courier picking up the hard drive? Can you tell me what happened?"

She succinctly covered the encounter.

The guy who wasn't a shrink pulled out a small notepad and began writing. Simmons saw a big gun nestled in a shoulder holster and realized the notepad was a charade. He'd wanted her to see the gun. This was going to get very bad.

"And your professor? When was the last time you saw her?" Frasier asked.

"Four days ago. The dean says she's on sabbatical."

The two men exchanged glances and Gun Guy wrote something in his notebook.

"The professor's report is incomplete," Frasier said. "Do you know why?"

She shook her head.

Frasier got up and went to the sink and brought her a glass of water. She noted it was in his artificial hand, which seemed to be capable of full articulation. You had to look very hard to see it wasn't real, so that was no yard sale on the prosthetics. She was pretty sure he did the eye for effect.

He handed it to her. "What happened to the professor? She's not on sabbatical."

Simmons drank some water and cleared her throat. "I don't know."

"Do you know why she scheduled the pickup for the drive a week early?"

"No."

"Did *she* schedule it?" Frasier asked.

Simmons squirmed in the chair. "No. When I found out she was gone, I followed the instructions in the binder. I scheduled it."

"Did you, Doctor Simmons?" Frasier asked, indicating he knew the story was incomplete.

"Debbie."

He smiled and actually seemed like a human being for a moment. She noticed he had very nice teeth. Government health care wasn't that shabby, was it? Then she looked at the eye and the arm and realized some of the government people really needed good health care given their job. She wanted to smile back but her gums ached, hell, even her teeth ached. Like she hadn't flossed in three days. And she knew where this was heading.

"Excuse me," she said and ran to the bathroom. She heaved into the toilet.

"You okay?" Frasier called out.

She stood straight and washed her mouth out. She pulled the afghan tighter around her shoulders; this would all be so much easier if she hadn't been naked at the start. She looked at herself in the mirror and started to laugh with a manic edge.

"Simmons?"

She realized she was losing it, so she took a towel and pressed it against her face. Slowed her breathing down. Got control. She walked back out. Frasier was standing near the door, a hint of concern on his face. Gun Guy looked like he could care less.

"Peachy," she said in a tone that indicated she was anything but.

"Did someone visit the professor?" Frasier asked. "Wanting the hard drive?"

"I thought I was doing the right thing," Simmons said. "The professor didn't give it to him."

"Not directly," Frasier said. "We found the professor's body last night. You might consider that a sabbatical."

Simmons ran to the bathroom again, heaving again, but there was nothing coming up.

Frasier was standing in the door to the bathroom. "Was his face scarred?"

"Yes."

"It's strange," Frasier said. "He could have made you give him the hard drive, couldn't he?"

She could only nod.

"Instead," Frasier continued, "he told you to move up the pickup."

She nodded again.

"And he paid you to do that, correct?"

She started to shake her head, but Frasier reached out and grabbed her jaw. "Speak." He let go of her. "I have to hear it."

Simmons licked her lips, swallowed, trying to get some moisture in her mouth. "Yes."

Frasier glanced over his shoulder at Gun Guy and she realized who was really in charge. Gun Guy cocked his head and looked at her and she got a cold chill and knew the gun wasn't for show. He'd as soon shoot her as write a note in that pad.

"Go sit back down, please," Frasier said.

She scooted past him, gripping the afghan tightly. She fell into the chair.

Frasier sat on the couch next to Gun Guy. "Strange that he did that," he repeated. "There is always a purpose to things. He could have done things so much more directly and simply if he'd wanted the drive. But he wanted a reaction."

Gun Guy finally spoke. "Your professor is dead. The Courier who picked up the drive is dead."

"An eighteen-year-old girl was used as bait to kill the Courier," Frasier added. He sighed. "Few people realize how serious life is. How our decisions, no matter how trivial, can have the greatest consequences. But you got very drunk last night because on some level, you know you did the wrong thing. You knew the professor wasn't on sabbatical. Your dean was covering for her while she was missing. And all of that would be fine, except you ultimately did it because he paid you."

Simmons felt as if she wasn't breathing, there was no more air to take in.

"How much did he pay you?" Frasier asked.

Gun Guy flipped shut his notepad and slid it into his inside pocket, once more revealing the big gun.

"A hundred thousand dollars," Simmons managed to get out. She looked out the window and saw a bluebird flitting among the branches of the tree. She envied that bird.

"I think I'm going to be sick again," she said, but she didn't get out of the chair. She felt that if she could stay exactly where she was, this would all pass.

Gun Guy put on his sunglasses, a not so subtle way of saying *we're done here*. Frasier looked concerned, but not overly.

He stared at her a long time, then turned to Gun Guy as he put on his sunglasses. "Let's go. Nothing more here." Frasier paused at the door. "Sorry to have disturbed your morning."

Then they were gone.

* * *

Ivar looked like he hadn't shaved in days, which was odd because he rarely shaved. He was one of those guys, the ones who got a little scraggly here or there, but a full beard would be an impossibility. Today, though, the look was deeper than unshaven: disheveled, slightly crazed, perhaps even manic. He'd been giggling to himself at times, which he found disturbing at first but no longer noticed. Then there was the whistling. He'd never been a whistler, but it seemed that had changed along with a lot of other things.

There was no tune to the whistle, just noise. It would have sent anyone around him climbing the walls, except the only person around was Burns and he didn't seem to care. He just sat in a chair looking at the monitor with his golden eyes, occasionally telling Ivar what to do.

Ivar sometimes stopped the whistling to look at what he was building. He wasn't sure what it was. He'd been through every lab in the building pilfering what was needed. The place was empty at night, and during the day he stayed in this basement lair.

He liked that word: *lair*. Much better than *lab*.

He'd even taken apart other people's projects to take what he needed. Probably ruined a few PhDs along the way, but this was big. Very big. Not big in a physical sense, although it did fill the center of the room, but he knew, on a very base level, that this was something very, very different, and that excited him.

Despite Burns, who'd put an explosive collar around his neck.

Despite the gun and the collar and the eyes, Burns was a lot easier to work for than Doctor Winslow. Which should have made Ivar wonder about the career path he'd chosen.

Ivar had felt this same drive as a kid when he'd decided to build the greatest fort ever in the dining room. He snuck into his sister's room and pulled the comforter off her bed without waking her. He'd pulled down his mother's new brocade drapes in the living room, something she still reminded him of in the mandatory weekly phone calls to maintain the illusion he had a family. If he talked to her now, he knew he could convince her that they had served a much better function being part of his fort than as curtains.

So the drive was familiar, even comforting because of that, but he wasn't building a fort. He stopped whistling for a moment and fingered an angry pimple on his neck, a thing growing as fast as the contraption in the center of the room. He saw the beauty in the mass of wiring and tubes and vacuum cases and batteries.

Fortunately someone had left their Prius parked behind the building overnight so he'd been able to pilfer the batteries protected by an orange cover that warned against touching or trying to do maintenance on them, as if they were some magical thing. High voltage, indeed. Of course the voltage was recharged by the brakes, so he'd had to improvise. He had appropriated the bike of Professor Whatever the Hell His Name Was, Ivar couldn't remember. The professor was known all over UNC for pedaling to and from campus every morning and evening in his spandex, his warning light flashing on the back of his helmet, and taking up his allotted three feet of space in the two-lane roads, causing massive backups behind him, lots of middle fingers and screams, and smiling all the way to and fro.

He'd miss the bike, and that made Ivar happy.

Of course the expensive bike had required some adjustments as suggested by Burns, who seemed to know exactly what Ivar was building, but wasn't sharing. In that, he was like Doctor Winslow. Ivar had rigged it to pedal backward as he was ordered. He wasn't quite sure why it needed to be that way, but he knew that there was no going forward anymore. The bike was cabled to the batteries, which were cabled to the mainframe, which was cabled to a huge glass incubator used for newly born rats that he'd had to go over to the psych labs to appropriate. They did some bad stuff in there to those rats, so taking the rats away from them made Ivar feel somewhat better. They used the pretty white ones that were sacrificed for science, not the ugly brown ones that were sacrificed by the exterminator.

The bike technically wasn't powering the batteries, as it was somehow part of the entire device, in between the batteries and the rest of it, in some way Ivar didn't comprehend.

At Burns's order, Ivar had gone back and taken some of the rats, saving them from their fate on the end of needles from grad students studying the latest way to flatten out the brain, get rid of the sine curves, the lows, and the highs, too, because you can't have one without the other.

He didn't know why he'd been ordered to get the rats, but like his mother's drapes, he knew they were essential and would fit in someplace because everything else Burns had told him to get was fitting someplace.

On his own initiative, Ivar had grabbed a large ziplock bag full of dog kibble from a grad student's locker who thought that if kibble was good for dogs, it must be just as nutritious for humans. Ivar had thought that weird six months ago when he first saw the guy eating it, but now he chewed a handful and tossed a few to the rats, and they seemed to like it, too.

Burns didn't seem to need food.

The rats, his nonhuman company, were watching him. He was sure that they turned their heads to the door as he left and seemed to wag their long pink tails whenever he returned, dragging a cart full of wires and circuits and whatever else he was told to scavenge.

He'd given a couple of them names although he didn't know which were girls or boys. The cute one who wiggled her whiskers at his every return he'd named after a girl he'd pined for in high school but had never spoken to: Susan. The one who looked big and strong he thought of as Ivar.

The other two he just thought of as the other two.

Ivar picked up an old half gallon of milk he'd found in the fridge in his old lab and took a big swig, pleased that it was nonfat and not rancid. A bit sour, but nothing he couldn't stomach.

He giggled again, realizing he was eating dog food and worrying about spoiled milk. Susan, the rat, stood and stared at him as he giggled, and he swore her little pink nose was wiggling and he felt happy. Tired, but happy. He was accomplishing something BIG here.

He had a feeling he was missing something important, between Burns from the government, the collar around his neck, and the thing he was building.

On order, Ivar got on the bike and started pedaling backward. It had been hard at first, but he'd finally gotten the rhythm of it down. He was able to go faster and faster. He heard a low hum. A golden haze filled the incubator.

Burns got up and grabbed one of the rats, one with no name, and tossed it into the gaping mouth of the incubator.

Ivar kept pedaling.

The rat scurried along the bottom of the incubator for a moment, claws scrambling for a hold, then the gold haze became more solid and coalesced around the rat's head. Which disappeared from sight. The glow moved along the body, as if consuming it, until there was only the quivering tail wagging frantically. Then even that was gone.

"Whoa!" Ivar said. "That was cool."

"Keep pedaling." Burns went over to the control panel and made some adjustments.

Ivar kept backward pedaling, faster and faster. The golden haze pulsed. Burns grabbed no-name number two and tossed it toward the incubator. This time the rat snapped out of existence as soon it hit the maw of the glass container.

Then he picked up Susan, her eyes full of trust.

"Not Susan," Ivar protested.

"'Not Susan,'" Burns mocked with a strange smile twisting his face, more blood seeping from wounds. "Then Ivar."

"Oh no," Ivar said, looking at the rat.

But Burns had his gun up, level, pointing right between Ivar's eyes.

"Ivar," Burns said. He paused as the gold pulsed larger than before and a rat came back out, a tiny one, a fifth of the size of the one that had just gone in. As they watched, it scrabbled up on the glass, and Burns, still keeping the gun pointed at Ivar, reached in and took it out of the incubator.

He placed it on a desktop and it expanded, filling out to normal size.

Burns smiled, drawing more blood from his wounds, but he didn't seem to notice.

"Ivar," Burns said, wagging the gun.

Ivar blinked, finally getting it. "No way, man!"

"Just put your hand in," Burns said. "It will do the rest. You'll be fine." He pointed at the rat. "It's fine."

Ivar swallowed.

Burns lowered the gun and Ivar felt a moment of relief, thinking he'd reconsidered. But Burns pulled a small device out of a pocket and flipped up the lid covering a toggle switch. "I wouldn't waste a bullet on you," Burns said. "I'll just pop your head off." He rested a finger on the toggle.

Ivar couldn't get his hand into the opening of the incubator fast enough.

The hand started shimmering and Ivar's eyes got wide as the golden haze climbed up his arm and then rapidly covered him.

With a flash, Ivar was gone and the golden glow went back to its original size.

Ten minutes later, a tiny human hand came groping out of the golden ball. Followed by an arm, and then a tiny Ivar, a foot and a half tall, stood in the incubator, clearly dazed and confused.

Burns reached in and lifted Ivar out, setting him on the floor.

Ivar's mouth was moving but no sound was coming out.

Ivar began expanding. He reached normal size in less than twenty seconds. And now he could speak.

"Fracking unbelievable!" Ivar exclaimed, blinking hard and shaking his head.

"Get on the bike," Burns ordered.

Ivar staggered, still dazed, but did as ordered. He got on the bike and began pedaling.

"What—" Ivar started to say something, but realized he had nothing cogent to say. He kept pedaling.

Thirty seconds later, another tiny human hand appeared out of the gold ball, scrabbling at the glass. An arm followed, then a head and torso.

"Oh frack!" Ivar exclaimed, stopping pedaling in his shock as he stared at a miniature version of himself. Burns helped it get out of the incubator, as he had done with the rat.

As he watched, it grew larger and larger, expanding until it equaled his size.

"Good job," Burns said. He went to the landline and dialed a number. Ivar only got to hear this end of the brief conversation:

"My friend," Burns said. "Your investment is working. But it will be threatened."

Burns listened, then replied. "I will tell you where it is this evening. Be prepared to defend it. There is still a lot of work to be done before it's truly ready."

Another pause. "I cannot tell you what it is. But you will be quite amazed." Burns looked at Ivar, the original, and smiled, more blood flowing, as if the two of them were in on something. Which they were.

"You will see tonight," Burns said and hung up the phone.

* * *

Ms. Jones had Pitr read the report to her one more time about the interview with Simmons.

"What do you think?" she asked when he was done.

"Burns could have made her give him the drive for the money, but he didn't."

"He wanted to take down the Courier," Ms. Jones said, "which means he wanted us to know about it."

"That doesn't make sense," Pitr said.

"We have to make sense of it," Ms. Jones said. "Remember Mister Eagle's Sherlock Holmes quote. Something is right in front of us and we're not seeing it."

"He's taunting us for firing him," Pitr said.

"If it were only that." Her eyes were closed. They often were, as if simply keeping them open drained her energy.

"Why didn't you make her wet?"

Ms. Jones eyes flickered open. "The girl? That was Mister Frasier's call. That is Mister Frasier's unique talent. That girl will never again stray."

"People are dead because of her."

"Ah," Ms. Jones said. "She was only one of seven things in Doc's Rule of Seven. She did not kill anyone. Burns killed them. For the innocents, they cannot imagine what a man like Burns is capable of. Nor can they imagine what we are capable of. The difference between us and Burns is Ms. Simmons is still breathing. What we must figure out is why is Burns acting this way?" She closed her eyes. "Has Support hacked into Doctor Winslow's phone yet? Made sense of those papers?"

"Not yet."

"Let me know the results as soon as they do."

"I will," Pitr promised. "Now you must rest."

Ms. Jones gave the ghost of a smile. "Another line from the team's favorite singer, Mister Zevon: *I'll sleep when I'm dead.*"

CHAPTER 22

"How do you guys feel about swimming?" Scout asked as she came in the door, Nada having pushed the piano out of the way as soon as over-watch reported her approach.

Nada was puzzled. "As a sport?"

"Hate it," Roland said.

"He sinks," Moms said with a smile. "The water isn't friendly to big muscles."

Roland blushed.

"Want to go swimming?" Scout asked.

"No," Moms, Nada, and Roland all said together.

"I wouldn't mind a dip," Doc said.

"You might in this pool," Scout said.

"Eagle, come down," Moms ordered over the net, then turned her radio off. She looked at Scout. "Pray tell, why is that?"

Scout did two cartwheels, ending up next to Roland and his stack of guns, magazines, and bullets. "Can I get one?"

"No," Roland said.

"Do I get paid?" she asked Moms.

Nada reached into his pocket and pulled out a money clip. "How much do you get paid for babysitting?"

"What do they pay or how much do I clear?" Scout asked.

Nada blinked. "What's the difference?"

"They pay me ten dollars an hour. But there are benefits."

"You steal?" Roland said.

"Dude! How direct. I use stuff. And know things. Like the Lindsays are in the middle of a month-long vacation. I like their pool best because it has a slide. Ours just has a pool." She looked at Nada's money clip. "So let's say twenty an hour, because this job is, like, dangerous, right, with Mac and Kirk and who knows who else getting hurt battling big Transformer-like things?"

"Where is the Lindsays' pool?" Moms asked. "And what did you see?"

Scout held out her hand. Nada peeled off five twenties and passed them to her. She stuffed them in her pocket, then held the hand out again.

"That's blackmail," Nada said. "We can find out where the Lindsays' pool is from Support."

"But you won't find out what I saw from your Support."

Nada peeled off two more bills and gave them to her. Scout frowned, then put them in her pocket. "Can I get one of those ear radio things you guys use? It would have been so fab to listen in last night."

"No," Moms said, shuddering at the thought of Ms. Jones eavesdropping with Scout on the net.

Scout did a backflip and dropped onto the couch with a heavy sigh. "You guys don't share well. What happened to the team? One for all and whatever?"

Eagle spoke up. "We're not the Three Amigos."

Scout laughed. "Love, love, love that movie. A plethora." She looked at Roland. "You have a plethora of guns. Seems you'd share."

Roland was frowning, which seemed to be his constant state around Scout. "A what?"

Eagle quoted: "*I know that I, Jefe, do not have your superior intellect and education. But could it be that once again, you are angry at something else and are looking to take it out on me?*"

"Oh, oh, oh!" Scout was literally bouncing up and down on the couch. Then she did three cartwheels, ending up in front of Eagle and holding her hand up, but restrained, not quite ready to high five. "*Do you know what Nada means?*"

"*Isn't that a light chicken gravy?*"

"Love it!" she squealed as she and Eagle slapped palms.

"I've been waiting to say that forever," Eagle said, with a worried glance at Nada.

The rest of the team was lost.

"So," Scout said. "Who wants to go swimming?"

Moms gripped the arms of the chair tightly and grimaced a smile. "Why would we want to go swimming in the Lindsays' pool?"

"Welllll," Scout said. "Earlier I went over there and noticed that the pool water kind of just slid over the edge into the grass and snatched a squirrel and, welllll, seemed to, like, just absorb it. Kind of gross. Seems like something up your alley. But maybe I'm wrong. Maybe golf is more your game?"

Roland had grabbed the iPad. "The Lindsays' house is three blocks over."

Moms got out of her chair. "Why didn't you tell us sooner?"

"Wellll, you're all so faaaabulous and on your super-secret mission, which you really haven't told *me* about, and were blowing up the golf course all night, so I thought you were kind of busy and when I saw you come back early this morning, everyone looked pretty beat, and it's not like the pool is gonna go anywhere.

And you guys aren't really sharing," she added, looking longingly at the pile of guns. "Sometimes it seems like you just got dropped in here like a nanny with a green card, 'cause you are so greeeen! I figured you knew about the carnivorous water."

"All right, all right," Moms said. "You've made your point."

"Points," Nada said.

"Tell us," Moms said with forced patience.

"It's kidney shaped, which is weird for here, but it's got the slide, which is fun, but also weird for here. It does have a deep end."

"What exactly did the water do?" Doc asked patiently, which seemed like an impossibility with Scout around.

"I told you. It ate a squirrel," Scout said. "How the hell should I know?"

"Don't curse," Moms said. "It's not pretty coming from girls."

"Her hair's blue and she can do a handstand longer than any of us," Nada said, as if that mattered.

"Thank you," Scout said with a smile.

Moms looked at Nada in consternation. "No more bantering. Especially from you. I'm not sure who you are anymore."

"Yeah," Doc agreed. "You're acting peculiar."

"Maybe he just likes me," Scout said. "People either love me or hate me."

"I hate you," Roland muttered.

"She's just a girl," Nada said.

"I don't think so," Doc observed.

"Fireflies can't go into people," Moms noted.

"What are Fireflies?" Scout asked for what seemed the twentieth time since the team had met her.

Moms gave a cold smile. "Nothing, dear."

"Great," Scout said. "You've finally become a Senators Club mom. 'Nothing, dear.' That means absolutely, positively there's something."

"Enough!" Moms snapped.

"Describe what happened," Doc said to Scout. "Please."

"It was like this tentacle of water lifted up, about five feet." Scout was using one of her arms to demonstrate, green-painted fingernails leading the way. "Then it moved horizontal, right over where this cute little squirrel was doing whatever it was doing, and then just shot down, all over the squirrel, which, let me tell you, was not happy. Then it just pulled back into the pool with the squirrel and everything was normal. Except no more squirrel."

Roland was on his feet, heading toward the door to the garage. "I know what to do."

They followed him into the four-car cavern. Roland pulled a portable generator out from its spot next to the wall. "What kills water?" He tapped the generator.

"Riiiight," Scout said. "Let's roll the generator over to the Lindsays' pool. No one will notice that. Even though most people are gone for the holidays, there's still enough around, and someone will notice in three blocks."

"You got any better ideas?" Roland challenged.

"Weelll, if you want to zap the pool," Scout said, "how about shorting out the pool light and letting the house current do it?"

"Maybe she isn't such a little girl," Nada said proudly, cuffing her lightly on the head, but forgetting once more about the curling iron.

"Oww, please stop with the head shit."

"Don't curse," Nada said.

"Fuck you," Scout said, and Nada smiled.

"This is getting weird even for us," Eagle said.

"Oh really," Scout said. "*Now* it's getting too weird? It sounded like Armageddon out there last night on the golf course."

Moms had her arms crossed. "To short the pool light, someone would have to get into the water. And probably end up however the squirrel ended up."

"I vote for the kid," Roland said.

"I'll do it," Nada said before he thought it through, which really scared Moms.

And that's when everyone finally accepted that Yada Yada Nada, with the glass half-empty and who hated everyone, really liked the runt with the blue hair.

"You're so brave," Scout said and Nada smiled, something as strange as squirrel-eating water.

"Just kidding," Scout said as she did a backflip to punctuate the moment.

"I hate to rain on everyone's solemn moment," Doc said, "but electricity doesn't kill water. Water conducts electricity. As far as we know, electricity has no effect on a Firefly."

"There we go with the Firefly again," Scout said.

"We could drain the pool with a shaped charge," Roland said.

"Brilliant," Moms said. "Our first priority is containment and you want to disperse the Firefly who knows where? Into the water table? Which flows where?"

"Cape Fear River Basin," Eagle said, as always knowing his geography.

"Let me think," Roland said.

"Oh, that's going to work," Scout said, and Roland's lips tightened in anger.

"Could someone shut her up for a minute?" Roland pleaded to Moms.

Scout started humming the theme song to the final *Jeopardy* round, and Nada took her by the arm. "Let's you and me get something to eat while they work this out. I'm hungry."

As they left the garage, Eagle and Roland were arguing about how to kill water, Mom refereeing, while Doc just sighed continuously.

As the garage door shut behind them, it drowned out the words.

"I don't eat during the day," Scout said as Nada went over to his rucksack.

"Give me a break," Nada said.

"Hey. Every woman here in Senators Club is size two. We either eat and puke or don't eat at all. I've got a lousy gag reflex."

"That will cause you problems drowning," Nada said as he opened the ruck and rummaged in it.

"What?" Scout said, taken aback for once.

"I used to teach at the Special Forces Scuba School in Key West," Nada said. "Everyone in scuba school drowns at least once."

"That sounds like fun."

Nada paused. "Well, Special Operations takes a lot of things that other people do for fun, teaches you how to do it on the government tab, then makes it miserable. I learned to scuba dive, parachute, ski, and some other things in the army. And it was rarely fun."

"And you're not in the army anymore, right?"

"Nice try," Nada said, pulling some meals out of his ruck. "Let's just say no one is in Kansas anymore on this op."

Nada couldn't figure it out as he read the labels on the meals. The kid was rubbing everyone the wrong way, especially Roland, and even Moms, but the kid rubbed him right. He had no idea why he gave a shit about her. Then he remembered the really smart dog he'd had as a child. It was brilliant. He could tell it which of the tattered stuffed toys to bring and it knew which one. Everyone thought it was just this barrio half-breed mutt, but it was smarter than most of the people wandering the streets shooting each other.

It bothered him that it bothered the rest of the team that he liked the kid. Like he wasn't supposed to like anyone? Didn't any of them think he could be normal? He knew he had more time on the team than anyone else, but that didn't make him abnormal. Did it?

"Hey," Nada said, holding up his favorite freeze-dried meal. "Eggs and ham." Everyone else on the team hated that one so he always had plenty. In fact, everyone in every unit he'd ever been in hated them. Which started worrying him again. Was he abnormal?

"Yuck," Scout said. "Gross me out."

"Give it a try," Nada said, and there was something in his tone that made Scout pause.

"All right," she said reluctantly as he led her to the kitchen.

He put a pot on the stove to boil water, something even he could manage in a kitchen. They waited in silence. Then he searched through way too many drawers and cabinets before he gave up and pulled out his mess kit and split it, one part for Scout and the other for him, although he did find a spoon for her. He broke the freeze-dried glop into two parts, one in each, then poured boiling water on it.

"I do have to admit," Nada said, "everyone gives me their eggs and ham."

"Gives, not trades?"

"Gives."

"And you gave Roland your other meal." Scout leaned over as the solid mass began dissolving in the boiled water. "Smells like someone already ate it and gagged it back up. Like mother birds do."

"I know," Nada said, and his face felt like it was breaking into a million pieces because he was smiling and he wasn't used to it.

"Oh," Scout said. "I get it. You eat it 'cause no one else likes it. You give them your other meals." Her feet were drumming against the wood base of the kitchen bar.

Nada froze, never having thought of that. It actually *was* kind of a lousy meal.

But Scout took a spoonful and put it in her mouth. She didn't start spewing, which he took as a good sign. Nada took a mouthful. They sat across from each other, eating the one meal everyone hated.

"Nada?"

He froze with his plastic spoon halfway to his mouth, which reminded him of how during Isolation before an op they used to tear apart their meal packages, tossing away the extra plastic spoons because they weighed too much and you only needed one spoon to eat. They stripped the meals down to the very basics before mission launch because they carried everything, and when it came between choosing to carry an extra meal or extra rounds or an extra plastic spoon, it always went in favor of the rounds. For the first time he also realized how weird that kind of math was.

"I can call you that, right?" Scout asked, bringing him back to the room and the present.

"Sure," he mumbled.

"Gross. Don't talk with your mouth full."

He sealed his lips and continued chewing, happy that she wasn't ten years older or else he'd be signing off another chunk of his pay to more spousal support. Maybe he should get a dog, he fantasized for a moment, but that made him think of Skippy and he swallowed hard.

"Where's the trash?"

Scout pointed to a cabinet.

"How can you tell? They all look the same."

"It's all in the placement," Scout said. "Are you going to throw out your eggs and ham?"

Nada nodded.

Scout smiled. "Great. Me too. But we'll use the garbage disposal. And you should have known it was bad when they couldn't even call it ham and eggs."

She took both parts of the kit and turned the water on. She scraped the food off and turned on the grinding disposal. When she was done, she washed them and dried them, then handed them back to Nada.

"That was an experience," Scout said as he put the kit back in his ruck.

She was twirling her hair with one hand and gnawing on the fingers on the other. "You aren't that different from this place, you know?"

"What do you mean?" He picked up his camouflage Camel-Bak and took a few deep slugs from the end of the blue hose.

"Can I have some of that?"

"Use the sink, I'm sure it's better water."

"I want that."

Nada stared at her, then walked over and handed it to her. "What did you mean?"

"I think you're hiding your real self behind all this 'Nada' BS like everyone around here hides behind baby grand pianos and golf courses and fancy cars."

Nada looked at the tiny girl with blue hair sipping from his CamelBak. He definitely had to get a dog when they got back to the Ranch, but then the problem was who would take care of it when they were on an op. Ms. Jones? Doubtful. "What?"

"You've got the same look on your face as when I first met you," Scout said. "Like you're someplace else and just existing here."

Nada blinked, but the door to the garage opened and Moms came in, followed by the rest of the team, still arguing. Nada was oddly grateful to the team for interrupting his conversation with Scout.

"We need to call in an Acme," Moms said. "I'll get Ms. Jones on it."

Roland groaned.

"You know how to kill a pool?" Moms asked.

"Blow it up." Which was usually Mac's response to every situation, but Roland liked blowing things up also.

"It's in the water," Moms said, "not the pool itself. Like I said, we destroy the integrity of the pool we spread the Firefly who knows where. It's never been in a liquid before according to our history. We go Acme."

* * *

While they waited for the Acme, Moms sent Roland and Doc over to recon the pool. They drove one of the SUVs and Doc dialed up a bunch of codes on a transmitter. It took him all of three seconds to turn off the alarm system for the house and get the garage door to go up. They pulled in, shutting the door behind them.

Roland had his machine gun, which Doc found rather amusing, since they were reconning water in a pool, but it was a comfort to the big man, and Doc had been on the team long enough to know not to make the big man uncomfortable. They wove their way through the enormous house, although it wasn't quite as big as the Winslows' since it was three streets down from the top of the ridge.

There were lots and lots of pictures. There was a framed photograph of presumably the Lindsays in snow gear and holding skis, and engraved on the frame: *Snowbird 2010.*

Roland was looking about, shaking his head. "They can't remember anywhere they been and what they done? They got to take pictures of every place?" Every member of the Nightstalkers was extremely camera shy. In fact, it was against Protocol for them to have their photo taken.

There was a psychology paper for the writing in here, Doc thought as they penetrated further into the house, going by photo after photo of the same people. Roland paused as they passed one door. Doc looked around him to see what had caused him to stop. It was the family room, with big-screen TV, comfy chairs, and a bunch of pictures. But what had grabbed Roland's attention was that an entire wall was covered by a map of the world.

"That's pretty cool," Roland said, walking over, machine gun resting on his shoulder.

There were a number of different-colored pins scattered around the map—four different colors, in fact—and there was even a legend set in the middle of the Pacific Ocean, north and west of Hawaii, explaining what the colors meant.

Green: Places the Lindsays have been.

Blue: Places the Lindsays have plans to go to.

Yellow: Places one or more of the Lindsays have been but not all.

Red: Places the Lindsays dream of going.

"What the fuck?" Roland muttered. He stepped back and looked at the map, noting the colored pins. "I've been more places than they even dream of going."

"Yes, but it wasn't for the tourism and you usually didn't land with the airplane," Doc noted. He pointed at some of the pins. "And it wasn't Hawaii or Sydney or Hong Kong. It was usually some place no one wants to go to. Note no pins in Iraq, Iran, or Afghanistan."

"I don't get this place or these people," Roland said as they left the room. Not for the first and probably not for the last time.

They reached the sliding glass door that opened to the backyard. The yard had a high, solid wood fence around it. The pool was indeed kidney shaped with a slide. It looked deceivingly tranquil, not like one that had eaten a squirrel earlier.

"How about I throw a frag in it?" Roland suggested.

"We already used our Fourth of July excuse," Doc said. "And remember what Moms said about dispersing the water."

"Maybe the girl is wrong," Roland said. "Maybe she made it up, just to get Nada to pay her?"

"You think?" Doc said, turning to look Roland in the eyes. "You think she would lie to us about this?"

The big man shifted his feet. "Well, no."

"Okay, then," Doc said. "I will tell you what, though. You feel like tossing the barbecue grill over there into the pool? Just to see what happens?"

That made Roland happy. He slung his machine gun over his shoulder and slid open the patio door.

"Careful," Doc warned. "Water can be pretty powerful. People underestimate it. Remember it killed hundreds of thousands during the tsunami." Doc pulled out his phone and began filming Roland's assault on the pool.

Roland got behind the grill, turned it toward the pool, and then ran a few steps pushing it, before releasing. The momentum carried it over the edge and it toppled in.

It promptly sank. Roland turned to Doc and shrugged, just as the pool ejected the grill up into the air thirty feet.

Roland dove out of the way as it crashed down exactly where he'd been standing. A half-dozen water tentacles rose out of the pool, groping toward Roland. He ran toward Doc, who slammed the door shut as he passed. The tentacles reached the glass door and began sliding about.

"Why don't they just bust it?" Roland wondered. "If it can throw that grill, it can bust glass."

"Fireflies have never been known for their smarts," Doc said, backing up and tapping Roland to join him. They moved away from the glass. The tentacles finally gave up and retreated back to the pool. Doc stopped filming.

Their earpieces came alive. "Sitrep?" Moms asked.

"We've got a Firefly," Doc said.

"Acme is coming in the gate. We'll meet you there."

The radio went quiet. "Keep an eye out," Doc said to Roland. "I will meet them in the garage."

He retraced his steps, the eyes of the Lindsays peering at him from numerous frames in every room. He got to the garage as Moms pulled in with Eagle, Nada, Kirk, and Scout. They piled out of the SUV as a Support driver in a Senators Club patrol car pulled in the drive. A man got out and Moms waved him into the garage as Nada hit the close button for the door.

"Doctor Kelsey?" Doc always took points with Acme. "I'm Doctor Ghatar." Doctor on doctor, it always worked better than Moms or Nada as Acmes tended to view the military as Neanderthals.

Kelsey was a surprisingly young man, one they'd never worked with before on a mission. He had black, thick-framed glasses and carried a briefcase tucked tight under one arm. They always carried briefcases.

"It was a surprise and a pleasure to be called," Kelsey said. "Very exciting. They picked me up right off the campus at Duke in a helicopter."

Behind Kelsey, Nada rolled his eyes and Scout giggled.

"Should that girl be here?" Kelsey asked, pointing at her. "I was told this could be dangerous."

"We gotta kill a pool," Nada said. "You let us worry about her. She's the one who figured it out."

Kelsey forgot about Scout just as quickly as he noticed her. "Yes, yes, the pool. I was given the rough parameters of the situation. A possessed pool. How exotic."

"It killed a squirrel," Doc said, "and it almost killed our weapons man. Threw a two-hundred-pound grill at him."

"Sounds like an angry pool." Kelsey laughed at his own joke. No one else did.

"Come on," Doc said, taking Kelsey by the arm before Nada pulled his machete out.

They trooped through the house to join Roland standing in the kitchen, staring out at the killer pool.

"Watch this," Doc said, taking out his phone and putting it in front of Kelsey. He played the grill assault.

"Fascinating!" Kelsey said when it came to an end. "The force required to move the water molecules like that in a coherent form. But I wonder why it simply didn't break the glass when it came after you?"

Roland shot Doc a triumphant grin.

"And you still don't know what this Firefly thing is that has caused this?" Kelsey asked.

"Not a clue," Doc said, which earned him a hard look from Kirk.

"I read the reports on your encounters in the form of Fireflies when I signed on," Kelsey said. "I must say, they act rather irrationally on all levels."

"We're not here to analyze it," Nada said. "We're here to kill it."

"Well, that is the key question, isn't it?" Kelsey said, and they all, except Kirk and Scout, who'd never worked with an Acme before, knew what was coming: the theories every Acme spouted, proving Kelsey had actually taken some science courses and earned his doctorate. They always went to the theories when standing around a group of people armed with guns and intent on killing something, because it made them very insecure at a primeval level. Like they had to prove themselves to the Neanderthals.

"It depends," Kelsey said. "Do we want spectacular or clever." It wasn't a question and no one replied. They knew they had to wait this through. "From a clever standpoint, I'd be tempted to add cornstarch or some other polymerizing agent. From the scientific standpoint, once the cornstarch polymerizes you have a non-Newtonian fluid. Which means that its viscosity increases with applied force. At the very least that would slow the pool down.

"You put enough in, in this case," he looked out the window, "I would say at least a thousand pounds, it would make it so that you could actually probably run across the surface."

"But until it solidifies," Doc said, playing his role, which was bubble-burster on bad ideas, "you're slowing it down, but you're also making it more powerful in potential force and coherence. So we could end with the water taking a more solid form and literally climbing out of the pool and killing us."

"Uh, well, yes." Kelsey recovered quickly. "And, frankly, we don't know how the chemicals that are in the pool will affect the process, so I'd say we move on from that idea. It was just a warm-up."

"Right," Roland muttered. He was fingering his machine gun, which Kelsey failed to note.

"Water is tricky. Evaporating it is a possibility, but that would require a ridiculous amount of energy."

"We can get a ridiculous amount of energy," Doc said, "if it would work, but I definitely would not want the Firefly to go into a single gaseous cloud, which it might be able to do if we evaporated the entire pool."

"Is ridiculous a scientific term?" Eagle wondered, which earned him a high five from Scout.

"Electrolysis," Kelsey said.

"Hey!" Roland stepped forward. "That's what I wanted to do."

"Not electrocution," Doc corrected the big man. "He said electrolysis."

Kelsey nodded. "Apply an electric field to the water and disassociate the H2O molecules into H2 and O, both of which are gases, but"—he quickly added with a glance at Doc—"not a cloud." As Doc was about to speak, he jumped into the breach once more. "However, it would be dangerous because it would become explosive, very quickly."

"Water explosive?" Roland said. "Mac would love that."

"Who is Mac?" Kelsey asked.

"Forget that," Moms said. "Continue."

"The other problem is," Kelsey said, "I don't know how to electrolyze that much mass." He nodded toward the pool.

"Whoa!" Eagle said, getting everyone's attention. "Check it out."

A column of water about six inches in diameter was rising out of the pool, straight up.

"Fascinating," Kelsey said.

The water went up, passing above fifty feet.

Moms was on the radio. "Support, we've got a situation here. You might get some calls on a column of water."

The column was now at a hundred feet. The level in the pool was now down appreciably.

"To keep coherence of that much weight in the face of gravity," Kelsey said, "is truly remarkable. And powerful."

The column reached over one hundred and fifty feet, then wavered.

A second later all the water came pouring straight down, splashing into the pool.

"Well, what the hell was that about?" Kirk asked.

"I don't like it," Nada said. "It's planning something."

"Planning indicates intelligence," Kelsey said. "The Firefly reports have never been—"

"How do we fucking kill it?" Nada demanded.

"Oh. Uh. As far as electrolysis, it would take more than this house is wired for anyway. Too much thermal mass in the water. Going back to the cornstarch, we could add a zeolite."

"A what?" Kirk asked.

"The stuff that comes in those little packets in things like baby diapers; my wife just had a little boy by the way. Those packets are stamped 'Do not eat' and it makes diapers ultra-absorbent. Hmm, you know, if you add a strong acid to water it becomes exothermic.

You can boil a pot of water just by pouring acid into it. Again, though, it would take several tankers full of acid to tackle this."

"I can get several tankers of acid here within an hour," Moms said.

"Cloud," Doc repeated. "With acid. Not good."

"Got it," Moms replied.

Kelsey was off in his theoretical wonderland. "For spectacular, there are things that react negatively with water. Sodium, lithium, and cesium all react violently and produce an explosion."

"That much water," Doc said, "and that much metal, we'd take out the entire neighborhood. And it would disperse the water everywhere and the Firefly might stay in part of it."

Kelsey sighed. "Supersaturated sodium acetate will instantly crystallize when added to water, but you'd need a lot."

"That still doesn't kill it," Nada said.

"How do you usually kill a Firefly?" Scout asked.

Kelsey ignored her. "More simply, how about we drain the pool into a tanker? That would contain it."

"Unless it decided to punch a hole in the side of the tanker," Doc said.

"We flame it," Roland said to Scout, ignoring Kelsey. "If it's in an animal or plant, we flame it. I usually do the flaming."

"What a surprise," Scout said.

"And if it's in a mechanical object," Nada said, also ignoring Kelsey in favor of the girl, "we blast it, like the other night on the golf course, until it's so structurally destroyed that even the Firefly can't keep it coherent."

"Be that as it may." Kelsey was getting irritated that the adults were talking to the child and not focusing on his words of wisdom. "Perhaps we could use Occam's razor. We don't know if the Firefly inhabits all of an object or part of it."

"Part," Nada said. "I chopped a rabbit in half and the Firefly kept the front going, but not the back."

"You killed a bunny?" Scout looked about to cry.

"It was a bad bunny," Nada said defensively.

"Kidding," Scout said with a playful punch into Nada's body armor. "Ouch."

"We divide the water into portions," Kelsey said, "trying to isolate the part where the Firefly is."

"I don't know," Moms said. "And while we're doing that? One of those tentacles could eat one of my people."

"Flame it," Scout said.

Roland was eyeing the pool. "I don't have enough napalm."

Scout shook her head. "What he said earlier," she jerked a thumb at Kelsey. "Baby diapers. They absorb water, right? A lot of water. But they can also be burned, right?"

Everyone stared at Scout.

"Get me Support," Moms said to Kirk.

"You're on," Kirk replied after tapping his PNR.

"Support. We're going to need a bunch of baby diapers. And tampons. Enough to absorb"—she looked at Doc—"how many gallons?"

Doc did some quick mental calculations and supplied the number.

"Roger," Support responded. "Diapers and tampons."

"I'm gonna need a lot more flamers," Roland said, smiling at the thought.

Moms clicked off the radio and smiled bitterly. "I remember the code line in the Special Forces resupply report for tampons. They used that as my nickname in the Q-Course."

"They were assholes," Roland said.

"Yeah," Scout threw in. "Assholes."

CHAPTER 23

Back at the Winslows', everyone was shedding their vests, armor, and outer clothes, which were saturated with a mixture of water and soot from flamed wet tampons and diapers. Roland had gone through fourteen flamers, another record in the secret history of the Nightstalkers. They'd dashed to the pool in relays, tossing in cases of diapers and tampons, while Roland flamed the surface.

The Firefly had fought back. Kelsey, cowering behind a lawn chair, had suffered a broken arm, and Support had taken him away afterward for medical treatment. Kirk, keeping his record intact, had suffered a dislocated shoulder when a tentacle grabbed his hand and tried to drag him into the flaming pool. He'd simply walked over to the wall of the house and slammed it back into the socket.

The Firefly had dissipated when they were down to three feet of water left and their copious supply of diapers, tampons, and napalm was running dangerously low.

"Maybe you need to go home, Scout?" Moms said as she noted the team in a state of half-undress.

"You know how to use the washers and dryers?" Scout asked. "They have one on every floor."

"Why?" Nada asked.

"You think anyone around here carries laundry up the stairs?" Scout said.

"I doubt anyone who lives here carries their laundry anywhere," Moms said.

From the room off the hallway from the garage they heard Roland cursing. "Anyone know how to turn this thing on?"

"See?" Scout said.

"Everyone get some pants on," Moms ordered, "while the kid dries our cammies."

The guys trooped upstairs while Moms and Scout gathered clothes off the floor.

"Thanks," Moms said as she removed magazines from a sopping combat vest, along with a radio, grenades, and other assorted goodies.

Scout looked over at her in surprise. "For what?"

"That was a good idea. More importantly, it worked and no one got killed."

Scout shrugged. "I just put what the guy was saying together."

"I know," Moms said, "but you did it quick. That's important. That's a talent."

Scout flushed. "You should see me ride. Now *that*, I'm talented at."

"I'd like to someday," Moms said.

The conversation was over as the team came back down dressed in their civvies, with bundles of sopping camouflage fatigues in their hands. Scout dispatched them to all three floors with orders to put them in the washers. Then she went from floor to floor, loading each machine with detergent and softener and setting them correctly.

The team sat around on leather sofas while their clothes began to whirl. A loud clanking sound came from the upstairs laundry.

"Eagle," Moms said. "Where's your Mark-23?"

"Just great," Roland muttered and he went upstairs with Scout and retrieved the wet gun from the washer. He sat down with it and ejected the magazine.

"Can you show me how to take it apart?" Scout asked, startling Roland.

"Sure."

So while the big guy and the little girl took a large-caliber pistol apart, the rest of the team decompressed. Roland didn't even realize he was rubbing his fungus-covered feet along a carpet that cost more than the house he grew up in. Doc was eyeing the bourbon in the crystal decanter, but decided he'd had enough of liquids that could kill him for the day. Kirk was looking at a photo that had been in his pocket and gotten soaked, setting it so it would dry but not be seen by the rest of the team. Eagle was upstairs on over-watch. Nada had taken out his machete to sharpen it, but realized he hadn't used it in the Great Water Battle, as they had decided to name it on the way back, so he put it on the coffee table that cost as much as his MK-23 pistol. Moms was typing up her after-action report.

Roland had finished taking apart Eagle's gun and then he walked Scout through the steps. Moms watched them, torn between pride and disapproval. When Scout did it correctly, on the first try, the girl did a flip, then went to a handstand in the center of the room on top of the coffee table next to Nada's machete.

"I'll give you a dollar to stop doing that," Moms said, feeling bad because she knew the real reason it bothered her was Scout's exuberance and energy. Moms couldn't remember ever feeling that way.

Scout was still on her hands and looked at Moms. "Do you mean four quarters or a hundred bucks?"

Roland looked up from the gun, stunned. "She's a gambler. That's what they call a hundred bucks."

Scout flipped and stood upright. "No. I don't gamble, but Doctor Carruthers, two blocks over, is a bookie. And his son, Tad, was my BF, for a while. And I think he was my BF because his dad was so interesting and he let me listen as he took bets. I like to listen."

"Of course you do," Moms said, running a hand through Scout's damp hair, avoiding her burn from the killer curler. "Four quarters. On my tab."

Scout sat down, yoga style, on the plush rug being invaded by Roland's fungus ten feet away. "Sure, but there's a vig on the tab." Then to no one and everyone she began speaking, the words rushing forth. "Did you know the term *vig* comes from *vigorish*, which is how they supposedly treated you when you owed money? Broke your knees with vigor?"

"No, I didn't," Nada said, with a warning look at the others, and they all realized what he meant. Scout was finally coming down off the action by talking and everyone had a different way of doing it.

"But Doctor Carruthers said that was mostly movie BS, because how's someone going to pay you if they got broken knees? He said the worst thing you can do to a degenerate gambler is cut them off from gambling. Which makes sense, right?"

"Right," Nada said.

Scout looked at Kirk, who was looking at the drying picture. "How's your shoulder?"

Kirk looked up, startled, his mind 990 miles away in Parthenon, Arkansas. "Huh?"

"Your shoulder?" Scout repeated.

"Oh." Kirk rotated it with a wince. "It works."

Scout nodded toward the picture. "Girlfriend?"

Everyone on the team went still, because no one ever asked personal questions.

"My kin," Kirk said.

"You guys don't seem like you have families," Scout said. "How many brothers and sisters do you have?"

Kirk didn't seem to notice the rest of the team, only Scout. "My older sister, Dee. Two younger brothers and little Becca. She's the baby of the family. Just turned six."

"I wish I had a brother," Scout said. "A sister, maybe not. We'd probably fight."

"Right," Roland said. "You not getting along with someone."

A bunch of dings started going off and Scout jumped up. "Washer to dryer. I'll take care of it." She ran up the closest set of stairs, not the ones Roland had taken.

Moms looked at her exhausted team. "We've got two Fireflies left. We were lucky we had Scout on this one. That stupid Acme would have blown us all up."

Doc made no protest, which meant assent, which was just piling on top of all the strange things the Nightstalkers were going through.

Moms pointed in the direction that Scout had gone. "We cover her ass. I want over-watch on her twenty-four/seven. Got it?"

"Got it," Nada and Doc and Kirk said.

Moms looked at Roland. "Got it?"

"Got it."

* * *

"You look funny," Roland said when Scout came in the door.

They'd sent her home, Kirk providing security, and now she was back. The team was geared back up, everyone much more comfortable in their cammies and body armor and combat vests.

Scout was geared up in her own way. Wearing boots and a little helmet and white pants and was so unlike the girl who'd rang their doorbell not long ago. But she still had blue hair.

She jerked a thumb at Kirk, who was hovering over her shoulder. "He says I can't go."

"Go where?" Nada asked.

"Duuuhhh," Scout said, twirling about. "I need to exercise Comanche. I haven't seen him since you guys dropped in. He's probably going nuts."

"Comanche?" Roland looked up from adjusting the trigger pressure on his MK-23 for the umpteenth time. "Why'd you name him that? Did you know that's the name of the horse that survived Custer's Last Stand? Captain Myles Keogh's horse?"

"Duh." Scout started humming "Gary Owen."

Roland shook his head. "You are one weird little girl."

"How do *you* know about Comanche?" Scout asked.

Once more the room fell silent, because Roland was exhibiting intellectual prowess, which was like Eagle throwing the hatchet. Dangerous.

"Myles Keogh was a distant relative on my mother's side of the family, the wild Irish side," Roland said.

"You have a not-wild side?" Scout asked, and Roland gave a hint of a smile, which was like a slab breaking off the Antarctic ice shelf.

Roland continued. "We didn't have much in my family, but we had this big Bible and in it were all these names and Keogh was there. From fighting in Ireland to Italy to the Civil War to dying with Custer. He was a warrior."

"His horse was the only survivor," Scout said. "I thought that was pretty cool. He was wounded and all, but they took care of him."

"Well," Roland said, military tactics and history being an area he actually spent brainpower on, "technically people have the whole Little Bighorn thing kind of wrong. The Seventh Cavalry was *not* entirely wiped out. Just half. Just the guys in the companies following Custer. Reno and Benteen held their ground."

"Most Medals of Honor ever given out for a single battle went to the men who crawled down to get water for the wounded," Moms said without looking up from the laptop, earning her a look from Roland that no one else could interpret. She went back to typing in the report for the Great Water Battle.

"How the hell do you know this stuff?" Nada asked Scout. "Most people don't even know where Little Bighorn is."

Roland thumped the table. "Bet she got a hippo—hippo-whatever as big as Eagle's."

"Hippocampus," Kirk said.

"I have all the books," Scout said. "And my dad took me there when I was twelve. My mom was, well, she was off at the time. It was soooo not what I thought, but it soooo made sense when I got out of the car and saw it."

"How do you mean?" Nada asked.

"Well," Scout said, "all the pictures and paintings are so wrong. It looks flat. The battlefield. Two-D. But when you get there you see it's all valleys and hills and rolling land. Three-D. You could hide Lady Gaga and her entire crew out there."

"Yeah," Nada said. "Cover and concealment. Critical to any battle. We had some shitholes in the 'Stan that—"

"No cursing," Moms said, still typing, and Nada's jaw flapped down.

"Why did Custer fascinate you?" Kirk asked.

Scout twirled her crop. "I guess I wonder what it would be like to have to follow him, follow his orders with no choice. Be one of his soldiers and they knew it was going to be bad and that he didn't care about them because he had his own agenda. I don't like the idea of not having a choice, of having no control over your own life. I just don't understand how those guys did that— follow orders and just go and die?"

Moms stopped typing and everyone got quiet.

"Oh! Sorry." Scout stopped twirling her crop and for once was still.

"I don't think they thought they were going to die," Kirk said. "Soldiers have hope. You gotta have hope or you can't do the mission."

"Sometimes they don't," Moms said, surprising everyone. "At Cold Harbor, the only battle Grant ever admitted he screwed up, there was a soldier who wrote in his diary: *June 3. Cold Harbor. I was killed.* Not much hope there."

Roland stood abruptly, dropping the gun to the table, parts spewing everywhere. "It might not be the Medal of Honor, but Moms was awarded the Distinguished Service Cross. I'd follow her anywhere, hope or no hope. She saved my life."

Moms shook her head, ignoring the looks everyone was giving her, and knew Roland had said it as much for Scout's benefit as anything else. "No personal stuff, guys. Roland, you drive Scout to the stables and watch over her. Like you'd watch over me."

Roland picked up the MK-23 parts and had it reassembled in fourteen seconds. "Yes, ma'am."

* * *

Roland and Scout came back twenty minutes later. Scout was pale and her lips were as blue as her hair. Her face was streaked with tears. Roland was literally twitching, gun in hand but shaking his head over and over.

"I didn't kill him," Roland said. "I didn't kill him."

Nada ran across the room and grabbed Scout, pulling her in tight to his chest, up against his body armor, his magazines and his grenades. Scout melted in his arms and he held her from collapsing on the floor. "What happened?" he asked, looking at Roland, who had the crazed look in his eyes of combat.

"I didn't kill him," Roland repeated.

"Good," Moms said, walking over. She put a comforting hand on Roland's shoulder. "Who didn't you kill?"

Nada realized it. "There's a Firefly in Comanche?"

Roland nodded, getting control. "The guy who runs the stables was hurt bad. I got him out. The horse damn near got us. Took out doors. Just kept kicking at us. I pulled the guy out. He got broke ribs, smashed jaw, but he's alive. Said the horse just went nuts. He was lying there dying for a day after he got hurt. Support got him now. He'll be okay. I didn't kill the horse. I didn't. I shoulda. I screwed up Protocol."

"Please, please," Scout said between sobs into Nada's body armor. "You can't kill him. I'd die if you killed him."

Nada looked down at the rag of a girl in his arms, her sobs wracking through both of them. "We won't." He easily lifted Scout up and her head rested on his shoulder.

"Swear?" Scout said.

"Protocol," Moms said. "We have Protocol. Containment. We have—" Then she stopped speaking, seeing the look in Nada's eyes.

Nada held Scout with one arm and patted her on the head with the other.

"Ouch!" Scout said in her misery. "Curling iron."

"Sorry." Nada gently lowered her and she looked up with tear-filled eyes.

"We might have to hurt him," Nada said, "but we won't kill him." Nada had snot on his combat vest from Scout. "It's going to be okay."

"The government will buy you a new horse," Doc said. "Support is already rebuilding the Lindsays' pool."

Scout got even more upset. "Comanche isn't a pool! I don't want a new horse. I want Comanche!"

Roland spoke up. "Well, he did survive Little Bighorn. He could survive this. Maybe we can, like, you know, evacuate him, quarantine him."

"Right," Moms said. "Get a chopper and sling-load a horse inhabited by a Firefly over the neighborhood to where? The goat lab at Bragg?"

They all, except Scout, knew what went on at the goat lab at Bragg. It was necessary to train Special Ops medics, but it was brutal. Each medic at the beginning of the lab phase was assigned a goat that they had to shoot. Wound only. And then nurse back to health. But they said goats don't have a nervous system that registered pain anyway; so they said. No one ever asked the goats.

"We'll just have to make the Firefly leave him," Roland said.

"You said you have to kill him and flame him for that," Scout whined.

"Well," Doc said. "Maybe not."

They all turned to him.

"We've never done a controlled kill," Doc said. "It's always been a—"

"Clusterfuck of a firefight," Nada said.

"Exactly," Doc said. "We do not know what Fireflies are, and we have only a limited knowledge of their parameters, and lately they have been pushing that. Whatever was going on inside the Rift in the Fun Outside Tucson was new. The backhoe trying to take out the Wall around here was different. Maybe we need to be different. Approach things in a new way."

"You still said *kill*," Scout said.

Doc knelt in front of her. "You say you've seen a lot of movies?"

Scout nodded.

"Seen *The Abyss?*"

Scout nodded.

"Remember where the woman drowns and they revive her?"

Scout's eyes grew wide.

"Do you trust us?" Doc asked.

Scout looked him in the eyes, and then at the other team members. "No."

"'Cause you think we're Custer," Roland said. "But we aren't Custer."

Nada nodded. "That can be our new Nightstalkers motto: 'We aren't Custer.'"

Scout wiped snot off her face. "But that's like saying we aren't Fetterman. Custer knew about Fetterman, they all did, from ten years before Little Bighorn, but nothing different happened."

"Who's Fetterman?" Kirk asked.

"Don't you guys read anything?" Scout asked. "Or watch the History Channel?"

Roland nodded. "She got us there. Fetterman was a lieutenant at Fort Kearny who went out to relieve a wood-cutting party that was attacked and disobeyed orders. Went beyond Lodge Pole Ridge because Crazy Horse sucked them into an ambush with a diversion. Ten years before Crazy Horse sucked Custer into the Little Bighorn."

"We ain't him either," Nada said.

Moms sat down with a deep sigh into a chair. "Do you see the irony of that statement, considering we're going to try to kill a crazy horse, dissipate a Firefly, and bring the horse back to life? Ms. Jones is going to kill me." She looked up. "And I am not speaking metaphorically."

Scout started crying again and Nada started to say something, but he knew his limitations. He was a soldier and he knew when to keep his mouth shut while his commander made a decision.

CHAPTER 24

The FedEx truck backed into the driveway with an irritating beeping.

The team was ready, combat gear on, locked, and loaded. Doc got on board the FedEx truck to check the gear he'd requested directly from Support, while the rest of the team piled into the SUVs with the tinted windows. The convoy rolled down the street and turned to the stables.

Comanche wasn't hard to spot. He was running around the white-fenced pasture, dirt flying under his huge hooves. Every so often he paused and struck out with one of his front hooves, mostly at nothing.

"Geez," Kirk said to Scout. "You ride that thing?"

Comanche was big. "Yes. He's always been peaceful," Scout said.

"Why hasn't he jumped the fence?" Eagle wondered, turning the wheel and pulling them up to the stable.

"Why didn't the pool Firefly break the glass door?" Moms said. She looked over her shoulder to Roland. "You ready?"

Roland was unhappy. His beloved M-240 was on the floor, next to his feet. He had a bolt-action rifle on his lap. "If they don't stop when we blast them and kill them, how are we going to stop them with just a drug? The Firefly will just ignore it."

Doc's voice came over the net. "Most likely. The drug will overdose the horse and stop his heart and that might not change anything. But you've read the binders, Roland. This has never been tried before. It's always been an all-out firefight between us and the Fireflies. Black or white. Maybe we've been wrong? Maybe there's a middle ground?"

"That's a big maybe," Eagle said.

Kirk was watching the horse through binoculars. "What if we're wrong?"

Moms sighed. "I know we're probably wrong." She looked at Scout. "We're going to try, but the chances aren't good. You have to understand that."

"You'll do it," Scout said, the words more confident than her tone.

"No," Kirk said, "what if we're wrong about our supposition about the Firefly?" He turned to Scout. "Watch the horse carefully."

The horse spotted them and neighed loudly. It kicked out once more, then raced hard in a counterclockwise circle. As it came to the fence separating the humans from the horse, it lashed out with its left front hoof and shattered the top board in the fence. It was shaking its head and its eyes rolled wildly. Roland had the rifle to his shoulder, but he also had the machine gun slung over his shoulder and the flamer on the ground next to him.

"It's the curling iron," Scout suddenly said.

Kirk nodded. "Right."

Roland's finger was on the trigger.

"What are you talking about?" Nada asked.

"Watch him," Kirk said. "Watch him kick. Notice anything strange?"

They all watched as the horse once more did a hard circle and several kicks.

"Same leg," Moms said. "Stand down, Roland. The Firefly isn't in Comanche. It's in the horseshoe."

Roland lowered the gun. "That's a fucking stupid Firefly."

"Language around the girl," Moms said absently, staring at the animal. "Actually, it almost got us to kill the horse and miss where it is entirely."

"This is new," Doc muttered.

"This is bad," Nada said. "But good," he added, looking at Scout.

"You have a tranquilizer?" Moms asked Doc.

Doc nodded. "Yes."

"Roland, switch out the round. We're going knock Comanche out. Kirk, get me Ms. Jones."

The radio clicked and it was as if Ms. Jones was somewhere close by, watching them as she responded immediately. "Go ahead."

"I'm going to need a blacksmith," Moms said.

"Did you need to use the resuscitation gear you had Support bring?"

Moms swallowed. "No, Ms. Jones."

"How interesting. Consider the blacksmith en route."

CHAPTER 25

There were four Ivars in the basement lab now, taking turns pedaling the bike backward. The really hard part for Ivar was that there were moments he wasn't sure which one he was. His mind was teetering on the precipice of going insane. Sometimes he blinked and he was on the bike, but he'd been the one tinkering with the device just a second ago.

There was only one Burns. But he was sitting in a chair, doing nothing, just watching the Ivars.

Ivar had lost track of what he was doing, but it was apparent at least one of the Ivars was paying attention, because Ivar watched that Ivar throw the switch and another mini-Ivar appeared in the chamber, crawled out, and began growing to normal size.

The Ivar who'd thrown the switch went over to a new machine, one the second Ivar had built, and opened a panel. He pulled out a circuit and held it out to the real Ivar. Then held up two fingers. Then pointed at the door.

"You need two more or two, which means just one more?" Ivar asked, because the labeling was a bit confusing in the sign language.

The other Ivar blinked as if processing that question through a long series of synapses, then put the circuit down on the table and pointed one finger at it. Then pointed at a blank spot near it with two fingers.

"He wants two more," Burns contributed.

Ivar was happy to leave the lab.

"Hey," Burns said. He held up the toggle switch.

Ivar nodded.

"See you soon," Burns said. Then he and the other Ivars suddenly stiffened. They all looked at each other.

"Only one is left," Burns said. "We must work faster."

"What—" Ivar began, but Burns pointed to the door. "Go. Hurry."

Ivar went up to Winslow's lab. It was late in the day and the building was mostly empty. The weirdest thing was that despite there being more Ivars and this getting really crazy, he was starving. As he raided the fridge, he noticed that the door to Doctor Winslow's office was ajar.

Ivar went over and stepped inside. As he reached for the light switch, he felt something metal press against his temple.

"Do not move," a man whispered, more hissed, "or I'll splatter your brains all over this place. Where is Doctor Winslow?"

"I don't know," Ivar said.

The metal moved away and the man stepped in front of Ivar. He had a gun in his hands with a bulky suppressor screwed onto the barrel. He was a tall man who spoke with the trace of an accent Ivar couldn't place. His face was expressionless.

"When did you last see him?" Stone-face asked.

"Three days ago." *Was it only three days?* Ivar wondered.

"What's with the Feds at his house?"

Ivar held his hands up helplessly. "I don't know anything about that or his house."

"What do you know?" the man asked, raising the gun so that the black hole at the end of the barrel was pointed directly between Ivar's eyes. "What did he buy that he needed five hundred thousand dollars for?"

Ivar couldn't blink. He was mesmerized by that black hole. He felt as if his entire being was being drawn into it.

"The hard drive."

"A hard drive cost half a million?" Stone-face shook his head. "I think Winslow skipped town with my boss's money. Where is this hard drive?"

"Doctor Winslow has it."

"Then he either ran with it or the Feds have it. How can a hard drive cost so much?"

"It wasn't the drive, it was what was on the drive," Ivar said. "A program."

"What kind of program?" Stone-face cocked his head, and for the first time Ivar noticed he had a little white wire running from inside his coat to his ear, like the Secret Service. "My boss is coming. He will not be asking as politely as I am. He is in a very bad mood."

Stone-face stared at Ivar. "What kind of program?"

"You'll have to see it," Ivar says. "I can't explain it."

"Where is Burns?"

"Downstairs in the lab. The program is running."

He waved with the barrel of the gun. "Sit down."

CHAPTER 26

Ms. Jones took Moms's report on the Killing of the Unlucky Horseshoe without comment. When Moms ground to a halt, an uneasy silence wavered over the radio waves for almost thirty seconds, then all Ms. Jones said was: "You have one more Firefly. Good hunting."

Ms. Jones opened her eyes and looked at Pitr. "I wish you wouldn't hover over me like that."

Pitr shrugged. "You can wish all you want. I am here."

"Winslow's notes?"

"Nothing new there. He made some adjustments on the Rift algorithm, but he actually changed it back to an old version. Of course he didn't know that. Whatever direction it was going in Tucson, he actually reversed, so either he was smarter than Craegan or—"

"More old-school with his physics," Ms. Jones said. "And the phone? I want to know how he contacted Mister Burns or, more likely, Mister Burns contacted him. It could have been a call or an e-mail and it would be on that phone."

"I'll check on that," Pitr promised.

"The team is changing," Ms. Jones said.

"I know. Do we need to start looking for a new team leader?"

Ms. Jones surprised Pitr with her answer. "No. The Rift in Tucson was different. The backhoe was taking out probes, showing a plan and intelligent behavior. The horseshoe bothers me, because the team was misdirected. They would have known it wasn't in the horse once they killed and flamed it, but they might not have flamed it enough to melt the horseshoe."

"What damage could a horseshoe do on an incinerated horse?" Pitr asked.

"That's not the point," Ms. Jones said. "We've always considered the Fireflies random in the way they occupied. But what if they're just trying different things? Experimenting?"

"To what end?"

Ms. Jones shook her head. "I don't know, but I don't like it. But that is why we will leave Ms. Moms in charge of the Nightstalkers. She, and the team, are evolving also. They killed the pool and saved the horse. Change can be good."

* * *

"Thank you, thank you, thank you, for saving Comanche." Scout's skinny arms were clinging to Nada's neck.

"Yeah, yeah," Nada said, prying her loose as they unloaded the gear in the garage. "Could you open the door?"

Scout ran over and did so as the team hauled their weapons and other gear into the house. The interior of the Winslow place was beginning to show the wear and tear of serving as a base of operations.

They'd seen a lot of action, one right after another, and everyone was tired. Moms could read it in the way they slumped onto the sofas and chairs.

"Good call out there, Kirk," Moms said. "Take over-watch and try not to move too much."

Kirk just nodded and checked the readings on his PRT before heading up the stairs. The lack of chatter bothered Moms. They'd done a good thing, killed a Firefly and kept the horse alive, even given it an entire set of new horseshoes courtesy of the well-compensated and confused blacksmith, but everyone just seemed done in, and Scout's squeals of happiness were putting everyone on the edge of whatever abyss they were staring into. Too much change, Moms realized. And also, there was the unspoken next and final op that they'd all been avoiding.

Scout ran upstairs and Moms relished the moment of silence. She powered up the laptop but had no desire to write the after-action report. Because no matter the fact that Ms. Jones had asked nothing during her verbal report, Moms knew she'd have to report the plan to resuscitate the horse, which violated Protocol. Telling the truth, after all, was in her own Protocol.

Instead she sent an RFI: Request for Intelligence.

Scout came running downstairs with a plastic bag full of something. "I found Mrs. Winslow's stash in the fridge in her closet!"

She proceeded to go around the room, passing out Fudge-sicles. No one refused the offer and soon everyone was peeling back the wrappers. Moms ignored her laptop and just bit into the frozen stick.

"Doesn't that hurt your teeth?" Eagle asked.

Moms shook her head. "Good enamel. I used to chew ice when I was a kid."

Everyone stared at her, not because of the ice chewing, but they had never envisioned Moms as a kid. She was Moms.

"Moms chews ice!" Scout said. "Lots of women do. No calories."

Moms wanted to tell the girl that wasn't why she'd done it, but decided to let Scout have her moment. She'd chewed ice like Roland's mother had made pine bark and needle soup. Because sometimes you make do with all you have.

Moms watched Scout licking her Fudgesicle and the way everyone on the team was working on their own, and was a bit amazed that this girl had taken them all, even Roland, over so easily. In a few years she'd be very dangerous. Right now she was like a frolicking puppy to them, but one day she'd be a woman. Moms experienced a momentary pang of jealousy for a girl who could so easily win over her team with just her spirit and gumption.

"What are you thinking?" Scout had noticed Moms's scrutiny.

Moms bit off the last piece of Fudgesicle and swallowed it. "What are we going to do about the house?" Moms said, not to Scout, but the team.

But Scout didn't realize what she meant or to whom she was talking. "You can hire a cleaning team. You get a good one and—"

"Going to be tough," Nada said. "The cameras have been tracking us every time we come and go. I think the yard is mined. And I bet there are a lot more surprises inside."

"I wonder what the owner is up to in there," Eagle said.

"I wonder what the Firefly is up to in there," Roland said.

"It's had time to adjust," Doc said. "You have to wonder if the dog was doing a recon of us."

"And testing the Wall," Nada added.

Scout's head went back and forth, like at a tennis match. "You mean Bluebeard's house?"

Moms nodded. "I suspect the last Firefly is in there."

"In there where exactly?" Kirk asked over the net.

"I'm afraid in the defenses," Moms said. "From what we've seen there's a very complex alarm and defense system built into the place. If the Firefly got into the computer system that controls it, then it controls everything."

"Fuck," Roland muttered. "An entire house?"

"An armed house," Nada corrected. "Just from what I've seen, there are steel shutters on the insides of all the windows. Motion and heat sensors backing up the cameras. I think there are Claymores on the lawn. Automated guns in some second-story windows."

"Who is this guy?" Eagle asked. "Why does he need that much security here, in the middle of a gated community?"

"Wrong question," Moms said. "The real question is why would someone pick a gated community to put their stronghold in?"

"Someone with something to hide," Kirk said.

"Drug dealer," Eagle said. He looked at Scout. "You said he had SUVs coming and going in the middle of the night."

"Not a drug dealer," Kirk said with conviction.

"How do you know?" Eagle asked.

Kirk's voice echoed out of the speaker. "My father cooked meth. This might be Senators Club and high and mighty, but from what I've seen, it's not operating like that. There's a pattern to things, and the issue with drugs is you can't control when you deliver, because when people need, they need."

"Could be a distributor," Nada said. "He's using the gated community as his outer defense."

"Like 'The Purloined Letter,'" Scout said.

Eagle shook his head. "Have you read everything?"

Scout pointed at the books behind glass. "I haven't read the book on bird watching in Bolivia."

Everyone laughed and the tension in the room evaporated just like that.

Moms nodded. "She's right. Best place to hide something is right out in front of everyone. Hell, nobody's come knocking on our door and we've destroyed part of the golf course and a pool."

"Nice neighborhood watch you've got," Roland said.

"Thanks," Scout said. "We like it."

"Let's just blow the house up," Roland said. "We could Excalibur it. Two ought to do the job."

"If the Firefly is in the security computer and has Internet access," Doc said, "it could escape. After the horseshoe, I think we need to be very certain of our target and guarantee the kill."

Moms wasn't keen on the idea either. "We blast it, we don't know whether the Firefly goes. We'll have debris all over the place. Concealment will be a bit hard."

Kirk's voice cut in. "We've got company rolling in."

Everyone started reaching for weapons.

"Friendlies," Kirk added. "Mac is back. I'm opening the garage and coming down."

Everyone went into the garage. Mac was not only back, but he was back in style, riding with Emily from the golf course, sitting next to her on her bar-cart. The door slid down behind them.

"What the hell are you doing here?" Moms demanded.

Mac gave his trademark smile. "AWOL, Moms." He held out his hands, wrists together. "You can arrest me if you like."

Moms went around the cart and put a hand on Mac's shoulder. He didn't shrug it off. "We're glad to have you back. We need you."

Mac got out of the car, but couldn't hide the wince of pain.

"I told him he needed to go back to the hospital," Emily said. "He called me from outside, needing a ride. I picked him up at the service entrance."

"I couldn't trust that Support wouldn't send me back to Womack," Mac said. "I remember Eagle told us he'd met another Asset," he smiled at Emily, "and, well, I'm back."

Moms stuck her hand out to Emily. "Eagle told us about meeting you. We're so sorry for your loss."

Emily shook Moms's hand. "My husband believed in the Corps. A person's got to believe in something or life isn't worth living."

Nada put them on task. "We gotta kill a house, Mac."

"Let me take a look at it," Mac said, and they all trooped inside.

Moms was the last out of the garage and she paused for a moment before entering the mudroom. They had a sixteen-year-old girl as their Asset and a war widow bringing back their demo man, AWOL, in a golf cart loaded with booze. Moms knew she should send both Scout and Emily packing, but Scout had shown her value over and over again. And Emily had brought them the man they most needed right now to take down a house. Moms was beginning to understand that once you broke Protocol a single time, it got easier and easier to break.

She wasn't sure if that was a good thing or a bad thing.

"Nada," Moms said, "tell us your thoughts about the house."

Nada pointed and began explaining their suspicions about the house being armed.

Nada ended, "We're going to have to go in."

"How the hell—" Eagle began but was cut short as Moms's computer dinged, indicating incoming e-mail. Ms. Jones was nothing but efficient, and she also had access to every intelligence apparatus under the umbrella of the United States government as well as overseas connections.

Moms scrolled through the intelligence summary.

"Bluebeard's name is Octavio Forrenzo."

"Fucking mafia," Roland said.

"Not," Moms said. "It's a cover name for a Russian, former KGB. Arms dealer."

"Worse than the mafia," Eagle said.

Roland was excited. "I bet he's got some good stuff in there."

"Yeah," Eagle said, "and it's all pointed at the windows and the doors, ready to blow your big head off when you stick it in."

"Any more Fudgesicles?" Nada asked Scout.

She shook her head. "Just a box of Creamsicles."

"Get me a couple," Nada said.

She looked at him and he said, "Please?"

"Me too," Moms said. "Please."

"Yeah," Kirk chimed in. "Please."

"Please?" Eagle said.

"Pretty please," Mac said. "And one for Emily?"

"Of course Emily gets one," Scout said. She headed for the stairs and paused, looking at Roland. He nodded his big head. She waited.

"Please," Roland said.

Scout scurried up the stairs.

Emily looked worried. "You aren't putting Greer in danger, are you? She's a good kid, and there's not many around here I can say that about."

"Scout's fine," Moms said.

"She's part of the team," Roland added, which caused everyone, especially Mac, to look at him in surprise.

Roland held his hands up. "She's, like, you know, uh, a mini-Moms."

"Not sure I like that," Moms said.

Nada brought them back to point. "What do you think, Mac?"

"Have you cut power to the house yet?" Mac asked.

Moms and Nada exchanged a glance. Moms looked at Kirk. "Get me Support."

Three minutes later, power was off to the house. They waited for a bit, and then as a car rolled down the street, a camera followed it.

"Firefly," Nada said.

"Or a generator," Mac said. "They cut in automatically. Still, though, I go with Firefly."

"Boots on the ground," Nada said. "We have to go in."

"It's always boots on the ground," Roland said, still excited about the idea of seeing the inside of an arms dealer's house. Sort of like a gingerbread house to him.

Moms was looking back at her computer. "The owner, Forrenzo, has been on Interpol's radar for a while. He was working out of Spain, but bolted before they could get to him. Three Interpol agents died getting into his house there and he wasn't even around. And there was no Firefly involved. He went off the grid for eighteen months."

"While his house got built here," Nada said.

"Apparently," Moms said.

"If the Firefly is in there," Kirk said, "what do you think has happened to Forrenzo?"

"Let's hope something very bad," Moms said.

"I could HALO onto the roof," Roland suggested. "Blast through, work my way down."

"You always want to land on roofs," Mac said. "Got a secret Santa fetish?"

Kirk was standing by the window, peering through his binoculars at the target. "You could die."

"How so?" Nada asked, joining Kirk.

"See the chimney?" Kirk asked. "It's not real. If this guy is that badass, he's looking in every direction, including up. Professionals know to look up."

"He had a Russian antiaircraft gun with a targeting radar on his roof in Spain," Moms said, looking at the screen.

"Man, that's cool," Roland said, ignoring the fact that it would have killed him if he'd gotten his way.

"What?" Scout was way behind on the conversation, with her bag full of Creamsicles. She passed them out. Emily was standing in the background, just watching.

"A Firefly is in that house somewhere, and a Russian arms dealer with an Italian cover name built it and lives there," Eagle summarized.

"I knew Bluebeard was weird," Scout said.

"Use the FedEx truck," Eagle suggested. "Pull right up, past the Claymores to the garage door. Ram through."

"What if it's rigged to blow?" Nada said.

Moms nodded. "Biggest worry ST-6 had taking down Bin Laden was whether he had a dead man's switch on him. After all, he sent plenty of other people out there to suicide themselves while taking out others."

"They're *homicide* bombers," Eagle said. "I hate when they call them suicide bombers. If they were suicide bombers, they'd go out into the middle of the desert and blow themselves up. Don't take others with you."

"We hit it from several directions at the same time," Nada said, nodding at Eagle's statement, but getting the team back on task. "Kirk takes out the chimney from here with a Javelin, while Roland does come in from above. Eagle in the FedEx truck through the garage with Mac in the rear with charges to destroy the house. I'll come through the back. Kirk, you follow up Eagle once he secures the—"

"You could use the tunnel," Scout said.

"—fuses for the Claymo—" Nada ground to a halt. "What tunnel?"

"Told you," Scout said. She nibbled a piece off the end of her Creamsicle and made a face. "Ow. That hurts my head. Don't know how you can do it," she said to Moms.

"Told me what?" Nada said.

"This guy, Forrenzo, he's, like, the, what do you call them, the meerkats? He built a getaway tunnel, so if someone comes in the roof or the garage or the front door, or all of the above, he can get out. I saw them build most of it one night. They put a tunnel in." She walked over to the window and pointed. "The rear right corner. He has a golf course lot, like my folks do. The tunnel runs from that corner to the sand trap just short of the eighteenth hole."

Everyone stared at her. "You saw them build this?" Mom asked. "How could he get away with it?"

"How did you get away with blowing up the eighth hole?" Scout asked. "I bet he paid off a lot more people than you guys are."

"He wouldn't booby-trap his escape route," Nada said. "He'd have to get out fast."

"So we can get in fast," Kirk said.

Moms turned to Mac. "We can't blow it up into a thousand pieces, because we won't know exactly what piece the Firefly is in. Besides, it would muck up our concealment."

"Implosion," Mac said, staring at the house.

"How are we going to implode it?" Nada asked.

"Like they take down old skyscrapers and stadiums," Mac said. "Blow up the internal support so it falls into itself. Also keeps dust and debris to a minimum so we can spot the Firefly dissipating." He nodded at Scout. "I go in via the tunnel. Plant the charges and rig them in sequence."

"No," Moms said.

"It's the last Firefly," Mac said. He looked past them at Emily. "We take it out, we empty your golf cart. Party like it's 1948."

Emily was shaking her head, having no idea what they were talking about, but not buying into it for a moment.

"We've got containment," Nada said. "Concealment, we do our best at. Mac's right."

"Mac's wounded," Moms said.

"I'm wounded," Kirk said. "So I go with him. We're expendable."

"*No one* is expendable," Moms said.

Ms. Jones's voice came over the radio and Moms glared at Kirk, realizing he'd opened the channel back to the Ranch.

"Do not be angry with Mister Kirk," Ms. Jones said. "You violated Protocol and I told him to keep the channel open. It seems the rules are changing. That is not necessarily a bad thing. I agree with Mister Mac. You will use the rest of the team to provide a diversion while they take down this last target."

Moms opened her mouth to speak, but the click indicated the channel was closed at Ms. Jones's end.

"All right," Nada said. "The rest of us have to provide a diversion."

"For a Firefly?" Eagle asked.

"It's been watching us," Nada said. "It'll be diverted." He looked at Moms. "What do you have in mind?"

Everyone turned to Moms, who regrouped quickly. "Football. I saw one in the garage."

"No one plays football in the streets here," Scout said.

"Exactly."

Mac turned to Emily. "May we borrow your cart to get to the sand trap? Ours got busted up."

She said nothing, but stood out of the entry to the mudroom and, beyond it, the garage. The rest of the team prepped their weapons and put them right inside the front double doors of the Winslow house. They changed into shorts and T-shirts. Mac and Kirk prepared the charges.

Moms got on the radio and, just in case, had the howitzer ready, loaded with an Excalibur round and five more on call. She called Support and made sure they had taken over the local fire department. Gas leak was going to be the reason Forrenzo's house imploded. It wouldn't pass muster with an expert, but Support had replaced all the experts.

Kirk went upstairs and propped the laser designator up and turned it on, aiming at the center of the house. Mac set up a Javelin in the garage behind one of the doors and gave Nada the remote for both the door and the Javelin.

As Mac and Kirk went out the back golf cart garage, the rest of the team went out the front door.

Roland carried the football as he went to the middle of the road with Nada, Eagle, Moms, Emily, Scout, and Doc.

"Go for a long one," Roland told Eagle.

Nada saw that the camera in the nearest corner of the house was panning over them, and as Eagle ran down the street, the one on the other corner tracked him. Roland let loose with a tight spiral and Eagle caught it.

"Traffic," Moms called out.

The same BMW came rolling down the street and slowed, window rolling down.

"Hey, Doctor Carruthers!" Scout called out.

"Hey," Roland waved. "Good to see you again."

"Yeah." Carruthers was looking at Nada and Eagle and Doc and it was just one ethnic group too many for him, here in Senators Club. "More relatives, Greer?"

"Oh, no," Scout said. "My uncle George here is a football coach and these guys played for him years ago. They're having a reunion."

Carruthers focused on Roland as he heaved another bomb to Eagle.

"I'd take the over on my uncle George," Scout said.

Carruthers nodded. "Hell of an arm."

"The over?" Moms asked.

"Hey, Aunt Betty," Carruthers said. He laughed. "Greer, have you been talking out of house about my hobby?"

Scout grinned mischievously. "My uncle might want to place some action with you later, if you're up for it."

Carruthers nodded. "As long as you vouch for him."

He spotted Emily. "I know you, don't I?"

"Not really," Emily said. "But I'm around."

A woman's voice echoed down the street from three houses away. "Everything all right there?"

Carruthers leaned his head out the window. "Friends of Greer's, Mrs. Jordanson. Everything's fine."

Mrs. Jordanson looked a bit doubtful, but went back into her house.

Roland walked over to the car and started talking football with Carruthers while Nada took a pass from Eagle. His earpiece crackled with Kirk's voice.

"We're in the tunnel."

* * *

Mac led the way, searching for booby traps and trying to shake the sand out of his gear. The lights were off in the tunnel and he had his night-vision goggles on. His backpack was loaded with charges and Kirk brought up the rear, carrying the rest.

Twenty feet in, Mac halted. The tunnel might not be booby-trapped, but Forrenzo wasn't stupid. Mac could see the unblinking red light of a video camera about forty feet ahead and a motion detector ten feet in front of it.

"We set that off," Mac was pointing, "the lights go, and the camera sees us."

"What do we do?" Kirk asked.

"I'll disable it. You wait here."

Mac put his pack down carefully, then went belly down on the floor of the tunnel and ever so slowly crept up on the motion detector.

* * *

Carruthers drove off, convinced he had Uncle George as another sucker willing to hand him money.

"Emily, take Scout inside and stay there. Things could get messy soon."

Emily and Scout went back into the Winslow house, but took up positions near the front window, watching. The four Nightstalkers looked very out of place tossing a football around, but the cameras were watching them.

"You like Mac?" Scout asked.

"He's nice," Emily said.

Scout looked at Emily. "He's cute."

"He's not what you think," Emily said. "He pretends real well. No one else on the team sees it. And that matters not in the slightest. He's a soldier. And he's putting his life on the line."

Scout nodded sagely. "They're very good at what they do, but in terms of the things they don't do, they're not the sharpest knives in the drawers."

* * *

Mac had the motion detector off-line in twelve seconds. It was hard working at close quarters using night-vision goggles and depth perception was off a bit, but he got it done. He walked back to Kirk and shrugged his backpack full of explosives back on. They moved down the tunnel, past the camera.

Forrenzo didn't leave his back door open. Mac pulled out his set of picks and tossed the tumblers. This took longer than usual as Forrenzo didn't go cheap in the lock department.

"We're in," Mac said, opening the heavy steel door.

And promptly got slammed back as a burst of automatic fire hit him in the chest, pounding into his body armor. Kirk dove to the floor, firing over Mac's falling body.

* * *

Nada heard the muffled sound of automatic fire and knew the charade was over. He raced to the house where Scout and Emily waited, handing weapons out as they ran into the garage, piling into the SUVs as the doors opened. They peeled out into the street and over to the golf course, tires tearing up the perfectly manicured grass. As Scout had said, a gaping dark hole beckoned in the sand trap, a trap door and a pile of sand to the side.

Nada led the way, the others following.

They got to the end of the tunnel where Mac was sitting with his back against the wall and Kirk was framed in the doorway, weapon at the ready.

"What happened?" Moms demanded.

"Mac took a couple of rounds to the chest. Nothing got through the armor, but he's pretty beat up." He jerked a thumb into the basement of the house. "Forrenzo had an AK-47 rigged to fire if the door was opened from the outside. I blew it apart."

Doc was kneeling next to Mac, peeling open his body armor. Ugly welts were already forming where the rounds had impacted. Mac ignored Doc and struggled to his feet.

"Let's blow this son-of-a-bitch up," Mac said. "My experience is that there shouldn't be any more booby traps inside the house. People don't like to trip over something in the middle of the night in their own house and kill themselves."

Moms issued orders. "Kirk, stay with Mac. You too, Doc. The rest, clear the house, make sure we're not taking any people with the house and Firefly. Watch out for Forrenzo if he's still alive and in here. He'll be armed and won't hesitate to shoot."

They moved into the basement. A concrete wall was in one corner with a large vault door on it. Forrenzo's stash of who knew what instruments of death. Roland looked longingly at it, but stayed on task.

Mac and Kirk moved in, headed for the first support column as Roland took point up the stairs, Nada, Eagle, and Moms following. They reached the door to the main level. Nada pointed at himself and indicated number one, then at Roland for number two.

Nada crouched down as Roland kicked open the door. They went in, Nada low and Roland, with one hand on Nada's shoulder, high. They quartered the room, a classic room-clearing technique as taught in the Killing House. Moms and Eagle followed, overwatch, scanning up and then hard to the sides.

In the basement, Mac was staring at a steel bracing going up to a crossbeam, slightly puzzled, explosive charge in hand.

"What's wrong?" Kirk asked.

"It's not right," Mac said. He began tapping on the column, ear pressed up against the side.

Above them, first floor cleared, they made it to the second floor with no sign of Forrenzo or anyone else.

"Why isn't the Firefly attacking us?" Nada asked as the paused in the wide hallway. The interior of the house was full of paintings, sculptures, and other items the newly rich acquired to prove to themselves and others they were rich. Or else they liked art.

"We're inside the security system," Moms said. "The Firefly has got to be in it, not in the actual house. Like Mac said, security is oriented outward, not inward."

* * *

In the basement, Kirk pulled out his knife and scraped away at the side of the pillar. "Doc, get out of here." He keyed his radio. "Moms, withdraw, withdraw, withdraw. Confirm? Over."

There was nothing but static. He looked up and saw that the steel sheathing covered the insulation. Forrenzo had shielded the room to prevent imaging from penetrating and also for giving him a tempest-proof area to work: secure from listening devices and taps.

Mac's digging yielded what he feared. A series of wires. "Kirk, go upstairs and get everyone. ASAP. They need to get down here and get the hell out."

As Doc hurried out the tunnel, Kirk took the stairs three at a time, ignoring the shooting pain from his broken ribs. He looked about the first level as he keyed his radio. "Withdraw, withdraw!" he called out over the radio.

"Withdrawing," Moms's voice said, and the thunder of boots running reverberated through the house. The team came down the stairs in a hurry, but orderly.

Kirk was staring at a bronze of a Native American on a rearing horse, a lance in one hand.

"Crazy Horse," Roland said as he ran by.

Kirk fell into the rear and they made it into the basement. Moms waved for everyone to hit the tunnel and came up to Kirk.

"You got all the explosives in place and wired it already?"

Mac didn't turn from what he was doing, but briefly waved his wiring pliers at his rucksack, which still bulged with explosives. "The house is already wired. Forrenzo wasn't going to leave any evidence if he had to bolt out of here. I'm amazed the Firefly didn't blow it down on top of us. Still could. Go!"

Moms ran to the tunnel door. She paused, looking over her shoulder at Mac hard at work, then followed the rest of the team. She stumbled out into darkness, where the team had gathered in the sand trap.

"What's going on?" Nada asked.

"The house is—" Moms began, and then there was a series of muffled concussions followed by a rumbling sound.

Looking back, the entire Forrenzo house shivered, then began crumbling inward, roof first, then outer walls.

"Mac!" Roland ran back into the tunnel.

"Roland, stop!" Moms called out, but it was too late.

A blast of dust and debris came jetting out of the tunnel a few seconds later.

Thirty seconds later a dust-covered Roland came out, once more carrying a protesting Mac in his arms.

Moms breathed a huge sigh of relief.

The last of Forrenzo's house crumpled inward.

Nada was watching carefully, along with Eagle.

"There!" Nada pointed. A Firefly lifted out of the rubble and then slowly dissipated.

* * *

In the lab, Burns and the four Ivars paused. "They'll be on their way soon."

The Ivars got back on task.

Burns checked his watch. The original Ivar had been gone too long. The kid was too terrified to not follow orders.

Which meant something had happened to him.

Burns went to the door and opened it. He stepped into the dark hallway, an emergency exit sign at the far end the only source of light.

He pulled out his cell phone and hit quick dial.

It was answered on the second ring. "Yes?"

"Mister Forrenzo. Please come to the University of North Carolina. The physics research building. Call me when you arrive outside. I will meet you."

"I want—" the Russian began to protest, but Burns hit the off button. He opened the steel door and laid his cell on the ground, wedging it open so it could still get a signal.

"Faster!" Burns yelled.

* * *

Roland laid Mac down, and Doc got to checking his latest wounds, which mostly seemed to be his old ones aggravated and some scrapes and bruises from being blown down by the blast in the tunnel. And the bruises from the AK rounds.

"We did it," Roland said. "We got 'em all."

Mac lifted his head. "He had the entire basement lined with incendiaries. Whatever was in that vault will be nothing but melted scrap."

There was a muffled explosion. "Secondary ignition," Mac said. "It's going to burn now."

"Looks like Fireflies aren't suicide bombers," Nada said. "It could have gotten all of us in there if it had set off the charges."

Two figures appeared out of the darkness: Scout and Emily.

"I told you to stay at the house," Moms said, but there was no disapproval in her voice.

"Did you get it?" Scout asked.

"We got it," Nada said.

A fire chief's Blazer came roaring up and Cleaner got out on his prosthetics. "Hell of a gas explosion," he said. He looked them over. "Need medevac?"

"I think we're good for now," Moms said.

Cleaner looked dubious, but got back into the Blazer and headed for the fire.

Emily knelt next to Mac. "Are you all right?"

"Just banged up a bit," Mac said, struggling to a sitting position. "I could use a cold one."

"I think we all could," Moms said.

Emily went to her cart and opened the cooler and passed out beers—and a soda to Scout.

Mac lifted the beer, wincing as he did so. "To the Nightstalkers." He tilted it toward Scout and Emily. "And Assets."

Everyone lifted their drinks to the toast. Except Kirk. He was staring at the house, shaking his head. An intense blaze was now roaring straight up.

"What's wrong?" Moms asked Kirk.

"Crazy Horse," Kirk said.

"That was a nice bronze," Roland agreed. "And I bet he had some good stuff in that arms room."

Kirk turned from the house and looked at everyone. "We've been chasing Crazy Horse."

Scout was the first to get it. "Fetterman. He chased the wrong thing. The real battle is somewhere else."

CHAPTER 27

"But—" Nada began, but then Kirk held up his hand with the PRT on the wrist and pressed a button. Ms. Jones's voice came over the net.

"Support got into Doctor Winslow's phone. Just before the Rift opened he was communicating with a student of his named Ivar. He was directing Ivar to place dampers on a computer at his lab. A computer that had a copy of the Rift program on it."

"Fuck me to tears," Nada said.

"Language," Moms said without any conviction. "But Ms. Jones, Support checked his lab. There was nothing suspicious."

"The number Doctor Winslow was calling wasn't to his regular lab. We've tracked the line. It's a landline wired into the basement of that building. He had a lab we didn't check out, where this Ivar was working."

Moms turned to the team. "Gear up. These were just the battles. We've got to finish the war now."

"There's something else," Ms. Jones said. "We tracked the money that was paid to Burns for the hard drive. It came from Doctor Winslow's account, but it was wired in there immediately before from another account. From Forrenzo's account."

Nada stared at the blazing house as the rest of the team began loading the SUVs. "Winslow went to Forrenzo for the money," Moms said.

"But Forrenzo's been gone," Nada said. "I don't think the Firefly would have peacefully coexisted with him, considering it shot Mac up."

"He left that night, remember?" Scout said. "I saw two SUVs drive away from his house in a hurry right after you guys got here."

"This doesn't make sense," Eagle said, trying to connect the dots in his huge hippocampus. "How would Winslow know about Forrenzo? And how did Forrenzo know to leave? We're missing something."

"We've been missing a lot," Moms said. "This whole thing here was to keep us occupied, making us think we were handling the problem."

"So where is Forrenzo now?" Eagle asked as he slammed shut the tailgate on one of the SUVs. There were sirens coming closer, Support with their fire trucks.

"Probably looking after his investment," Nada said.

"What do you think is going on in that lab?" Nada asked.

Moms grimaced. "A Portal. Let's just hope it hasn't opened yet."

"All right," Nada said. "Let's move out."

"You're not leaving me behind," Scout said.

Nada turned to her. "There are no more Fireflies here. You'll be safe. This is our duty, not yours."

She didn't notice that behind her, Moms had pulled out a syringe. As Scout began to protest, Moms slapped her on the shoulder with it.

Scout jumped. "You *did not* just—"

Nada caught Scout as she crumpled and lifted her in his arms. He carried her limp form over to Emily's golf cart, her blue hair contrasting sharply with his cammies. "Make sure she gets home?"

Emily nodded. "I will. And make sure you all get home."

Roland was next to Moms and leaned close. "Do you think he'll forget her?"

"Would you?" Moms asked. "Let's load up!"

* * *

Ivar wondered if Burns or the other Ivars would come looking for him, since he'd been gone a while, but he had a feeling they weren't operating as well as the machine they were working on. He was more concerned that Burns might simply flip that toggle switch.

The man with the gun hadn't said a word after asking a few more questions. Hadn't moved. Still as stone, while Ivar fidgeted on Doctor Winslow's couch. As out of tune with the rest of the people around here that he was, even Ivar had heard some of the stories about what happened on Winslow's couch with some of the more aspiring female postdocs.

The doors to the lab banged open and Ivar started as a man wearing an expensive camel-hair coat walked in, followed by eight men dressed all in black fatigues with combat vests and carrying automatic weapons and other assorted weaponry.

"Your Doctor Winslow betrayed me," Forrenzo said. "He brought the Feds into his house but I did not see him get arrested. He put a virus into my home security system and I barely got out with my life." He walked over to Ivar and leaned forward until his dark eyes were just inches from Ivar's. "I want my money and I want whatever he bought with my money. And I want it now because I have a plane waiting at the airport and I am leaving this shithole of a country. And I want Winslow."

"I don't know where the money or Doctor Winslow is," Ivar said. "And as I told him," he nodded toward Stone-face, "Doctor Winslow has the hard drive."

Stone-face finally spoke. "Mister Forrenzo. He says it is the program that is on the drive that is important. And he says they made a copy."

"Where is this copy?"

"In the basement." That wasn't the only thing copied, Ivar thought.

Forrenzo pulled out his cell phone and dialed.

Burns answered and without preamble got to the point. "You're inside the building, Mister Forrenzo. I told you to call from outside. And you have the student, don't you?"

"I do," Forrenzo said. "He is under my control."

"No," Burns disagreed. "He's under my control. See that collar around his neck? You've seen similar."

Forrenzo looked at Ivar, saw the collar, and began backing out of Winslow's office, indicating for Stone-face to stay with the student.

"What do you want?" Forrenzo asked. "What is this great program that cost me five hundred thousand dollars? Where is Winslow?"

"I'll answer all your questions soon enough," Burns said. "But first, we need just a little bit more time. We might have it before the Feds catch on. But if they're as smart as I know them to be, they're on their way here now. A small, elite team. I need you to stop them from getting in this lab down here."

"How long do you need?" Forrenzo asked.

"Forty-five minutes. And they'll begin their assault by parachuting someone, if not the entire team, onto the roof. They'll come top down. It's their Protocol." A manic burst of laughter came over the phone. "They always follow Protocol. Forty-five minutes, and everything will be different. You will be paid back many times over, I promise, Mister Forrenzo."

The phone went dead.

* * *

Moms looked over her shoulder and thought of Custer as they sped down the road toward the FOB. Kirk was having trouble breathing with broken ribs. Mac had been rebandaged, but she could tell he was near his limit, no matter how many happy pills Doc fed him from his tackle box of good stuff. She didn't think he'd go Burns on them, but he just might collapse. Roland was, well, Roland. But then again, his ancestor Myles the warrior had followed Custer and that didn't turn out well.

Eagle had a thoughtful look on his face, but then he always looked like that.

Nada was off his game, the girl having affected him. Nothing had ever affected Nada.

Doc was the only one excited. He wanted to see what was in this lab.

As Eagle drove, those who could scrambled as best they could to pull their cammies and body armor and other gear on over the civilian clothing. They pulled into the FOB.

Support already had the camo nets off the Snake. The team ran up the ramp, Eagle jumping in the pilot's seat, no time for a preflight check, having to trust in Support. He began powering up the engines as the ramp shut. Moms had the iPad out, checking the information forwarded from the Ranch by Ms. Jones.

"This is our target," Moms said, kneeling in the middle of the cargo bay, the rest of the team, minus Eagle, bending over in a circle around her. "Physics research building, University of North Carolina. Should be empty this time of the night."

"Except for whatever is in that lab," Doc said.

"No," Kirk said. "Wrong. Forrenzo the arms dealer wasn't in his house. He gave Winslow five hundred thousand to buy that hard drive from Burns. I'd think Forrenzo is somewhere in the area."

"Arms dealer?" Roland was intrigued about going up against them. Even if they killed him with the latest weaponry, it would still be fun.

They all staggered slightly as the Snake lifted.

"It's six stories high and the target is in the subbasement," Moms said. "Will take a while to clear our way down." She looked up. "Roland and Nada, go in high onto the roof via HALO. Clear the top floors. Rest of us fast-rope in after them onto the roof, link up, and clear down to the basement and finish this thing."

"Whatever this thing is," Eagle said as he banked the Snake to the north, the lights of Chapel Hill glittering ahead.

"No," Nada said, surprising everyone. "That's Protocol. We've used Protocol so far every step of the way on this mission until we ran into Scout. And we were making mistakes, including one very big one, being lured into a diversion."

"We're ten miles out," Eagle said. "Six minutes until we're on target. If you want me to gain altitude for a jump, I need to start doing it now."

Everyone looked at Moms. She tapped the iPad. "See this? Right outside the lab?" She slid her finger over slightly. "And this? Great infil point."

She stood and began unbuckling her body armor. "We go in like normal people for once."

* * *

Six Russian mercenaries scanned the night sky. One had the latest generation Russian-made surface-to-air missile—the SA-24 Grinch—on his shoulder, finger resting lightly on the trigger. It was a fire-and-forget system, in that once the firer got the sighting system to acquire the target, he pulled the trigger and the missile did all the rest of the work getting there.

All the way below them, in the subbasement, Forrenzo reached the landing, one of his men prodding Ivar twenty feet ahead of him. The other merc covered Forrenzo's back.

They walked down the hallway. The steel door was shut.

Forrenzo saw no need for subtlety. "How many people are in there?" he asked as he slammed Ivar up against the wall outside the steel door.

"I don't know."

Forrenzo pulled a gun out from under his expensive coat and pressed up into the soft part underneath Ivar's jaw. "Stop toying with me, boy. Is Doctor Winslow in there?"

"No! I swear."

"Who is? Burns?"

"Yes."

"Who else?"

Ivar swallowed, which hurt because the muzzle pressed into his chin. "I can't explain."

Forrenzo pulled the hammer back on the gun, which wasn't necessary as it was double action and only something they did in movies, but he figured the kid watched movies.

Ivar's eyes bulged. "Just open the door. You'll see!"

Burns's voice echoed out, through the steel door. "You must give me a little more time, Mister Forrenzo. Just a little more time, then all will be made clear to you. Are your men ready for our visitors?"

"They're ready," Forrenzo shouted.

He gestured and let go of Ivar, who slid down the wall to a sitting position. The two mercs faced back the way they had come, weapons at the ready.

* * *

The team was dressed in their Senators Club camouflage: golfing shorts, shirts, khakis—a hodgepodge of civilian clothing. Roland had a large, sky-blue canvas bag with the UNC logo on the side packed full of goodies slung over his shoulder while the rest of the team had their MK-23s under their shirts.

Eagle brought the Snake low over a cemetery in the middle of campus on South Road, several blocks from the research building and the clock tower that was the center of the UNC campus. The side doors slid back, fast ropes were tossed out, and they were all on the ground in five seconds. The ropes were cut loose and the Snake disappeared, flying low away from the target.

The team rendezvoused at the edge of the cemetery.

Moms looked at her team. She managed a smile. "We survived Senators Club. We can do this. Some of you even went to college, right?"

"I—" Doc began, but Mac cut him off.

"Went to a whole bunch of colleges and got a whole bunch of degrees. We know."

"I went to Harvard," Eagle said, surprising everyone. "They partied hard there."

"Then let's party," Moms said.

Roland hefted the UNC bag. Moms looped her arm through Kirk's as much to look like they were a couple as to help him with his injured side.

The Nightstalkers began walking down the street. The physics building wasn't in sight yet. They passed the student stores. The Wilson Library with the clock tower to their left.

"Showtime," Moms said.

Roland began bellowing "Lawyers, Guns and Money." Moms and Nada did "Roland the Headless Thompson Gunner," and to add southern charm, Kirk added a country tune.

None of them sang well and they began to stagger as if drunk.

* * *

Inside the lab, the golden sphere was changing shape, becoming an iris. Expanding, growing taller, wider. Burns and the other Ivars were kneeling in front of it, like worshippers.

* * *

On the roof, the Russian mercs spotted the group staggering down the sidewalk, singing something awful, very loudly.

One of the mercs spit over the edge of the building. "Drunken American fools." He pointed up. "Keep watch."

* * *

Eagle had the Snake at a hover a half mile away, equal in altitude to the roof of the building. "You were right, Nada," he said over the net. "I've got six hot on the roof." He flipped a switch and the chain gun extended out of the nose of the Snake.

* * *

The team went past the front of the physics lab building, then staggered into the parking lot.

Two big SUVs were parked near the back doors of the physics building, away from the parking lights in the shadows.

"I think Forrenzo is here," Nada said.

Roland was still singing loudly.

"What's in the lab is the priority," Moms said, "not the arms dealer."

"He's an arms dealer," Nada said. "He's probably got guns that can shoot at us."

"Then shoot back," Moms said.

With efficient hand and arms signals, Moms moved the team toward the open doors.

Roland stopped singing and opened the bag, passing out MP-5s and strapping on his flamer.

They sprinted toward the back doors.

* * *

On the roof, the Russians heard the sudden cessation of singing. One ran to the edge and looked down. He saw the last of the team disappear into the building.

"They're in!" he yelled over his own team's radio.

The six mercs rushed to the stairwell on the corner of the roof. They jammed in, hurrying to get down to support Forrenzo.

Which is when the stream of thirty-millimeter bullets from the Snake tore through the wall and the stairwell became their grave.

* * **

"Scratch six," Eagle reported.

Moms didn't acknowledge.

"Drop your weapons!" Moms yelled as she peeked around the edge of the stairwell door into the corridor, spotting two men holding automatic weapons. Not that she expected them to, and Roland was a trigger ahead of her anyway. They were Russian arms dealers after all. Weapon dropping was not part of their repertoire.

As the two mercs brought them to bear, Roland stepped past Moms and blew them against the wall with a well-controlled and precise burst from his MP-5. They crumpled to the floor in bloody heaps.

Nada took out Stone-face with a double-tap to the forehead. Which left Forrenzo holding his gun to Ivar's chin.

The Nightstalkers spread out, surrounding Forrenzo.

"We don't care about him," Nada said, nodding at Ivar, "so you can kill him or not, you're not getting out of here."

"Actually we don't even really care about you," Moms said to Forrenzo. "But you are a bad man…"

* * *

Inside the lab the iris reached from floor to ceiling. It was pulsing and the color was shifting, from gold to something darker. And deep inside, as if it had distance far behind the room and they were looking into a very long corridor, something was stirring. Something that looked vaguely human, but wasn't.

The golden glow in Burns's eyes was flickering. The cactus spike next to his right eye, through which the sixth Firefly from the Fun Outside Tucson had gotten into his brain, was vibrating. The spike pressed forward, tearing into his eye, and he didn't feel it.

His face was fixed with a rigid, insane grin, blood seeping from the slashes across it. It was the mask of a man controlled by something far more powerful and dangerous than even the human brain.

* * *

"I want a car and—" Forrenzo began, but the team had no time for him.

Nada double-tapped and Forrenzo dropped like a sack of potatoes. No dying finger twitch, another thing Forrenzo should have known was false in the movies.

Ivar screamed like a girl.

"Mac," Moms said. "The door."

Mac reached for his ruck and pulled out a shaped charge. He put it over the lock on the steel door. "Clear!" he yelled, and the team backed up as he pressed the igniter.

The charge blew the lock out.

Kirk reached out and pulled the door open, the rest of the team ready with their weapons as they entered.

Burns faced them, his face scored with blood, a thorn poking out of his right eye. The left eye was completely gold.

Behind him, three Ivars stood shoulder-to-shoulder, eyes glowing golden. Another was on the bicycle, furiously pedaling backward.

"Fuck me," Nada muttered as Roland fired, hitting Burns and all the Ivars.

With no effect, except to stagger them slightly as their bodies absorbed the bullets.

Behind them, the team could see the thing in the Rift. Like they'd seen in Tucson, but bigger, closer.

"Doc!" Moms yelled.

Burns's mouth opened wide, wider than a human's mouth can open. A golden spark flew out of it right into a fire extinguisher hanging on the wall. The red tube burst off the wall toward the team.

It slammed into Kirk's unprotected ribs, shoving the ragged, broken edges into his lungs. He went down in a heap.

"Doc!" Moms yelled. "Shut it."

Doc fumbled for his laptop in its case as Burns's mouth opened wide once more. Another spark flew out, flashing past the team into the hallway.

Mac wheeled and saw it fly into the fire hose. He fired, shredding the hose, but it lashed out like a snake, wrapping around him, an anaconda of heavy canvas. Nada whipped out his machete and began hacking at it.

Blood was bubbling out of Kirk's mouth, his lungs torn from the broken ribs.

Moms kept her focus on the Portal. The thing inside was coming closer, stalking forward through whatever hell that iris was opened to. It was big and it emanated anger and hate.

"Doc," Moms said, "shut the Portal. Roland, get ready to flame."

"Flaming isn't going to help," Doc said. "They're not human. We've got to send them back." He was on his knees, laptop open, small dish pointed at the Portal, the FireWire already in place. "Working on it."

Just for the hell of it, Moms let loose with another burst from her MP-5 at the Ivar on the bike. It seemed mildly perplexed by the intrusion but kept pedaling.

Kirk was on his side, blood dripping out of his mouth. "Doc," he gasped.

"Yes?" Doc was focused on his screen.

Behind them, Mac was slammed into the wall by the fire hose as Nada gave a powerful swing of the machete and cut the hose in two. Which didn't help, as the part wrapped around Mac began to tighten down around his body.

Kirk reached out and grabbed the blood-spattered and cowering Ivar's ankle. "Your turn on the bike."

Moms was moving forward toward Burns as his mouth opened wide once more. Roland was on her shoulder. "We kill whatever comes out of there," Moms said.

A sign of desperation as they couldn't even kill what was already in the room.

Kirk tightened his grip on Ivar's ankle. "You're the only one who can do it."

Ivar looked at the soldier holding on to his leg, blood dripping out his mouth, his face pale. And then Ivar did a most un-Ivar-like thing.

He stood up and walked into the room.

Burns's mouth let loose another golden spark. It bounced off the wall, circled, then settled in a tank of acetylene.

"Oh shit," Moms muttered.

In the hallway, Mac's left arm cracked from the tightening hose. Nada dropped the machete and tried to muscle the hose off him, tearing loose fingernails in his desperation as a piece of the hose went around Mac's neck and constricted.

Ivar walked past Moms and Roland and Burns and the other three Ivars, up to the Ivar on the bike.

The Ivar on the bike looked at the real Ivar, and then simply gave up his place. Ivar got on the bike and looked at Kirk, who was going into shock on the floor. But had enough presence of mind and enough strength to lift his hands and rotate them.

Ivar nodded, getting it right away.

He began pedaling, but forward this time, not backward. Everything in the room froze for a moment except for Ivar pedaling.

Then the thing forming in the Portal lunged forward.

And collapsed.

The four copy Ivars wavered, then began to shrink, one by one, in reverse order of their entrance into Earth. When they hit their entrance size, they were sucked back into the Portal and were gone.

The golden spark in the acetylene tank and fire extinguisher rose up and went back into the Portal. And then the one in the hose flickered out and was gone. Mac collapsed to the ground, gasping for air.

All that was left was Burns and a diminishing Portal.

Moms took a step forward, then spun, letting loose a high kick that hit Burns's face and knocked him back. Up against the golden iris.

"No!" Burns screamed.

"Yes," Roland replied, firing an entire magazine from his MP-5 into Burns. The bullets didn't kill him, but they pushed him back and then he was sucked into the iris.

The Portal flickered, pulsed, and then snapped out of existence.

"Doc, help Kirk," Moms ordered as she went over to Ivar. "You can stop pedaling."

He didn't hear her, pedaling faster and faster until Moms slapped him with a syringe and Roland caught him as he tumbled off the bike, unconscious.

CHAPTER 28

The team was on the Snake, all the equipment from Doctor Winslow's secret lab strapped down in the middle of the cargo bay. Ivar was seat-belted in, still unconscious, not aware he was going to a new job. Kirk was stable, Doc working on him the entire way.

Eagle brought them down onto the taxiway just outside the hidden hangar at Area 51. He lowered the ramp and Support personnel came in and carted off the equipment and Ivar on a stretcher. Eagle brought the ramp back up and took off. He flew them to the Ranch and lowered the Snake back into the Barn.

"Home again, home again," Eagle said, because he always said that when they got back from an op.

They piled in the Humvee, Roland taking the fifty-caliber and singing "Werewolves of London" because he liked the howling part. Moms was in the passenger seat, Eagle was driving, and the rest were jammed in. Kirk complained about Mac jabbing him in the ribs with his MP-5, and Mac warned if he complained any more he wouldn't get his three-beer successful mission allotment of Pearl when they got back to the Den.

Moms turned in her seat and spoke over the team net. "Mac, you took two extra Pearls during Kirk's naming ceremony."

That shut Mac up for a moment. "Sorry, Moms."

"Just don't do it again, all right?" Moms said.

Mac nodded.

Moms looked at Nada, crunched into the back corner of the Humvee. "You going to be okay?"

Roland stopped singing, and the only sound was the diesel engine and the tires rolling down the road.

"Yeah," Nada said. "But I am going to miss her."

Roland howled from the hole: "*Aahoo! Werewolves of London!*" And the rest of the team howled with him, the sound echoing across the Ranch so loud that they must have heard it in Area 51: "*Aaho! Aaho!*"

* * *

Ms. Jones read the debrief from the Ivar Incident one more time, then tossed it aside.

"This is not good," Pitr said.

"It is never good, but we will deal with it," Ms. Jones said. "Just as we deal with every challenge we are faced with. Do you have the other file?"

Pitr extended a painfully thin file.

Ms. Jones opened it and quickly read the contents. The ghost of a smile crossed her face. She snapped it shut, then extended it with her scarred and burn-streaked hand to Pitr.

"File it under priority possibles."

"What title?" Pitr asked as he took the file. "Her name is—"

Ms. Jones forestalled him. "File it under Scout."

ACKNOWLEDGMENTS

Profound thanks to Debbie Cavanaugh for her invaluable streams, her font of 'useless' information, the horseshoe, and her incredible patience.

To Craig Cavanaugh for Riley K., the lab at UNC, and his imagination and working to invent the tricorder.

To ODA 055, 2d Battalion, 10th Special Forces Group (Airborne), the A-Team I had the honor to command.

My mates at Western Command Special Operations, JFK Special Warfare Center, and other units in my journey in that world.

And, of course, to you, the reader.

ABOUT THE AUTHOR

New York Times best-selling author, West Point graduate, and former Green Beret Bob Mayer weaves military, historical, and scientific fact through his gripping works of fiction. His books span numerous genres—suspense, science fiction, military, historical, and more—and Mayer holds the distinction of being the only male author listed on the Romance Writers of America Honor Roll. As one of today's top-performing independent authors, Mayer has drawn on his digital publishing expertise and military exploits to craft more than fifty novels that have sold more than 4 million copies worldwide. These include his best-selling Atlantis, Area 51, and Green Beret series. Alongside his writing, Mayer is an international keynote speaker, teacher, and CEO. He lives in Knoxville, Tennessee.

16107262R00185

Made in the USA
Charleston, SC
05 December 2012